## "Wha [P9-DLZ-232] if I asked you out again?"

"Yes" hovered on the tip of Maggie's tongue. It was what she *wanted* to say. But then she remembered the f.p. factor. *Father potential.* No matter what Nick Sorenson said, he wasn't the marrying type. She could feel it. "No," she said. "I'm sort of involved with someone else."

"With whom?" he asked.

Maggie knew she was stretching here. But she needed some excuse. She couldn't let herself fall for a guaranteed heartbreaker. "His name is John."

"John?" He blinked at her as if she'd suddenly grown two heads. "John who?"

"You don't know him," she said. "I met him on the Internet."

* * * * *

Great! Now he was competing against himself.

Nick sat at his desk, going over some paperwork, although in reality he was doing nothing more than wondering how he'd managed to strike out with Maggie again. The night had been going so well. He'd easily recognized the signals she was sending—they told him he wasn't alone in his attraction. Yet when he'd gone for the close, she'd shot him down. Because of "John."

And he couldn't even ask what "John" had that he didn't!

Dear Reader,

Set in Sacramento, California, where I live, this book
was especially fun to write. I drive the streets Maggie
and Nick drive, I frequent the same places, I use the bike
trail. Against the backdrop of such familiar territory, I guess
it was inevitable that this story would seem more real to
me than any other. But as you read *Dear Maggie*, you'll
understand why there were times when "real" wasn't such
a good thing! I often spooked myself into looking over my
shoulder as I jogged along the American River or double-
checking my windows and doors at night.

Though there is definitely an element of suspense
running through this novel, it's still about relationships and
trust and finding the one person in life who completes us.
Nick, an undercover FBI agent, and Maggie, a newspaper
reporter, are perfect for each other, but there are plenty
of obstacles standing in their way—Maggie's background
and childhood experiences, Nick's job and his fear of
commitment…and a serial killer.

I'd love to hear from you. You can write me at P.O. Box 3781,
Citrus Heights, CA 95611. Or simply log on to my Web site
at www.brendanovak.com to send me an e-mail, enter my
monthly draws, join my mailing list, check out my book
signings or learn about upcoming releases.

Happy (and safe <G>) reading!

*Brenda Novak*

P.S. I hope *Dear Maggie* helps you "get caught reading"
something you can't put down!

# Dear Maggie
## Brenda Novak

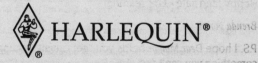

# HARLEQUIN®

TORONTO • NEW YORK • LONDON
AMSTERDAM • PARIS • SYDNEY • HAMBURG
STOCKHOLM • ATHENS • TOKYO • MILAN • MADRID
PRAGUE • WARSAW • BUDAPEST • AUCKLAND

ISBN 0-373-70987-0

DEAR MAGGIE

This edition published by arrangement with Harlequin Books S.A.

® and TM are trademarks of the publisher. Trademarks indicated with
® are registered in the United States Patent and Trademark Office, the
Canadian Trade Marks Office and in other countries.

Visit us at www.eHarlequin.com

**Printed in U.S.A.**

To Pam,
For being more than a sister.
For being a lifelong friend.

And to Joy,
For exactly the same reason.

## ACKNOWLEDGMENTS

I'd like to thank Dixie Reid and Ted Bell,
staff writers at the *Sacramento Bee*, for giving me a tour
of the newsroom and helping to answer my questions
about a cop reporter's world.

# *PROLOGUE*

FOR THE FIRST TIME in her life, Maggie Russell wasn't sure she wanted to be a police reporter. She'd always known she could, and probably would, be faced with situations like this, but somehow the reality was far worse than she'd ever imagined. Maybe it was because she was a single mother now. Maybe it was because her three-year-old son was sleeping soundly in his bed only a few blocks away.

Shivering despite the warm Sacramento night, she tried to block out the flashing police lights, and the stench—God, the stench was cloying, sickening—and concentrate on the snippets of conversation she overheard as the evidence recovery team worked carefully and cautiously to preserve the scene. This was her first big story. She couldn't wimp out now.

"It's a female, been here maybe three days," the coroner announced, bending over a body so badly decomposed Maggie couldn't bear to look. "She's been stabbed, repeatedly."

"Watch that piece of plastic, Rog," someone else muttered. "The lab might be able to lift some prints from it."

Two detectives stood off to the side frowning. Maggie recognized them as Detectives Mendez and Hurley from the Sacramento Police Department, because it was her business to know who was who on the force. But she'd never had any direct contact with them. Most of her tips came from the police dispatchers who handled the calls as they came in. And most of her stories centered on domestic violence, insurance fraud or embezzlement. She'd once reported on a convicted felon who'd escaped from Folsom Prison, and she'd paid close attention when Jorge, a fellow cop reporter for the *Sacramento Tribune,* followed a rash of armed robberies. But she'd never been involved with a murder—especially such a brutal murder.

The homeless woman who'd discovered the body while rummaging through the Dumpster behind a small Midtown office building sat on the asphalt parking lot, rocking. Her hair was long, matted and dark, her thin frame buried beneath several layers of clothing. She carried her belongings in a plastic grocery bag and wore a sober, intense expression on her face. Maggie thought she recognized a glimmer of intelligence in her eyes, but when Detective Mendez had tried to talk to the woman, she wouldn't respond. Afterward, Maggie had heard him mutter to Hurley, "Man, the lights might be on, but nobody's home."

"See anything that could've been used as the murder weapon?" someone asked.

"No, that kind of damage can only be inflicted by a pretty big knife. Nothin' like that in this Dumpster. We'll have to spread out, check the surrounding shrubbery and garbage cans."

Maggie shot another glance at the homeless woman and moved closer. Maybe Mendez had approached her too soon. Maybe he hadn't been patient enough...

"Hi, there," she said.

The woman didn't even look up.

"You must be feeling terribly frightened after stumbling onto something like that. I'm sorry you had to see it."

No answer.

"Do you hang out here every night?"

Nothing.

"The police think the woman you found was murdered about three days ago, but the body could've been dumped as late as yesterday. Any chance you saw something that might help them?''

Again, nothing.

''Ma'am? I'm talking to you, and this is pretty important. Do you hear me?''

*The lights might be on, but nobody's home....* Maggie sighed. She'd started to walk away when the woman finally spoke. ''What?'' she asked, turning. ''I couldn't hear you.''

The bag lady's gaze latched onto her face. ''It could happen to you. It could happen to anyone,'' she said.

# CHAPTER ONE

"HE'S WATCHING ME AGAIN. I can feel it." The hairs on the back of Maggie's neck stood on end as she peered over the partition that separated the corridor where she stood from her friend Darla's cubicle. She refused to turn around for fear she'd find herself nose to nose with Nick Sorenson.

Darla, a staff writer for the Entertainment section of the *Tribune,* frowned and stood up, too.

"Don't!" Maggie said above the static of the cop radios on her desk a few feet down the corridor, the droning televisions, clacking keyboards and voices that surrounded them on all sides. "Sit back down, or he'll know I'm talking about him."

"Relax," Darla muttered. "He can't hear us."

"He can see us!"

"He's there, all right," her friend reported. "At the end of the hall, about twelve feet away." She shook her head. "Ooo la la, he's gorgeous. But he's leaving now. Looks like he's on his way to the photo editor's desk."

Maggie seemed to know whenever Nick was around. She could feel his presence, sense his interest. Just after he'd started working for the paper almost three weeks ago, he'd asked her out, and she'd turned him down. A man like him would have no serious interest in a woman like her. She'd learned that lesson the hard way, clear back in high school when Rock Tillman and the other jocks used to throw spit wads at her in class and make fun of her braces, her acne,

her red hair, even the heavy load of books she toted everywhere. Her appearance had changed considerably since then,
but one failed marriage later, the girl inside remained the
same, right down to her contempt for cocky hard-bodies who
thought the world should bow at their feet for the price of a
wink or a grin.

Fortunately, when she'd refused his offer, Nick hadn't
pressed the issue. Every once in a while, she'd look up to
see him watching her, usually from a distance. Only he didn't
turn away or smile when she caught him. He wore his devil-
may-care disposition like a leather jacket and studied her with
thick-lashed tawny eyes as though…as though he *desired*
her. Which was unsettling enough. Add to that the obvious
strength of his tall, athletic body and her own small size in
comparison, and he made her nervous as hell.

"What do you think he wants with me?" she asked.

Darla chewed her lip and squinted in the direction Nick
had gone. "You know what he wants. He wants a date."

Maggie braved a quick glance over her shoulder to find
the hallway empty. "If I thought that was all he wanted, I'd
probably go out with him. Lord knows he wouldn't want a
second date, so I'd be rid of him. But I'm afraid he wants to
forego the date and get right down to business. He looks like
the type who's had a lot of experience, which definitely puts
him out of my league."

Darla raised her brows. "That can't be all he wants. Prac-
tically every available woman in this office has made a play
for him, but he treats them all the same, with a hands-off,
don't-approach-me attitude. And I've seen him treat Susie
with something closer to contempt."

Maggie shrugged. "Oh well, we can't hold that against
him. Who doesn't treat Susie with contempt? She's slept with
every guy in the office. Even the publisher."

Leaning an elbow on the partition, Darla propped her chin

on her hand. "Maybe you should tell Frank that Nick makes you nervous."

"No, I don't want to bring his boss in on this. I don't really have anything to accuse him of. What do I say, 'Nick's looking at me.'? He'll think I'm a sexual-harassment case just waiting to happen. Half the time I think I'm imagining it myself."

"Maybe your job's getting to you. Listening to all those cop radios and working at night is creepy."

"A cop reporter is *supposed* to report on crime," Maggie retorted. "How would I know what was happening without my radios?"

"Don't you like this better? You should thank Jorge for taking the day off and trading shifts with you. Look at the sun shining outside. During the day you don't have to worry about simple things like walking to your car."

"Jorge didn't take the day off for my benefit. He's having knee surgery. Besides, you know how hard it is to get a start in this industry. I'm lucky to be where I am."

Darla stooped for her handbag, her fake nails clicking against its contents as she rummaged through it. A minute later, she pulled out some red lipstick, liberally applied it, then tossed the tube back where she'd found it. Her purse followed with a soft thud. "So what about that murder last week? You still think that's your big story?"

"Yeah. But there's definitely something strange going on with that."

"Do the police know who did it yet?"

"No, and they're being very tight-lipped. They've given me a press release with a few pat quotes, but they're holding back. I can tell. There's something about this case they don't want me to know." She smiled. "So, of course I'm going to dig until I find out what it is."

Darla grimaced and ran her nails through her long blond

hair. "Well, don't feel obligated to share the details with me once you discover them. I, for one, have heard enough about the poor woman in that Dumpster. Everything about that crime is sickening and proves my point that nothing good happens after midnight."

Nick Sorenson walked by, and Darla's gaze followed him.

"That is, nothing *good* happens after midnight unless you're spending the night with him," she mouthed after he'd passed.

Maggie noted Nick's long, confident strides, and fought her own appreciation. "Looks do not make a man," she said to remind herself as much as Darla. "Jeez, you really have a thing for him, don't you? Too bad he doesn't ask *you* out."

Her friend gave her a wicked smile. "Too bad is right. There's that dangerous glitter in his eyes, you know? And there's the scar on his temple and the way his hair falls across his forehead, like he doesn't care how he looks. And yet he still manages to look better than chocolate." The audible breath she took did even more to express her admiration. "What a package. And he's intense. I can tell."

Maggie raised a doubtful brow. "'Heartbreaker' is written all over him, along with 'catch me if you can.' I'm not up to the challenge." She'd spent too much time and energy carefully building her self-esteem to risk losing it on a man like Nick.

"You only think that because you're a single mom. Single moms can't be too careful."

"True."

"Should I *ask* him why he's been staring at you?"

Maggie raised a hand. "No, don't embarrass me."

"All right. He probably just thinks you're attractive, anyway. What man doesn't?"

"Sometimes it's very apparent that you haven't known me long," Maggie said. "But just for starters, what about Tim?"

"He married you, didn't he? And let's face it, in the end, *you* left *him.*"

A call blared across one of Maggie's radios. Instinctively she tensed, listening to the dispatcher's gravelly voice, then relaxed when she realized it was only a 5150—the call for a crazy person doing something stupid but certainly not newsworthy.

"I *had* to leave Tim," she responded to Darla. "If it weren't for Zach, I probably would've hung on, forever grateful that he'd deigned to marry me in the first place. But my son deserves a father who wants him." She sighed heavily. "Provided I can ever find him one."

"So that's what's happening." Darla's expression softened. "The singles scene has finally gotten you down. Is that it?"

Unexpected emotion clogged Maggie's throat and stung her eyes. What a baby, she thought. Millions of people were lonely, and they didn't cry about it. But here she was with her nose starting to run, at work, of all places. "There's just no time to meet anyone. I'm here almost every night and taking care of Zach all day, and let's face it, spending my afternoons hanging out at McDonald's Playland isn't exactly the best way to meet a single guy, you know?"

"You're working today, so you're going to have Friday night off, aren't you? Why don't you let me watch Zach so you can go dancing?"

Dancing? Dancing was Darla's idea of fun. Maggie didn't have much experience with nightclubs.

"I'm not sure a nightclub is the right place to go," she said, knowing Darla would never understand her phobia about such places. Typical reporters were like Darla, confident and bold and, professionally, Maggie fit the image. For the most part she'd buried the awkward, self-conscious person she'd been as a young girl. But all too often, when it

came to her personal life, the old Maggie reasserted herself.
"I don't have a single tattoo or body piercing," she joked.
"I'd probably be a wallflower."

"No, you wouldn't," Darla argued.

An unruly, copper-colored curl tickled Maggie's cheek,
and she tucked it behind her ear. "Anyway, you can't baby-
sit for me. You need to get out, too. You told me you wanted
to get married this year."

"I did until I decided to swear off men for good."

"You swear off men every Monday. This is only Wednesday. By Friday you'll be ready to dress up and go out again."

Ray, from sports, grinned as he strutted past them on the
way to Frank Buckley's office. "Ladies."

They murmured a quick hello, then rolled their eyes because Ray considered himself such a lady's man.

"This time I mean it," Darla went on. "That last loser I
hooked up with stuck me with over five hundred dollars in
long-distance bills."

"Ouch." Maggie grimaced. "You're as unlucky in love
as I am. Maybe we'd be smarter not to hang out together."

Darla waved her teasing away. "Enough already. We'll
each find someone eventually." Sitting down, she swiveled
to face her computer.

"Wait a second before you go back to that," Maggie said.
"I received something in the mail I want to show you."
Crossing to her desk, she opened the top drawer, retrieved
the white envelope with the red heart on the front and returned to Darla's cubicle. "What do you think of this?"

"What is it?"

"An advertisement for a dating service."

Darla cocked an eyebrow at her, looking far from impressed. "What do I think? I think you're nuts. Anyone as
attractive as you shouldn't have to pay to get a date."

If only Darla understood how painful that whole process

was for her—getting out and meeting someone, all the little rituals and deceptions… "I kind of like the idea of the questionnaire. You get to skip the first part of dating, where everyone's kind of checking other people out." She flattened the paper against the partition. "Look, it's right here. You answer these questions so the service can match you up with someone who's compatible."

"And they use a crystal ball to decide this? Or do they simply include a 'no weirdos allowed' clause in their contract?"

"Come on, Darla. They obviously can't protect their clients from every possibility, but if Tim and I had filled out one of these we would have known right from the start that we weren't meant for each other. He didn't tell me until after we were married that he didn't want any kids."

Maggie didn't add that she'd been so happy to find a man to love her that she hadn't pressed him on anything, and he simply assumed she'd accommodate his plan for their lives. In the end, her inability to go along with his refusal to have children had come as a big surprise to both of them. "It took me several years to change his mind, and the result was disastrous. He resented Zach from day one," she said.

"But you could meet someone pretty scary through an outfit like this," Darla complained. "You could wind up dating a rapist or a murderer."

"We'd have a greater chance of meeting someone like that at a club. This route takes patience, something rapists and murderers typically don't possess."

Darla scowled. "Tell the woman in the Dumpster that. I'll bet some murderers show incredible patience. Isn't that what 'premeditated' is all about?"

"Come on. We could be going out with guys who have the same level of education, the same goals, the same marital status—"

"Pathetic bordering on desperate? Why would I want to meet someone like that?"

Maggie considered the questionnaire again. "We could always tick the 'I make over $100,000' box under annual income and insist on being matched up with someone who makes that, too."

"Now you're talking," Darla said.

NICK STRETCHED OUT in his chair, crossed his legs at the ankle and closed his eyes. He wanted to photograph Maggie Russell. He wanted to dress her in a white sundress that fell off the shoulder on one side and see her through his lens, laughing and barefoot, her thick auburn hair blowing in the wind, her eyes slanting up at him.

It would have to be evening, he decided. That was when the light would be perfect and he'd be able to capture her nearly flawless skin in a warm, gentle glow. The dusting of freckles across her nose, and her mouth, slightly larger than most women's ideal, added to the earthy beauty of her face. The sun behind her would provide just enough of a shadow to hint at the shape of her body, naked beneath the cotton dress. And he'd shoot her on a beach, where surf the color of her eyes crested in the background and shimmers of heat rose from the sand beneath her feet.

Somehow Maggie Russell managed to combine innocence and vulnerability with an incredibly high dose of sex appeal. The effect was very intriguing. And he could capture the essence of it on film; he knew he could. Someday he'd put her photograph on the cover of the coffee-table book he hoped to publish—when he had the time to pursue his love of photography more seriously.

Right now he had to get back to work. The FBI's Ogden field office hadn't sent him to Sacramento to pose as one of the *Tribune*'s staff photographers so he could waste his time

lusting over the beautiful female reporter he was here to protect. The owner of the paper—someone Nick had met just
once—was the only one the bureau had clued in to his true
identity and purpose. Besides heading the small task force
assembled by the Sacramento P.D., Nick had the added burden of performing at the *Trib* in a manner convincing enough
to fool the photo editor who was his boss, his co-workers
and everyone else, which meant he had to make the most of
every minute.

Sitting up, he reached inside his desk for the file that contained the coroner's report on the victim found in the Dumpster almost a week ago. He'd studied it exhaustively, but
every time he read it, he hoped he'd find something he'd
missed before. Something that would illuminate the series of
brutal murders that had started along the eastern seaboard
almost four months ago, then traveled to Missouri and Colorado and finally the west coast.

The victim's name was Sarah Ritter. Her death brought the
body count to seven. A Caucasian woman in her mid-thirties,
she was attractive in a professional, polished way and held a
master's degree in English from the University of California,
Davis. She'd taught second grade at an elementary school in
the suburbs, had a three-bedroom, two-bath tract house, two
children, a dog, and an insurance salesman as a husband.

Unfortunately, she'd also been brutally attacked, raped and
stabbed, her body tossed in a Dumpster. How she'd gotten
from her house, nearly twenty miles away, to Midtown, was
a mystery.

Nick pinched the bridge of his nose. *Why her?* The other
six victims were younger, including the Seattle reporter.
Three were single, one had a live-in lover, the last was sep-
arated from her husband. All were in their mid-twenties.
What had specifically attracted the murderer to these women?
What put them at risk?

It certainly wasn't accessibility. These were difficult murders to commit. The victims hadn't been living on the street. They weren't drug addicts or prostitutes. They had homes and jobs, and some had families. Beyond that, they had no obvious connection to each other—they didn't belong to the same book club, graduate from the same school, attend college together or correspond for private or professional reasons. As far as Nick could determine, they didn't know each other at all. The only thing they had in common was the fact that they'd become victims of the same murderer.

Random targets, except Lola Fillmore, the reporter in Seattle. That had been personal.

Nick shuffled through another file and came up with the letter that had brought him to Sacramento in the first place. Received at FBI headquarters almost a month ago, it had been printed on regular copy paper by a standard Hewlett-Packard DeskJet. Nothing of particular note there, at least nothing that was going to help him. But the letter itself shed some light on the psychology of the killer.

April 13th
Seattle, Washington

"Dear Sirs, or should I say Madams? Welcome to the investigation. For all the challenge local police have given me, I assume most forces are now run by a bunch of women, but be that as it may, I've decided to let you join the fun. I've tired of Seattle and all its blasted rain—makes working out of doors rather miserable, if you know what I mean—and have decided to move to California. But where? Los Angeles is entirely too big. With all the different jurisdictions, etc., it would be too easy for local law enforcement to bungle the investigation, and it's certainly no fun outwitting one's opponent so easily. I considered San Francisco, but no one would much care if I murdered women there, now, would they? They have no use for the fairer sex, anyway. So I think Sacramento is the place. River City, isn't that what they call it? Well, we shall soon see what the river turns up.

Catch me if you can…

Dr. Dan

Dr. Dan was famous for his letters. He sent them to local law enforcement, taunting their failed attempts to catch him. He sent them to the FBI, bragging about his superior intellect. And when the police and FBI kept them from the press, he started writing to newspapers, hoping for headlines. He'd sent two letters to Lola Fillmore at the *Seattle Independent,* right before he killed her.

Fortunately, as far as Nick could tell, no one at the *Sacramento Tribune* had received such mail. Yet. After what had happened in Seattle, his instincts told him it would come, and he guessed Maggie Russell would be the recipient when it did. The *Trib* was the major newspaper in town, and she was the only female cop reporter on staff.

He shoved the letter back into the file and went for the profiler's report instead. Ms. Lalee Wong, one of the FBI's best, had analyzed the letter, along with all the others, and deemed it genuine. But she hadn't come up with as much as Nick would have liked. She said the perp was a man, probably fairly young, most likely short and balding, with sexual hang-ups to spare.

*No surprises there.*

Dr. Dan's utter contempt for women, evident in the letters but even more in the violent and cruel nature of his killing, fueled his murderous rage. Perhaps he'd been abused by his mother or a strong maternal figure in his youth. Perhaps his wife had left him.

Or maybe he'd killed her, Nick thought. There could be

another body out there. Maybe more than one. Most serial killers didn't go from zero to sixty in a matter of days. They started slowly, usually with animals, and built up from there.

Skipping further down the report, Nick skimmed the final paragraphs. Wong doubted Dr. Dan was truly a doctor, but she hadn't ruled out Daniel as the man's first name. She felt certain he was educated, most likely to the college level, and that he was Caucasian, possibly British, judging by his formal and rather stilted use of language. Going by the normal statistics on such violent criminals, as well as the tone of his writing, she guessed he was in the age range of twenty-eight to thirty-five.

The last sentence of her report Nick knew by heart because he'd come to the same conclusion himself. *Considering how quickly and efficiently Dr. Dan removes certain internal organs, he probably has some working knowledge of anatomy. If he's not a doctor, he could be a nurse, an EMT, a medical student, a veterinarian or a butcher.*

"He is definitely a butcher," Nick growled. Dr. Dan seemed to think of himself as some sort of modern-day Jack the Ripper, but Nick planned to put an end to it. He was going to find this bastard and nail him to the wall if it was the last thing he did. No one traveled across America killing wives and mothers and got away with it. Not on his watch.

He heard Maggie's laugh and looked up to see her standing at the water cooler, talking to another photographer. She was very attractive in her gray tailored business suit and crisp white cotton shirt. She had the most kissable lips he'd ever seen, the most incredible bedroom eyes….

But none of that mattered. He was a federal agent. His interest in her was strictly professional. Even if she never became one of Dr. Dan's targets, she could dig up something that might prove helpful to his investigation. Actually, chances were good she'd do exactly that. She tracked all calls coming in after ten o'clock.

And Dr. Dan always struck at night.

# CHAPTER TWO

WHAT WAS GOING ON? Lowell Atkinson, the county coroner, had always been helpful to Maggie before. She'd sent his wife Mary Ann flowers when she'd delivered her last baby. She'd gotten Zach and the Atkinsons' Katie together for a picnic last summer. She could hardly believe he'd treat her so impersonally now. When she'd arrived at his office to request a copy of the coroner's report on the Dumpster murder, he'd claimed he hadn't finished it, said he'd call her when he had. But when she'd pressed him for a verbal explanation of his findings, he'd told her he hadn't even done the autopsy yet.

Bull. Maggie knew better. The police were under a lot of pressure to solve such a high-profile case. They wouldn't let Lowell store the victim in his morgue for over a week. They'd probably had his report in their hands the following day, but her police contacts weren't talking, either. And to top it all off, Ben, her editor, was riding her hard, expecting a follow-up to the story they'd run last week—a follow-up she couldn't conjure from thin air. She needed answers, and she needed them fast.

Frustrated, she set her purse on the desk and slumped into her seat, wondering where to go from here. Detectives Hurley and Mendez had the case. She doubted they'd talk to her when no one else on the force would, but it was worth a chance.

She fished her police roster out of her drawer and dialed,

but Lopez, the sergeant at the front desk, said they were both out. She considered leaving a message, decided against it and hung up, hoping to catch them later. In the meantime, she'd get organized.

She was clearing off her desk when she noticed a sticky note from Darla attached to the partition directly in front of her, next to her photographs of Zach.

"Before we join a dating service, let's try some online sites," it said. "They're free."

Maggie had never actually gone into a singles chat room before. She'd surfed the Web a lot and grown compulsive about e-mail, but she wasn't sure online dating would work. How could she and Darla meet men via the Internet who lived close enough for dating purposes? What if she found a man who seemed interesting and he lived in Florida, for Pete's sake? A pen pal wouldn't exactly fill the gap in her life.

Still, she liked the idea of socializing from behind the safety of her computer screen while Zach played at her feet. No baby-sitter needed. No fuss. No awkward moments. No fears or worries if she stayed in control of the situation. Visiting chat rooms might help pass the long, lonely evenings before she went to work. And it certainly wouldn't hurt that she could subsidize the fun with some frozen yogurt from her own freezer.

"What do you think?" Darla asked, coming into her cubicle before Maggie had a chance to make a firm decision.

"What about the risks? We could end up attracting weirdos. Cyber nuts," she said, determined to consider every angle.

Darla frowned. "That might be true. I've heard some scary stories. We'll just have to be careful."

"How will we know when it's safe to reveal our name and number?"

"We'll get to know the guy first."

"And how will we determine when we 'know' him?"

"We'll just have to play it by ear, I guess."

Maggie rested her head in one hand and regarded Darla skeptically. "You're going to get me in trouble, aren't you? I can tell already."

Darla smiled, sorted through Maggie's side drawer and helped herself to a piece of gum from the pack she kept there. "I think it's time to mix things up around here. I think it's time for a little trouble," she said and headed back to her own desk.

"What are friends for?" Maggie muttered, but Darla couldn't hear her. She was gone for a moment before popping back in to hand her a new sticky note.

"Here. This is where we'll go. Log on tonight at eight. I'll meet you there."

Maggie read Darla's loopy handwriting directing her to a chat room called Twenties Love. "You might be only twenty-six, but I just turned thirty," she protested. "I have no business in Twenties Love."

Darla shrugged. "Okay. Older men are fine by me. We'll go to Thirties Love, then."

"I don't know." Maggie rubbed her pencil between her hands until the friction warmed her palms. "I'm still leaning toward the dating service. Their questionnaire asks what I'm looking for in appearance." She grinned. "I was planning on checking the box 'moderately attractive' so the guy wouldn't hold my red hair against me."

"Your hair isn't red. It's auburn, and it's beautiful."

"No one likes red hair."

"Men are crazy about red hair."

"Tim was paranoid our baby would have red hair."

"Tim was always trying to hurt you."

Her ex had definitely succeeded there. But he'd toughened her a lot, too, and Tim was old news, anyway.

Maggie pulled the dating service's questionnaire out of her desk. "Well, I was also planning to check the box that said I was moving in six months, you know, as sort of a safety precaution."

Darla propped her hands on her hips. "So, what you're saying is, you've already decided to lie on almost every question."

"Not every question. They don't ask about my weight."

"Like you'd need to lie about your weight." She shook her head. "Okay, what would you put under 'athletic interest'? Very active, active, occasionally active or does not matter?"

"Very active, of course."

"You call grocery shopping once a week very active?"

"No, but everyone knows an active woman is more appealing than an inactive one."

"You see, Maggie? Doesn't that tell you anything?"

"Yeah, that I'm not stupid enough to put 'inactive.'"

"No. That other people are probably doing the same thing you are, giving answers they think the opposite sex wants to hear, instead of the truth."

Maggie chewed her lip. Darla had a point. What if men were putting "advanced degree" when, in reality, the only thing they'd ever graduated from was juvenile hall to the state pen?

Grabbing the note with the chat room information on it, Maggie scratched out Twenties Love and wrote a big 3-0, then tacked it up on her wall so she wouldn't forget. "Okay. We go with the Web. It's no less safe, and it's free, right?"

"Right." Darla tossed her hair over her shoulder. "See you in virtual reality."

How would he know when she logged on?

Nick sat in front of his laptop computer, his dog's muzzle on his leg, reading the comments of people already in the chat room and hoping he'd be able to recognize Maggie's "voice" when he heard it. He'd logged on around seven-thirty, wanting to be there when she arrived, figuring that the timing of her appearance would somehow tip him off if nothing in her screen name or comments did. But it was after eight now, and he doubted she was anyone he'd met so far.

Was he in the wrong place? He glanced down at the note he'd snatched from Maggie's cubicle. He had the right server. Twenties Love had been covered by a numerical Thirty, but after scanning all the chat rooms, he decided it could only mean Thirties Love. So where were they?

They could have changed their minds about coming, but that didn't seem likely. He'd heard Darla talking about the chat room in the parking lot after work—and so had anyone else within a block radius. Darla kept nothing secret. He smiled at the many comments the tall blonde had made about him, both good and bad, not realizing he was listening to every word. He wondered if she'd be embarrassed if she knew, then decided she wouldn't bother with anything as inhibiting as embarrassment.

Maggie, on the other hand, would be mortified to learn he'd heard so much of their conversations. He knew he made her nervous, that she didn't want anything to do with him. Her flat refusal to go out with him had told him that. But he couldn't protect her *and* his cover as one of the *Trib*'s photographers unless he drew a little closer. So, with any luck, he was about to become her best friend—

Hey, Mntnbiker, you just lurking or what? You the shy type?

Dancegirl was talking to him. She'd been flirting with several of the men. She'd said she was from Washington, but Nick had no idea if she meant Washington state or Washington DC. At that point, he'd known she wasn't Maggie and started skimming.

Just quiet, he wrote.
Dancegirl: Well, join the fun. Tell us, if you had to liken yourself to an animal, which one would you pick?

Two new names appeared on his screen, one right after the other, and Nick smiled. Zachman and Catlover could only be Maggie and Darla. Maggie had a son named Zach. His pictures covered her whole office. And no one was crazier about cats than Darla. He relaxed, knowing he'd found them, and answered Dancegirl.

Mntnbiker: I'd be a Rottweiler.
Dancegirl: A dog? Why?

*Because it's the first thing that came to my mind.*

Mntnbiker: They're smart and loyal and fierce in a fight.

He scratched behind his dog's ears. Rambo opened his droopy eyes to acknowledge the touch, looking anything but fierce, then went back to dozing.

Mntnbiker: What about you?
Dancegirl: I'd be a horse.

Nick knew his next question was supposed to be why, but he wasn't the least bit interested in Dancegirl. So he moved to edge out a guy named Pete 010, who was welcoming Maggie to the chat and trying to draw her into a conversation about skiing.

Mntnbiker: What about you, Zachman?

Zachman: I'm sorry. I'm new at this. What was the question?

Mntnbiker: If you had to liken yourself to an animal, which one would you choose?

Catlover: I'd be a Siamese cat.

Zachman: I suppose I'd be a mourning dove.

Pete 010: Why a mourning dove?

Catlover: Because they mate for life, right, Zachy? You're so sentimental.

Mntnbiker: There's nothing wrong with that.

Unless you were like him and had no plans to marry and settle down.

Zachman: Beats the heck out of being a lioness and having to do all the work.

Catlover: I kind of fancy a black widow myself.

Pete 010: Watch out, guys.

Catlover: Just joking. I'm a nice girl, I swear.

Redrocket: Okay, enough inane drivel about animals. It's time to spice things up. Let's rate our last lovers.

Pete 010: I've forgotten. It's been too long since I've had one.

Nick chuckled to himself. Either Pete 010 was trying to garner sympathy, or he was just too honest for his own good.

Dancegirl: On a scale of 1–10, I'd give mine a 5. He was more interested in watching television than he was in me.

Catlover: Mine wasn't so bad in bed, but he was hell on my long-distance bill.

Wondering what Maggie's love life was like, Nick waited for her to comment. When she didn't, he joined the conversation to keep it alive. He didn't relish the idea of talking about Irene, or even thinking about her, for that matter—he hated the wave of guilt that engulfed him every time he did. But he answered honestly, anyway.

Mntnbiker: I thought I was in love with mine. That made the sex great.
Zachman: What happened?

Apparently he hadn't been as in love as he'd thought. When their relationship progressed to the point where she started pressing him to marry her, he'd finally agreed, then bolted the day of the wedding. The reception had to be canceled, all the gifts returned. Irene hated him now, and he didn't blame her. But neither did he regret his decision to call it off.

In the end, we weren't right for each other, he typed, wanting to keep things vague. He certainly wasn't proud of what he'd done, but at least he understood himself better now. He might flirt with the idea of marriage, but deep down he wasn't willing to make the sacrifices such a commitment would require. His job wasn't very conducive to permanence in anything, which contributed to the problem.

Zachman: I'm sorry.
Mntnbiker: What about you, Zachman? How would you rate your last lover?

Zachman: That's tough to say. I've only had one. I don't have anything to compare him against.

Catlover: Come on, I've heard enough about him to know he couldn't be more than a 2 or a 3.

Pete 010: All women say they've only been with one or two partners.

Catlover: With Zachman it's true. She's the shy, inhibited type. She doesn't know what good sex is all about.

Zachman: Someday I'll find the right man.

The image of Maggie as he'd like to photograph her came instantly to Nick's mind. He took a deep breath and reminded himself that he was in Sacramento to catch a killer, not to volunteer for a sex-education course.

Pete 010: Hey, you don't need love for good sex. I don't know why women always think that.

Zachman: Maybe some people don't, but I do.

Redrocket: What happened to your 2 or 3, Zachman? He's gone, I take it.

Zachman: I wanted a child. Tim initially agreed but ultimately wasn't interested. I couldn't take the indifference or the neglect.

Mntnbiker: Do you regret pushing for a child?

Zachman: No, I'd rather have Zach. One hug from him is worth more than anything I ever got from Tim.

Catlover: That's because Tim withheld affection as a form of punishment.

Zachman: Jeez, are these chats really supposed to get so personal? What happened to our discussion about animals?

Dancegirl: Yeah, no one ever asked me why I wanted to be a horse.

**Redrocket: Wait, I haven't rated my last lover—**

Redrocket and several others expounded on the strengths or shortcomings of their past partners for a few minutes, then Nick saw Zachman disappear from his screen. Catlover left soon after. Evidently, they hadn't found the chat room to be the singles haven they were looking for. But he didn't mind. He'd met Maggie, discovered her personal e-mail address and established a frame of reference so he could contact her again.

For now, that was enough.

ON FRIDAY NIGHT, Maggie kicked off her slippers, which were too hot for a Sacramento summer, and sank down in front of her computer. She lived in Midtown, in an old home she'd bought with her divorce settlement when she left Los Angeles two years ago. Half the buildings on her street had been converted to small offices or retail establishments, creating a mixed neighborhood that included tenants, owners and residents from many different nationalities, along with some of Sacramento's homeless. There were no large grocery stores, no sprawling shopping centers, only small independently-owned corner grocers, trendy coffee shops and a spattering of secondhand stores. But Maggie liked where she lived. Midtown had color and character. It had old-fashioned architecture that wasn't quite as impressive as that found in the Fabulous 40s, several streets of beautiful old homes just a few miles away, but the neighborhood had plenty of potential. Her own house only wanted a good coat of paint and some work on the worn-out, shabby yard—something she intended to do when she had enough money and time. Meanwhile, she was removing the wallpaper in her bedroom, large bunches of faded pink roses that looked very much like something her great-aunt Rita would have chosen.

Actually, the whole house looked like Aunt Rita—aging under protest—but Maggie had big plans for it. She gazed at the black night outside and wondered if she should start by taking down the iron bars that covered the front windows. According to her neighbor, the previous owner was an old widower, who had wanted to install them all around, but when he passed away, his son inherited the house and didn't finish the job. Maggie thought the bars were quite an eyesore, but then she remembered that Sarah Ritter's body had been found only a few blocks away and decided she'd keep the ones she had.

Glancing at her watch to make sure it wasn't too late, she called Detective Mendez on his car phone. She hadn't been able to reach either detective since Lowell Atkinson had put her off two days ago. She always got routed to voice mail, and they hadn't responded to her messages. Still, she was determined to lay hands on the coroner's report, even if she had to camp out in Lowell's front yard starting tomorrow morning.

"Yo, Detective Mendez here."

Maggie sat up in surprise. Evidently miracles did happen. "Detective? This is Maggie Russell with the *Sacramento*—"

"*Tribune.* I know who you are. Dammit, don't you people ever let up? It's nearly ten o'clock on a Friday night."

"If you've checked your voice mail, you know I tried to reach you earlier. I called at least five times today. Yesterday it was eight."

"And the day before that it was three. I got your messages, Ms. Russell, but I'm a busy man. What can I do for you?"

"I'm doing a follow-up article on the Ritter murder and was hoping I could ask you a few questions."

He hesitated. "Sure. And here are my answers: it's an

isolated incident. We're making progress. We'll catch the bastard.''

What? "I wasn't going to ask if it was an isolated incident, Detective Mendez. Why should I?"

"How the hell would I know?"

"You anticipated the question. You must have had some reason."

"Don't twist my words, Ms. Russell. I've already given you my statement."

"So you have. And it was gem, let me tell you. There's just one more thing. I'd like to see a copy of the coroner's report."

"Oh, yeah? Well, excuse me. I'll drive it right over."

Maggie ignored his sarcasm. "Fax would be fine. Or I'll pick it up at the station. You name the day and time."

"I'm booked up through next week. How about the following Friday?"

What was this guy's problem? "At least your buddies on the force are *pretending* to cooperate with the press."

"I'm not going to insult you by playing games."

"Well, you're doing a good job of insulting me without it. So what's the big secret?"

"No secret. A woman was killed. We're looking for her murderer. I have enough to do without chronicling my every move for you."

"Sorry, I don't believe this murder was an isolated incident—at least not anymore. Who else was killed, Detective? Has there been another victim?"

Mendez cursed, then the phone clicked and he was gone.

What a jerk, Maggie fumed. If this guy thought he could shut her out that easily, he had a shock coming his way. This story might very well be her ticket to a promotion, a raise and some respect. And after what she'd sacrificed to make

Tim happy, heaven knew she'd do almost anything to be able to take a little pride in her work.

"Mommy? I have to go potty."

Zach stood in her doorway, rubbing his sleepy blue eyes. Earlier they'd watched a Disney movie together and he'd fallen asleep before she could help him through his nightly routine. Smiling at his tousled blond hair and round soft cheeks, she scooped him up and carried him to the bathroom.

When she'd tucked her son snugly into bed, she returned to her bedroom and cranked up the air-conditioning unit in the window. If it was this hot at night on the first of June, she was going to be in trouble later. The wallpaper, the yard, the paint, everything would have to wait until she paid for central air. She couldn't take another summer like the last one. Zach had a fan in his room, but it would never be enough.

Sitting down at her computer again, she signed on to the Internet, intending to pull up newspapers from around the country. Mendez had claimed Ritter's murder was an isolated incident, but he'd volunteered the information before she'd even asked and he'd said it in a defensive tone. Why? Was he afraid she might connect this attack with something else? There'd been nothing like it in Sacramento, at least not since she'd come to town, but perhaps there'd been other murders elsewhere. If so, the police could very well have a serial killer on their hands. And that would certainly make them cranky.

"You've got mail," her computer cheerily informed her.

Maggie clicked on her mailbox to find a message from her mother in Iowa, a joke from Aunt Rita, who lived with her mother, spam from travel agencies and credit card companies and a whole bunch of junk mail forwarded to her by Darla. At the very bottom she found a message from someone called Mntnbiker.

Who was that? she wondered, but before the message appeared on her screen, she remembered. *Oh, yeah, the guy from the chat.*

Zachman,
You seemed a little shy the other night, so I thought I'd drop you a line to see if you might be interested in getting to know me via e-mail. I don't usually join chats and think it's pretty hard to decide what people are really like in that forum. Those rooms can get crowded and noisy, and the subjects people talk about can be either boring or a little over the top. Anyway, if you're already involved with someone or you're not interested, no problem. Just thought I'd make contact.
Friends?
John

"Well what do you know," she murmured. "Mntnbiker's name is John." She hit the reply button but before she could type anything, an instant message popped up from Darla.

Catlover: What are you doing tonight, Mags?

Maggie thought about telling Darla she was planning to scour the country for articles of murders like Sarah Ritter's, then decided against it. Darla didn't have the stomach for the gritty details involved with following the cop beat, and Maggie was probably wasting her time, anyway.

Zachman: Just messing around on the net.
Catlover: Anything fun?
Zachman: No.
Catlover: Nick Sorenson talk to you last night?
Zachman: He wasn't in the office.

Catlover: Oh, so you know he was out. You keeping tabs on him now?

Maggie didn't want to admit it, but glancing down the hall toward Nick's desk was becoming a habit.

Zachman: Of course not.
Catlover: I can't believe you don't think he's a babe.

Maggie didn't have to think he was a babe. She *knew* he was.

Zachman: I just don't want him to get too close. He makes me uncomfortable.
Catlover: You need to loosen up, have some fun.
Zachman: What makes you think I'd have fun with him?
Catlover: Are you kidding? Is there any question?

Maggie chuckled.

Zachman: He's too hard-bitten for fun. He's focused, driven.
Catlover: Yeah, and just imagine what it would feel like to have all that raw masculinity turned on you.
Zachman: For what? One night? What good would that do me?
Catlover: Forever the realist, aren't you? Okay, forget Nick. You going to do the dating service?
Zachman: No, I'm going to save up for an air conditioner.

Maggie stretched, feeling the effects of working all week without getting enough sleep.

Zachman: I'd better go. That murder's kept me pumped full of adrenaline since it happened. I'm just now starting to come down.

Catlover: Gee, how do you get all the good stories?

Maggie returned the sarcasm.

Zachman: By leaving all the award-winning baton twirlers to you.

Catlover: Very funny.

Zachman: Sorry.

Catlover: Get some sleep. Zach wakes up awfully early in the morning.

"No kidding," Maggie muttered to herself. She signed off the instant message with a friendly goodbye, then stared at the blank screen addressed to Mntnbiker. Now what? Should she really answer him?

Why not? Anonymity was empowering. If he wrote back and turned out to be a fruitcake, she wouldn't answer him again. If he bothered her, she'd change her e-mail address. It wasn't as if he knew where she lived. After two years in Sacramento without any romantic interludes, she was ready to expand her horizons, and e-mail seemed the perfect forum.

Dear Mntnbiker:

I'd be happy to get to know you, although I'm not sure I'm ready for anything more than friendship.

Big lie there, but she definitely didn't want to sound desperate.

Tell me a little about yourself, who you are, where you live, what you do.

You might remember that I'm a single mom. I have one little boy who's three and a half. I'm 5'5", 115 lbs, have red hair, freckles and green eyes. And if that doesn't scare you off, maybe this will: I work nights as a cop reporter and am currently following a murder. At any given point, my life is filled with the details of abuse, rape and other forms of violence. But in the meantime I try to be an average "girl." I'm a bit of a health nut, but when I'm splurging, I like to eat coffee ice cream and chocolate-covered strawberries (not necessarily together <G>). I also like lying on a warm beach and reading romance novels, probably because what I deal with at work is so harrowing. I like happily-ever-afters. I hate to wait for anything and can't cook a can of soup or sew on a button, but I can change my own oil and mow my own yard.

Now that you probably know more about me than you ever wanted to, it's your turn:)

She signed it simply *Maggie,* hit the Send button, and went onto the Internet, where she quickly forgot about Mntnbiker as she scanned the major newspapers throughout the country, beginning with the *New York Times.* Some of the crime stories were horrible enough to curl her toes, particularly those that involved child molestation or abuse, and it wasn't long before she decided to give up. The violence was making her heartsick, and without the coroner's report, she knew so little about the condition of Sarah Ritter's body that it was difficult to draw any connection between her murder and any others. She was wasting her time, just as she'd thought.

Yawning, she decided to get up early and head to Lowell Atkinson's house with a big bag of donuts and several freshly roasted coffees. A horse came more willingly to a handful of sugar, right? The same might hold true for Lowell.

She climbed into bed but couldn't get to sleep. The murders she'd read about had her spooked. The shadow of the trees outside fell across her carpet, their knotty, intertwining branches sometimes taking on the shape of a man, and she wondered if someone could remove her air conditioner and crawl through the hole it left behind. Then again, they wouldn't even have to go to that much trouble. Because of the heat, there were several windows open in other parts of the house, even a few of the ones without bars, just so she could get a breeze going through.

For a few moments, Maggie held her breath, thinking she heard something rustling, the creak of a footfall in the living room....

*It's nothing,* she told herself. She pulled the sheet up to her chin, resisting the urge to duck her head beneath it, too, and turned her thoughts to other things.

Fortunately—or unfortunately, depending on how she chose to look at it—Nick Sorenson came readily to mind. She tried to imagine what it would feel like to kiss a man like him, someone so completely opposite to Tim, someone who was all fire and no ice. But memories of Rock Tillman kept intruding on her fantasy. The way they'd gotten to know each other that one summer, the hope and attraction she'd felt from the start, and the way he'd treated her once school started—like she had the plague.

So she pretended to be outgoing Darla and quickly forgot all about Rock. Then she had no more problems imagining Nick's kiss—or anything else.

# CHAPTER THREE

BINGO! SHE'D TAKEN the bait. Nick smiled at Maggie's message, finding the personal touches more interesting than he should have. She loved chocolate-covered strawberries and coffee ice cream and sandy beaches. Those preferences, taken together with the fact that she couldn't cook or sew, meant they had a lot in common. Fortunately, he was damn good at ordering out. And he could certainly do worse than hooking up with a woman who knew how to change her own oil.

*Hooking up with Maggie?* Who was he kidding? She thought he was someone he wasn't. Ethically speaking, he couldn't touch her. And he was heading back to Ogden as soon as he caught his killer, anyway.

"Forget about touching her," he growled at himself. Rambo, who'd been sleeping curled up at Nick's feet, raised his head off his paws and cocked his ears. Nick absently patted the dog's head as he tried to think of a response that would draw Maggie into friendship. He needed to get to know her and her habits.

He needed to do his job.

He read her message again. What could he write that would make him look like a soft, sensitive guy? Women loved men who were in touch with their feminine side, didn't they?

Maybe. Only, as a cop, he didn't see himself as having much of a feminine side, and somehow it was important to him that Maggie like him for himself. Maybe it was the challenge of overcoming her initial rejection. Maybe it was something more. But he decided to be as honest as his cover would allow. He told her what he truly liked, what he hated and what he dreamed about. Then he sent the message. She might have turned him down when he'd asked her out before, but he was hoping "John" would be able to slip beneath her defenses.

"MOMMY, I'M AWAKE!"

Maggie squinted at the round face leaning over hers and groaned. "Zach, it's not even light yet."

"Can I watch cartoons-s-s?" he added.

Maggie smiled at his lisp, longing for the day Zach would be able to work the television without her assistance. Then she thought of how fast he was growing up and regretted the fleeting wish. At three years old, he was at the perfect stage— out of diapers, cribs, and high chairs, but still cuddly and generous with his hugs.

Dragging herself out of bed, she hauled him into her arms for a big kiss, then deposited him on the couch in front of Disney's *Ducktales* while she started the coffeemaker and put a frozen waffle in the toaster. It was actually later than she'd realized; when she opened the blinds, she saw that the sun was already up. She needed to get showered so she could begin her siege of Atkinson's house.

"Hungry?" she asked Zach.

He didn't answer. He was already engrossed in his cartoons, so she prepared his waffle with peanut butter the way he liked and brought it to him on a tray.

"I'm going to have a shower, okay, buddy?"

"Okay." Silence, then, "Mommy?"

"Hmm?"

"I'll be right here," he said, digging in to his waffle.

Maggie ruffled his hair, then hurried to her bedroom, but

before she turned on the shower and stripped off her night-gown, she checked her e-mail to see if Mntnbiker had written back.

Sure enough, there was a message from him, right at the top of the list.

Dear Maggie—
You sound beautiful, and sweet.

Beautiful? How did he get beautiful out of what she'd sent him? Or sweet? This guy was either an eternal optimist or extremely lonely, but despite that, the flattery felt good.

As for me, I like mountain biking, sailing, sand volleyball and legal thrillers. I hate spinach, regardless of its food value, clueless drivers and people who try to convince the rest of the world that men and women have to be the same to be equal. I like our differences.

I grew up in a large Catholic family of three sisters and two brothers, a stay-at-home mom and a father who was manager of a large copper mine in Utah before he retired about four years ago. My parents were strict, but we knew they loved us, which has probably saved everyone a fortune in therapy. Right now, my parents are hoping I'll find a nice girl and settle down to have a bunch of kids; but don't let that worry you. My job is pretty demanding. I doubt I'll be getting married any time soon—

Mntnbiker: Hi, Maggie.

Maggie blinked at the blue box that had suddenly appeared on her screen. Mntnbiker was sending her an instant message. She felt a moment's panic because she'd been out of the dating game for so long, then shook it off. She wasn't sixteen anymore. She wasn't that girl with braces and clothes so well made they'd last a century, and this guy was a total stranger. She didn't need to impress him. She didn't even know where he lived.

Zachman: Hi, John.

Mntnbiker: Did you get my message?

Zachman: I was just reading it. I have to admit I like the part about me being beautiful and sweet the best, although it would certainly have been more convincing if you'd seen a picture of me first.

Mntnbiker: I have a good imagination.

Zachman: Then send me a photo because I don't have a clue what you look like.

Mntnbiker: Does it matter?

Zachman: I'm curious.

Mntnbiker: I'm 6'2", 195 lbs., brown hair, brown eyes.

Zachman: Do you still live in Utah?

Mntnbiker: Yes.

Zachman: How old are you?

Mntnbiker: 33.

Zachman: Divorced?

Mntnbiker: No. Never married.

Zachman: Any close calls?

Mntnbiker: I've been engaged once.

Zachman: To the woman you mentioned in the chat?

Mntnbiker: Yeah.

Zachman: How long ago was that?

Mntnbiker: Three years.

Maggie tapped a fingernail on her front tooth, thinking. She hated to come on too strong, but she didn't want to waste her time with a guy who was still in love with someone else. Emboldened by the anonymity of e-mail communication, she decided to get right to the point.

Zachman: Are you over her?

Mntnbiker: I think so. Are you always so direct?

Zachman: Usually. I'm a journalist, remember? It's my job to ask tough questions. So, do you ever see her anymore?

Mntnbiker: No, she's married.

Zachman: I'm reading between the lines here, but the break-up sounds like it was pretty rough on you.

Mntnbiker: I wish I had taken the brunt of it. Unfortunately, I think it was rougher on her. How about you? Anyone special in your life?

Zachman: Just my son, Zach.

Mntnbiker: Tell me what he's like.

Maggie stared, disbelieving, at Mntnbiker's words. He wanted to know about Zach? For some reason, she hadn't expected him to ask about her son. Maybe Tim's attitude had colored her view of what most men were like. Maybe Mntnbiker—John—was different.

Smiling, she told him that Zach had a lisp, that he was blond and big for his age and that he loved basketball. The two of them played in the backyard all the time, using a pint-sized hoop and ball. Zach could already dribble.

Mntnbiker: He sounds like a great kid. What happened to his father?

Zachman: After I got pregnant, Tim demanded I get an abortion. He said he wasn't ready, after all. But I refused to terminate the pregnancy, and that was pretty much the last straw in our relationship.

Mntnbiker: What does Tim do?

Zachman: He's a podiatrist now. When we were married, he was going to school.

Mntnbiker: You supported him?

Zachman: Yeah.

Mntnbiker: As a journalist?

Zachman: Not exactly.

Maggie hesitated. She wasn't proud of this part of her life. She'd sold out, plain and simple, and she'd done it because Tim had asked her to. He had a way of making her career seem inconsequential next to his and, for a while, she'd actually bought into it.

Zachman: In order to get on at the paper in L.A., I would've had to intern for several years, which doesn't pay anything. We needed money for Tim's schooling, so he convinced me to hire on at one of the tabloids. We weren't living too far from Hollywood, so our location was perfect for that sort of thing.

Mntnbiker: You sound like you regret it.

Zachman: I do. It certainly wasn't the kind of writing I'd aspired to in college, but Tim can be very persuasive. He craved success more than anything, and he had a plan to achieve it. The only catch was that his plan depended on me making a sizable salary. Kids weren't initially part of the deal, and he wasn't happy he'd relented on that.

Mntnbiker: So is he successful?

Zachman: I guess. He has his practice, a new wife, a fancy car and a huge house.

Mntnbiker: And you have...

Zachman: An old house that needs central air and paint, a job that can eventually lead me in the direction I want to go, and Zach. Zach is worth all the cars and houses and money in the world. I actually feel kind of sorry for Tim. He's missing out on so much.

Mntnbiker: Don't feel sorry for him. He probably doesn't

deserve it. Does he pay you child support, have any relationship with Zach at all?

Zachman: No. He never really wanted Zach and wasn't interested in visitation rights, so I didn't have the nerve to ask for child support. I thought it was better to make a clean break and to do what I can for Zach on my own.

Mntnbiker: What did you ever see in this guy?

Zachman: We met in college. He was driven, ambitious, successful, confident. I fell in love with him almost right away. I fell out of love with him shortly after the wedding, for the same reasons.

Mntnbiker: And now? Are you seeing anyone?

Zachman: Oh, yeah. Lots of guys. On weekends, they form a line at my door.

Mntnbiker: How long's the wait?

For the right man? Maggie sighed in longing. There'd be no wait for Mr. Right, but she didn't have any hope of finding him soon.

"Mommy, you doing your e-mail?" Zach interrupted, coming into the room.

"Yeah, babe."

"Can I have s-s-some more milk?"

"Just a minute, honey." When her son drew close enough, she pulled him onto her lap and shifted him to one side as she considered her response to Mntnbiker.

Zachman: It depends.

Mntnbiker: On looks or personality?

Zachman: Definitely personality.

Mntnbiker: How am I doing so far?

She chuckled.

Zachman: Better than most, but we probably live a thousand miles apart.

Mntnbiker: We might live closer than you think.

Zachman: What if we do?

Mntnbiker: Who knows? Maybe we'll meet someday. Maybe I'll show up with chocolate-covered strawberries and coffee ice cream and whisk you away to the beach.

Zachman: Are you asking for my address?

Mntnbiker: No, because I don't want you to give that kind of information out over the Internet, to anybody. Ever. It's too dangerous.

Maggie raised an intrigued brow. This John guy seemed nice—caring and responsible. Maybe he was someone she could really like.

Zachman: I can trust you, though, right?

Mntnbiker: With your life.

Zachman: What do you do for a living?

Mntnbiker: I guess you could say I'm sort of a security guard.

A security guard? That wouldn't appear too impressive on a resumé. Tim would have laughed and told her she was stupid to befriend a $5/hour rent-a-cop. What kind of breadwinner could he be?

Good thing she and Tim had never measured success the same way. Good thing she wasn't looking for a meal ticket. She could earn her own money. She might never be rich, but she'd get by. She wanted a man who cared about life and love and didn't forget the simple things. Someone who valued her above his new BMW.

I'm having a good time, she wrote, marveling at the fact that she really was, but I have to go to work right now. Can we talk later?

Mntnbiker: You have to go in on a Saturday?

Zachman: I usually work graveyard, Tuesday through Saturday, but this week I traded with the guy who has the day shift on Wednesday, which gave me last night off and enough sleep to tackle some things I have to get done.

Mntnbiker: Like chase down that story you mentioned? The murder?

Zachman: Yeah.

Mntnbiker: How does a journalist track a story like that?

Zachman: It's not easy. Right now, the county coroner isn't being very helpful. He won't give me any information on the body that was found last week, so I'm going to head over to his house with breakfast and see if I have better luck.

Mntnbiker: Maybe the police told him not to say anything.

Zachman: I'm sure they did.

Mntnbiker: But you're a reporter. You're not going to let that stop you, huh?

Zachman: Sort of. It's my job to get the truth.

Mntnbiker: What if there's a good reason for keeping you out of the loop?

Zachman: I'm not sure I'd buy it. Sometimes the police try to manipulate the media, just to make the department look good.

Mntnbiker: Everybody has a different perspective, I guess. Are you going to send me a message later?

Zachman: If you want.

Mntnbiker: I want. Do you work tonight?

Zachman: Yeah, I start at ten.

Mntnbiker: Then log on around seven o'clock, and I'll take you on a cyber-date.

Zachman: What's that?

Mntnbiker: You'll see—I hope. I'm making this up as I go along.

Maggie typed LOL, the symbol for "laughing out loud," then, teasing, told him she insisted on going Dutch. After that, she signed off.

MAGGIE HAD PLANNED to have her seventy-one-year-old neighbor, who normally watched Zach, come and sit with him while she visited the Atkinsons. But a denture crisis sent Mrs. Gruber off to the dentist, and Maggie decided that taking her son along might actually work to her advantage. She certainly couldn't look too threatening with an endearing three-year-old in tow, not when he was carrying a box of donuts and she was toting a tray of coffee and hot chocolate. Besides, she *liked* having him with her.

She parked beneath one of the big, leafy trees that lined most of 36th Avenue, turned down the cop radio in her car and surveyed Lowell Atkinson's house. She'd always admired it. It wasn't large by modern standards but it definitely had class. Small, detached garage, well-tended shrubs, lots of flowers, big shady trees, and a new coat of paint on everything, including the fence. Maggie thought she might like to live in this neighborhood, if she could ever afford it. It was the kind of place where people bought and stayed. They mowed their own lawns, drove family cars and remembered to wave at the neighbors.

"Can I have another one?" Zach asked, lifting the lid and eyeing the donuts as she cut the engine. His face and hands were already covered with chocolate icing. Maggie considered his almost-clean shirt and decided not to tempt fate a second time.

"I think we've done enough damage already, buddy." She retrieved a napkin from the glove box and did her best to spit-polish him, the way her grandmother used to do with her. When his patience ran out half a second later and he started squirming too much to make further improvements, she said, "Let's go."

Tall and willowy, Mary Ann Atkinson answered the door in her robe, but she looked as though she was in the process of getting ready, not getting up. Her dark hair was brushed back off her face and she'd already applied mascara and violet shadow to her brown eyes. "Hi, Maggie. Lowell said you'd be over today."

"He did?"

"Yeah. Would you like to come in?"

Maggie didn't answer right away. She was too busy wondering how Lowell might have known to expect her. She was a reporter, and he'd been dodging her questions. He could have made a simple assumption, but it was a little surprising that he'd been so specific about the day.

"How did Lowell know I was coming?" she asked.

Mary Ann smiled. "You didn't call him?"

"No. Is he here?"

"I'm afraid not, but that's no reason to let those donuts go to waste." She stepped back. "Are you coming in?"

"Sure. Zach would love to see Katie. It's been almost a year since we had that picnic."

Katie, Mary Ann's five-year-old, peered shyly through the railing of the balcony above as Mary Ann showed them inside. Mary Ann waved her daughter down and led them through a comfortable-looking brown-and-green living room, where her six-month-old son was sleeping in a battery-powered swing, to a large screened-in porch. They sat at an iron table on chintz-upholstered seats while Katie hung back, regarding Zach with wariness. Her reserve vanished, how-

ever, the moment he caught sight of her tricycle and appro-
priated it for his own use.

Mary Ann put a halt to her daughter's indignant cries and
found a smaller riding toy for Zach. Then she and Maggie
watched their children play on the flagstone patio.

"The weather's been great, hasn't it?" Mary Ann asked.
"I love this time of year."

"It's going to be a hot summer," Maggie replied.

"Every summer is hot in Sacramento."

"I'm finding that out."

"Did you get air conditioning? I remember you spent last
summer without it."

"I decided to save two thousand bucks and bought a fan
instead."

Mary Ann laughed. "You should have saved the twenty
bucks you spent on the fan because it won't be nearly enough
in another two weeks."

"Even after I get an air conditioner I'm hoping to open
my windows at night and use the fan to keep my electric bills
down, at least on the nights I'm home."

"Then you're a braver woman than I am. After that Ritter
murder, I'm keeping my doors and windows locked."

Maggie set the cups of hot chocolate aside to cool for the
kids and selected a tall Starbucks cup from her cardboard
tray for Mary Ann. Then she opened the donuts. "Don't let
that scare you. Most murders are committed by a friend or
relative, so unless someone close to you is unstable, you're
pretty safe." She selected a chocolate cake donut and sat
back to eat it. "In Sarah Ritter's case, I'm guessing it was
her husband. She was probably going to sue for divorce or
something, so he freaked out and stabbed her with a kitchen
knife."

Mary Ann helped herself to a maple bar. "Except that she
wasn't killed with a kitchen knife. The murder weapon

was sharper than that, the grooves different, more like a hunting knife."

Maggie nearly choked on her first bite of donut. "What?" she said, coughing.

Mary Ann sent a furtive glance at her daughter and took a sip of coffee. "Lowell sometimes brings his work home with him, just like anybody else."

"So the autopsy's finished?"

"Of course. It was finished the same day they found the body. Lowell didn't get home until almost midnight."

"And? Did he find anything unusual?"

Mary Ann hesitated. "My husband left so he wouldn't have to talk to you. He told me to play dumb."

"I still don't understand how he knew I was going to show up here."

"Someone called. I thought it was you."

"Who else could it have been?"

"Someone from the force, maybe?"

Her appetite gone, Maggie pushed her donut aside. No one on the force knew her plans for this morning. How could they have alerted Lowell? Had they been following her and guessed where she was heading? Why would they waste the manpower? Mendez must have realized his gaffe the other night and had let the others know. "What's going on, Mary Ann?" she asked. "Lowell's never felt he had to dodge me before."

"He says the police are really worried about this case. They don't want him to say anything to the press."

"It was a brutal murder that needs to be solved as soon as possible, but why all the secrecy?"

"I don't know. To tell you the truth, I think it's wrong. I think people should know. The women of Sacramento should be warned to lock their doors and windows at night and to set an alarm, if they have one."

Maggie studied Mary Ann's agitated face. "Is it that bad?"

She nodded.

"Are you going to tell me why?"

With a sigh, Mary Ann lowered her voice so the children couldn't hear. "That poor woman had her tongue cut out," she said, her gaze pinning Maggie to her seat as effectively as her words. "Lowell said he's never seen anything like it. He said whoever did it knew how to use a knife."

Maggie cringed. "A hunter or a surgeon, maybe?"

"A serial killer, a wacko," Mary Ann replied. "And the most frightening thing of all is that this guy has already struck six times. The first victim was a woman in Boston."

So Maggie's hunch had been right. She hadn't found what she was looking for online last night, but she hadn't searched very long, and she hadn't known what she needed to track down—a monster who removed his victims' tongues. That was certainly enough to earmark a murderer. "When?" she asked.

"Ten months ago, and he still hasn't been caught."

# CHAPTER FOUR

"SO THE BLUE FIBERS are from some sort of blanket?" Nick propped the phone on his shoulder so he could thumb through the pictures of the murder victims again. They'd all been killed away from where they'd been found, and they'd all been transported, wrapped in a blanket for the journey. Evidently, Sarah Ritter had been no different.

"That's what the tests say." Tony Caruso's Jersey accent carried across the line even though he'd lived in Virginia and worked at the FBI's crime lab in Washington DC for almost twenty years.

"What kind of blanket?"

There was some paper shuffling on the other end. Caruso covered the mouthpiece to speak to someone else, then came back on the line. "Sorry about that. A new one, unfortunately. Otherwise, we might have had more luck finding something else, a strand of hair maybe, to help us. I'm still hoping for a DNA profile on this guy. But, as it stands, we know only that she was wrapped in a cheap, fuzzy blanket, the kind you can buy almost anywhere."

"What about the other fibers? The tan ones?"

"They're consistent with the kind of carpet found in the trunk of most cars, usually the cheaper models."

"So if this guy is a doctor, he's not a very successful one. He's not using a BMW or a Mercedes to haul bodies around."

"I'd guess he's driving an economy car," Tony agreed. "He could have purchased it for just this purpose."

"Maybe." Nick pushed his reading glasses up and rubbed his eyes. Economy cars were a dime a dozen. Cheap fuzzy blankets did nothing to narrow the field of his search, either. When was Dr. Dan going to slip up and make a mistake that would really tell him something? "Did you find anything in what the coroner scraped out from beneath Sarah Ritter's nails?"

"No skin or anything like that. If she put up a fight, she didn't manage to scratch him. There was soil in what you sent, but it was consistent with the samples you included from her yard. I'm guessing she had a garden of some sort. Am I right?"

"She'd just planted tomatoes." He remembered seeing them in the back, along the fence, when he'd visited the house to search for evidence of forced entry, evidence he'd never found. The tomato plants had been tender and young and vulnerable, just like Sarah Ritter's son. The memory of the shock and grief apparent in his small face made Nick clench his jaw. He had to bring down Dr. Dan. Before he killed again...

"There was also some sand," Tony went on.

"What kind of sand?"

"Rocky and uneven. The kind that usually appears on the shore of a lake, or maybe along the banks of a river."

*...we shall soon see what the river turns up...*

"There're two rivers that aren't far from where the body was found. I'll send you soil samples from each. Maybe we can get a match."

"I'll be expecting them."

The American River originated somewhere in the Sierras, descended through the foothills and cut through the Sacramento suburbs to meet the Sacramento River, which came from the north to downtown, near Discovery Park. The American River had something like thirty miles of bike path along one bank and was by far the more accessible. If Nick had to choose, he'd guess Dr. Dan had killed Sarah Ritter somewhere along it. Down by the water, there were plenty of places where screams might not be heard, where foliage would easily conceal two people. Especially at night. Car bridges spanned the river, but they were miles apart, and the bicyclists who used the path so religiously by day were gone once the sun went down. A murderer could conceivably move, undetected, from car to bike path to footpath and back again—with a woman or a body. The only question was why. Why didn't Dr. Dan simply kill her and dump her body in the river instead of dragging it downtown?

The lock jiggled at the front door, and Rambo jumped to his feet, ears forward, tail wagging. A glance at the clock and Rambo's eager response told Nick it was Justin, the thirteen-year-old neighbor boy Nick paid to feed and walk Rambo every day. Justin filled in for potty breaks when Nick had to work long hours, too. Fortunately the pair had taken to each other right away.

"Anything else?" he asked Tony, waving as the boy came in.

"That footprint you found in Lola Fillmore's flower bed? The size 12? It was a Nike knock-off."

Justin retrieved Rambo's leash from the kitchen and fastened it to his collar. "We'll be back in about an hour," he whispered.

Nick acknowledged his words with a nod and the door closed behind the boy and the dog. "What about wear, Tony?"

"There wasn't any. The shoes were brand-new."

Nick slammed his fist down onto the desk. "Dammit! Can't we get a break?"

"Sorry, I should have called the moment we identified the shoes, but I knew it wasn't going to help you, anyway. Not without wear."

"How expensive were they?"

"You can get 'em for around twenty-five dollars at the cheaper stores."

There was a long silence while Nick sank into his chair and digested this disappointing information. Everything about Dr. Dan reeked of *common*. They'd found nothing unique or unusual enough to track.

"You think Dr. Dan is a poor man?" Tony asked, surprising Nick out of his thoughts. Tony was a technician and usually too busy to involve himself in conjecture. That was for the field agents, who sometimes had to take risks based on instinct alone.

"No, I think he's smart," Nick answered. "He's taking his time and doing everything right. What I need is a witness." He sighed. "What I'm afraid I'm going to get is another victim."

THE FIRST TIME Nick remembered his date with Maggie, it was nearly five o'clock. He'd spent the day gathering the samples he'd promised the lab and combing through the statements in each victim's file, comparing and contrasting them with those he'd collected on Sarah Ritter. He had a whole chalkboard full of similarities and differences. But now, sitting in the sparsely furnished apartment the agency had rented for him with only Rambo as company, eating a late lunch of Chinese takeout, he was eager to get his mind off Dr. Dan's sick deeds. He wanted to replace the blood he saw, even when he closed his eyes, with the sweetness of Maggie's smile.

Fleetingly, he wondered how she'd reacted when Lowell Atkinson had stonewalled her this morning, but he felt no guilt for interfering. He was only doing his job. He didn't mind letting Maggie dig up something he didn't already know, but he was holding his own cards close to his chest. The last thing he needed was the press divulging everything the investigation uncovered, keeping Dr. Dan one step ahead of him.

Besides, Nick thought, finishing his chow mein and setting it aside, if she ever learned his true identity, she'd have much bigger things to forgive him for than placing a call to Atkinson.

His cop radio hissed and sputtered in the background as one of the dispatchers announced a possible robbery attempt. Rambo barked at the noise, but Nick ignored it. He used the radio to keep a pulse on what was happening around him, but listening to it was second nature to him now. It took no energy or focus.

Plugging his laptop into the phone line, he signed on to the Internet to shop for interesting places to take Maggie on their date. He considered having her join him at a site where they could watch a movie together and communicate via instant messaging. But he knew it would fall far short of the real experience. There'd be no giant screen, no smell of popcorn and no Maggie sitting next to him. He needed to take her somewhere more exotic. Knowing that he had no hope of getting an arm around her to see if her skin was really as soft as it looked, no hope of even a chaste kiss good-night, he needed to find a place that was fascinating enough to distract him—and intrigue her.

Twenty minutes later, he found it.

"MOMMY, WHEN'S-S-S Mrs-s-s. Goober coming over?"

"Mrs. Gruber?" Maggie corrected. "Soon." She was sitting at the kitchen table, preoccupied with the various newspaper articles she'd copied off the Internet a few hours earlier. According to what she'd found, six unsolved murders reported over the past year had enough common characteristics for investigators to assume they were committed by the same person. The victims were all Caucasian women ranging in age from twenty-four to thirty-nine. They'd been stabbed repeatedly with something resembling a butcher knife. And they'd had their tongues removed after death.

That last gruesome detail was as good as a signature—and was more than enough to make Maggie feel ill. What kind of sick bastard was this guy? It terrified her to think of him circulating among the people of her own city. He could be the guy smoking outside the café where she bought her coffee each morning. He could be her newspaper carrier or the house painter down the street. He could be anyone. And it appeared he could go anywhere. One victim was murdered in Massachusetts, one in Missouri, two in Colorado and two in Washington state. As if what she'd found wasn't unnerving enough, she noted that his last victim, before Sarah Ritter, had been a reporter for the *Seattle Independent*.

"Gads," she whispered. "What are we facing here?"

"Mommy! When's Mrs-s-s. Goober comin' over?" This time the frustration in her son's voice finally broke Maggie's concentration. Crayons were scattered across the table next to her, along with several scribbled pictures. She'd tried to entertain Zach while she worked, but he was bored with it all.

She glanced at her watch. Where had the time gone? Her "date" with John was in twenty minutes and she still needed to feed Zach.

"Where is everyone? All the lights you got on in this place, you'd think electricity didn't cost money." Mrs. Gruber shuffled into the kitchen, an overnight case heavy on her arm, but probably no heavier than the industrial-sized purse she carried in the other hand. Maggie had no idea what was in her purse, but she knew the contents of the suitcase by heart. She watched Mrs. Gruber pack it up each morning. A bag of gumdrops—her diet staple and probably the culprit in her denture disaster—a pair of reading glasses, a jar of cold cream, a toothbrush, a hair net and an entire medicine cabinet of vitamins. She'd tried to get Mrs. Gruber to leave her things in the guest bathroom, but her neighbor felt more comfortable carting it all back and forth. So Maggie had given up trying to convince her. Mrs. Gruber was a fantastic baby-sitter—more like a grandma to Zach, really—but she was accustomed to certain things. She always let herself in, said whatever came to mind and considered it her personal mission in life to see that nothing was ever wasted. She collected aluminum foil, washed and reused disposable flatware, birthday candles and plastic bags.

"Mrs-s-s. Goober! Mrs-s-s. Goober!" In his excitement to see her, Zach launched himself from the kitchen table and nearly tackled the old woman.

Mrs. Gruber told him to settle down and mind his manners, but her gruffness did nothing to stifle Zach's enthusiasm. He knew she loved him.

She held him close, then delved into her overnight bag. "Look at this," she told him. "I brought you something."

It would have been a rare night had she *not* brought Zach a small present—a pretty rock for their collection, a quarter for his piggy bank, a new toothbrush. Maggie filed the disturbing newspaper articles away, planning to take them to the office with her, before tossing a look over her shoulder to see what Mrs. Gruber had brought him today.

"Pajamas-s-s with a cape!" Zach shrieked, immediately stripping off his clothes.

A widow who lived alone, Mrs. Gruber survived on social security and what Maggie paid her. She had no business spending her money on Zach, and Maggie often told her so. But that didn't change a thing.

"He's getting too tall for his football pajamas," she explained, a defensive note creeping into her voice when Maggie cocked a brow at her. "And they were on sale."

"I'll pay you back."

Mrs. Gruber scowled and helped Zach pull the top of his new pajamas over his head. "They didn't cost enough to worry about."

"That's what you say about everything you buy him." Maggie started rummaging through the cupboards, wondering what to feed Zach, but Mrs. Gruber nudged her aside.

"What are you lookin' for?"

"Something for dinner."

"I brought dinner. Zach loves my spaghetti and meatballs." Before Maggie could respond, she added, "And don't tell me not to bring food. It was leftovers. What did you want me to do, let it go to waste?"

She took out a plastic container with enough spaghetti and meatballs to feed an army, and Maggie knew darn well that it wasn't leftovers. She'd made it for them, probably today.

"You're spoiling us," Maggie said, shaking her head.

Mrs. Gruber harumphed. "It's just leftovers," she said again.

"What are you doing here so early?" Maggie asked, changing the subject. "I don't have to be at work until ten."

"You were gone most of the day. I thought you might want to take a nap. You don't get enough sleep. You don't eat good. It's going to catch up with you one day."

Maggie smiled. Mrs. Gruber foretold her physical collapse on a daily basis. She was too thin. She worked too hard. She should be getting out more, making more friends, eating more vegetables. Today Maggie would've liked to take her up on the nap, but she wasn't about to postpone her meeting with John. She'd been looking forward to it all afternoon. "I can't sleep," she said. "I have a…date."

Mrs. Gruber's face brightened beneath the tight, perfect rows of short, bluish curls. "Is it that nice garbageman who takes my trash out to the curb each week? I've told you to introduce yourself to him. He'll probably start getting your trash now, too."

Maggie didn't tell her that there was no nice garbageman. She lugged the trash cans out for both of them when she got home from work on Tuesday mornings. "No, it's someone I met online."

"On what?"

Maggie laughed. "Online. On the Internet. We met at a chat, and now he's e-mailing me."

Mrs. Gruber propped one age-spotted hand on a bony hip. "He's sending you messages? That's *it?*"

"Well, no, not exactly. He's taking me on a cyber-date tonight."

"But you've never seen him? Never heard his voice?"

"Nope."

"You're going to stay in your house and he's going to stay in his?"

"Yep."

"That's too bad," she said. "You can't neck with a man online."

MAGGIE LEFT ZACH EATING spaghetti and playing Candyland with Mrs. Gruber and hurried to her bedroom so she wouldn't be late for her date. She couldn't believe she was actually nervous about "seeing" John again. What did she have to be nervous about? It was a cyber-date. It was nothing.

Her modem screeched through the familiar pattern of tones as Maggie hooked up to the Internet. She'd added John to her buddy list and expected to find his screen name listed there, but a quick glance told her he wasn't online yet. She found a message from him instead.

Maggie—
When you're ready for tonight, just click on the link below.
See you there.
John

The link John had sent consisted of a bunch of letters and numbers highlighted in blue. Maggie had expected another instant messaging session as their date, but apparently John had something else in mind. Pointing her mouse on the link, she clicked, and a moment later the picture of a beautiful island village filled her screen. Then a voice came through the speakers of her computer.

"Hi, Maggie. You said you like sand. Welcome to paradise."

Was that John's voice? she wondered. If so, she wished she'd been able to hear it more clearly. Her speakers weren't the best. Whoever it was sounded tinny and unnatural.

Mntnbiker: Are you always so punctual, or dare I hope you're excited to see me?

The words appeared in an instant message box in the upper left of Maggie's screen, making her smile. John had arrived.

Zachman: Where are we? This looks great.

Mntnbiker: We're vacationing in the Caribbean. Have you ever been here before?

Briefly Maggie remembered Tim and his many promises. "After I graduate, we'll…" She'd worked her heart out to put him through school, but it was his new wife, Lucy, who was cashing in on the trips to Europe, Hawaii and Asia they'd planned to take. Or, rather, Lucy was cashing in *if* Tim actually took the time off. Knowing him, he never would. In his mind, the good life was always just beyond the next professional hurdle.

Zachman: I've never been anywhere, except Boston, to visit Tim's family when we were married, and Iowa to visit mine.

Mntnbiker: Then you're going to like this. Click the start button.

Maggie did as he said and heard a new voice through her speakers, a woman with a heavy Caribbean accent. Reggae music played in the background.

"Welcome to the beautiful island of Barbados in the East Caribbean, a land of warm seas and fertile earth, a tropical paradise unlike any other…."

A video tour showed shimmering aquamarine seas, white sandy beaches, dark-skinned locals, some wearing dreadlocks, and lush wet countryside. Through instant messaging, John pointed out sights along the way and summarized the history of the island, which was something the guide didn't cover. Maggie was thoroughly impressed.

Zachman: This is really cool! I love it. How do you know so much about the sugar plantations of Barbados?
Mntnbiker: I worked there for a while.

*As a security guard?*

Zachman: Then you moved back to Utah?
Mntnbiker: Yeah.

Maggie felt a twinge of excitement at the thought that they could meet if they wanted to. Twelve hours by car wasn't exactly close, but it wasn't across the country, either.

Zachman: I live in California.
Mntnbiker: Is that where you were born?
Zachman: No, I was born in Iowa.
Mntnbiker: Did you grow up there?
Zachman: Until I graduated from high school. Then I left for UCLA.
Mntnbiker: Is that where you met Tim?
Zachman: Yeah. We were married right before I got my Bachelor's in journalism.
Mntnbiker: Tell me about your family.

Maggie told him about Ronnie and her mother, the only family she had left. When prompted by a few more questions, she shared what it was like growing up with a brother who was ten years older, what it was like having parents who were already forty-five when she was born and hadn't been planning on any more children. She told him she'd been the apple of her father's eye—until he died of a heart attack a year before she married Tim. She even admitted the terrible guilt she felt for going to UCLA and leaving him behind, how painful it was that she didn't get to see him before he died. She'd received the bad news by telephone, returned for the funeral, and that was it. In her first great bid to make something of herself, she'd lost the one person who'd given her a firm foundation on which to build.

Mntnbiker: I'm sure he knew you loved him, Maggie, and that's all that matters. I bet he was very proud of his little girl.

Maggie couldn't help the tears that slipped from the corners of her eyes at that statement. Her father had never seen her as the ugly duckling she was—the acne, the skinniness, the knobby knees. He'd looked at her and seen a swan from the moment she was born.

Zachman: At least he wasn't around to see my marriage fail.

Mntnbiker: That wouldn't have lowered his opinion of you.

Zachman: I hope not. I just wish he'd lived long enough to know Zach.

Mntnbiker: I'm sure that would've been the highlight of his life. Where is Zach today? What do you do with him while you work?

Ah, a happier subject. Maggie told John about Mrs. Gruber and her spaghetti, the balls of aluminum foil, the sweater she wore over her dresses even in the heat of the summer, and the old Cadillac she drove without much concern for inconsequential things like "right of way." By the time she was done, John indicated he was laughing by the LOL—laughing out loud—symbol, and she felt surprisingly close to him.

Zachman: You seem like a good man. I'm glad we met.

There was a longer pause than usual.

Mntnbiker: I'm not always sure I'm a good man, but I'm glad we met, too.

Zachman: Do you have a scanner?

Mntnbiker: No.

Zachman: Then would you go to Kinko's or some place and scan me a picture of yourself?

Mntnbiker: Why? I thought looks didn't matter.

Zachman: They don't, really. I just want something to imagine when I close my eyes and think of you. I know you're tall and definitely not overweight. And you have dark hair and eyes. But that's it. Aren't you curious what I look like?

There was another pause, this one even longer than the first.

Zachman: John? Are you still there?

Mntnbiker: Sorry. Listen, I have to run, but I'll write you later. Okay?

Maggie frowned at her screen. They'd been together online for ninety minutes, but there was still a good hour before she had to leave for work. She wasn't ready to let him go and couldn't figure out why he'd suddenly turned cold.

*Jeez, I'm lonelier than I realized,* she thought. *Now I'm clinging to a man I've never actually met.* She groaned and smacked her forehead. *Snap out of it, Mag!*

Zachman: Sure. I have to get to work, anyway.

WHEN MAGGIE ARRIVED at the office, she found Nick Sorenson slouched in her chair, his legs stretched out in front of him, his eyes on her pictures of Zach.

Surprised, she drew to a halt and gaped at him over the partition that divided her small space from everyone else's. "What are you doing at my desk?"

He smiled and stood. "Waiting for you."

"For me?"

He handed her a slip of paper. Maggie glanced at it and immediately recognized the scrawl—Jorge, the cop reporter who had the shift before hers—but she didn't take time to read his note. Nick was talking, explaining.

"Jorge's son is having his fourteenth birthday tonight. Whole family's going to be there. He wanted to take the call but couldn't miss the party. So it's your story now."

"If I want it." She forced her gaze away from Nick's rugged face and looked more closely at Jorge's note.

*Police on their way to the burger stand at Broadway and 14th Avenue. Drive-by shooting. Don't know details. Call just came in.*

She raised her brows in speculation. Broadway and 14th. Oak Park. It was the roughest area in Sacramento.

"Let me guess," he said. "You want it."

She eyed him narrowly. "Let *me* guess," she said. "You're the only photographer available for this."

His grin showed white teeth contrasted against a day's beard. "Yep. Don't you trust me to get the pics right?"

Maggie didn't trust him, period. She drew a deep breath,

trying to put a finger on what was bothering her tonight. Nick had invaded her personal space, which was presumptuous, even rude, especially since he was still so new. But it was more than that. He acted as though he was in complete control, even in a place where he should've been out of his element. He was obviously someone who enjoyed the upper hand, she decided, someone who was used to having it, like Rock Tillman. But after Tim, Maggie had promised herself that she'd never let a man take control of her life again. And she meant that. Any man who stepped on her toes was going to hear about it.

"Just one thing," she said.

"What's that?" He watched her from beneath thick dark lashes, the perfect frame for the unusual color of his eyes. Not quite brown, not quite gold, they were somewhere in between, like tortoiseshell.

"The next time you feel the need to wait for me, do it at your own desk."

Maggie had expected him to bristle at the firmness in her voice and was prepared to stand her ground. But he only chuckled softly. "Anything you say, Maggie."

Her name sounded strangely intimate on his lips. She almost demanded he call her Mrs. Russell but immediately realized how silly that would be. Everyone in the office called her Maggie. Her gray-haired ex-mother-in-law was *Mrs*. Russell.

He brushed past her and headed down the aisle, and for a moment, Maggie swam in his scent. Whether it was his aftershave, soap, cologne or shampoo, she didn't know, but whatever the combination, it was more evocative than she would have expected and caused a butterfly-like sensation in her stomach.

"Oh, God. Not Nick Sorenson," she muttered to herself,

trailing him at a distance. "Think John. Nice, tender, sensitive John, who tells you your father would be proud of you, who takes you on creative and thoughtful cyber-dates." Just because he wouldn't send her a picture didn't mean he looked like a monster. He was just more enlightened than most. He understood how little looks truly mattered in the overall scheme of things. She understood that, too.

So why, then, was she having such a difficult time keeping her eyes averted from the physical perfection of Nick Sorenson's butt?

## CHAPTER FIVE

THE VICTIM WAS a young black male, probably no more than fifteen.

Maggie stared down at the limp form sprawled on the sidewalk, watching as the paramedics worked to resuscitate him, and couldn't help imagining his mother's grief. No doubt the poor woman would want to know how her child's life could end this way. What had happened? Why?

They were the same questions Maggie would have to ask but for different reasons. She would ask because it was her job.

"This kind of tragedy makes me sick," she told Nick, who was standing next to her.

"Gangs," he replied, a frown tugging down the corners of his mouth.

Maggie clenched her fists at her side and prayed silently that the boy would live. *Come on, come back,* she chanted, *you should have another sixty years.*

But it was only a few minutes later that the two paramedics rocked back on their haunches and stared at each other in silent communication. It was over. He was gone. There was nothing else they could do. Their faces grim, they loaded the boy on a stretcher and transferred him to the ambulance. The motor rumbled, the siren wailed, the lights flashed and soon only a dark puddle remained beneath the streetlights, along with four firemen, their bright red truck, and a gathering crowd of spectators.

*Distance yourself,* Maggie commanded. She couldn't think about the violence, the senseless suffering, the mother's bewilderment—or she'd be too angry to be objective.

Nick put his hand on the small of her back and looked down at her. "You okay?"

For a moment, Maggie forgot that she didn't want anything to do with the *Trib*'s new photographer. She forgot about his arrogance, his fantastic body, his "love 'em and leave 'em" aura. She even forgot about Rock Tillman. After what they'd witnessed, nothing other than the basic issues of life and death seemed to matter. She turned her face into his chest and let him stroke her back. Then she took a deep breath and gathered the willpower to do her job and to let him do his.

"HAVING A HARD TIME staying awake?"

At the sound of Nick's voice, Maggie lifted her head off her arms and glanced up at him, wanting to curse him for looking so alert at four o'clock in the morning. They'd gotten back to the office around midnight. She'd found a message on her desk from Ben, her editor, demanding her follow-up to the Ritter murder and had spent the next two hours trying to get hold of someone at police headquarters to confirm what Mary Ann had told her. But no one would go on record, least of all the two detectives working the case. So she'd been forced to write the story using an unidentified informant as her source.

Despite that, she was pleased with the way it had turned out. And she was glad to have it behind her. For the past hour she'd been incapable of accomplishing anything more industrious than monitoring her scanners. "I've been up too long," she said.

"Why don't you go home and get some sleep?"

Maggie rubbed her cheek, hoping she didn't have waffle face. "Because it's my job to stay here until the morning shift comes on. And because that guy who killed Sarah Ritter might strike again. I don't *want* anyone else to get hurt, but if it's going to happen, I can't miss the story. I have to justify my paycheck somehow.'' She shoved a copy of her latest article at him, and his eyes cut to the headline: RITTER LATEST OF SEVEN.

''Ritter's murderer has killed before?'' he asked, his expression pensive.

She nodded.

''How do you know? The police tell you that?''

''Not in so many words. Other sources—and a little research—confirmed it.''

''What other sources?''

Maggie gave him a sly smile. ''A good reporter never reveals her secrets.''

''Seems I've heard that line in the movies. But we're on the same team here, right?''

A call came crackling through one of her scanners, and Maggie adjusted the volume so she could hear it better. Sounded like a domestic violence case. She certainly wasn't about to rush out of the office for that. If she reported on every man who struck his wife, there'd be no room in the paper for anything else.

Evidently, what she'd seen because of her job was making her a little cynical. ''Don't worry, I'll let you know when to take the pictures,'' she said, returning to their conversation.

He leaned an elbow on the partition surrounding her desk. ''Want me to help you stay awake?''

Yawning, she supported her head with her hand. ''I don't think anyone could do that.''

This statement elicited a wolfish grin. ''Maybe I'm better at keeping a woman's attention than you think.''

Maggie didn't doubt his capabilities; in fact, it was his

potential for late-night entertainment that scared her. "What did you have in mind?" she asked hesitantly.

"I don't know. We could play a game."

"Like checkers? I'm afraid I don't keep board games in my desk, and frankly I'd be a little surprised to find them in yours."

"I was thinking of something like Truth or Dare," he said with a chuckle. "Doesn't require any props and it can be very interesting, depending on who you're playing with."

Maggie rolled her eyes. "I'd be crazy to play that with you."

"Why? Got a few skeletons in your closet?"

"No, I just don't feel like doing anything stupid. Eating coffee grounds or something."

He scowled. "Eating coffee grounds is something a twelve-year-old would think of. I can tell you haven't played this game for a while."

"And you have?"

"No, but I can think of more exciting things to have you do than eat coffee grounds."

Maggie felt an unexpected tingle go up her spine at the thought of what some of those things might be. "I think that might be the problem," she admitted.

"I'm hurt you don't trust me."

"Why should I trust you? I barely know you."

He pushed away from the partition to steal a chair from the cubicle next to Maggie's so he could sit down. "That's the beauty of this game. It'll help us get to know each other. Come on, I'll let you go first."

Maggie regarded his six-foot-plus length folded in the chair beside her, long legs stretched out in front of him. Where was he going with this?

Wherever it was, she wasn't sleepy anymore. She had to give him points for effectiveness.

"Okay," she said, unable to resist the opportunity to have him at her mercy, "truth or dare?"

He pursed his lips and held her gaze. "Truth."

"Why did you ask me out a couple of weeks ago?"

"Isn't that obvious?"

"No. There are a lot of women in this office. Why me?"

"Because you're beautiful and driven and a little shy. I like the combination."

Maggie tried that on for size. It was a far cry from some of the things she'd been called in high school. Even though twelve years had passed since those days, she sometimes found it hard to rid her head of the echo. "Wow," she said. "Okay. Maybe this game is going to be fun."

He laughed. "Except that now it's my turn. Truth or dare?"

Maggie tucked her hair behind her ears, stalling. Truth was always safer, wasn't it? "Truth."

"Why did you turn me down?"

"Um, you're not my type."

He cocked an eyebrow at her. "You said yourself you barely know me. How do you know what type I am?"

"From hard experience."

"What does that mean?"

"Nothing. Anyway, I have a son."

"And you have a wall of pictures to prove it. Your point is?"

"I'm not interested in the type of relationships you are."

He stiffened in surprise. "What kind of relationships am I interested in?"

"Never mind."

"No, I'd like to hear your take on this."

"I'm just saying you're probably used to certain… activities with the women you date, and…and I'm really not that type, and...um...never mind. Your turn's over. Truth or dare?''

"I'm not sure I want to let that go, but I'm not sure I want you to elaborate, either, so...truth.''

"How many women have you had sex with?''

*"What?"*

"I think the answer to this question will explain what I mean about your type of relationships.''

"Can I change to dare?''

She smiled smugly. "Nope.''

"Well, I'm not as reckless as I used to be, and I don't think the distant past should count against me.''

"Just answer the question. This was *your* idea, remember?''

"Come on. Let's limit it to the recent past. I'm not the same now as I was say, ten years ago.''

"Okay. How many in the past three years?''

"One.''

"Liar.''

"It's the truth!''

"Maybe in the past three *months,*" she grumbled.

"Uh, uh, uh, that's not nice," he said, wagging his finger at her. "And it's my turn, thank heaven. Truth or dare?''

"Truth.''

"Again? What a chicken.''

Maggie folded her arms across her chest. "You've chosen truth every time yourself.''

"Okay, fine. Answer this: if you did agree to go out with me, where would you want to go?''

"You're setting me up, aren't you?''

He brought a hand to his chest. "Me? Of course not. I can respect *no.* I'm just saying, 'what if?' ''

"Do I have to be practical?''

"No. That's the beauty of this game. The only rule is that you tell the truth."

"Okay. Hawaii would be nice."

"Let's see, it takes five hours to get there and five hours to get back, so if we're going to see much of the islands, you're definitely talking about spending at least a week together, right?"

Maggie gulped, envisioning a long romantic getaway with the dangerous Nick Sorenson. "I was only teasing. I'd like to go water skiing at Lake Folsom—an all-*day* event. I haven't been on a pair of skis since college. But you probably don't own a boat."

"I could always rent one."

Maggie shook her head. She wasn't going to fall for it. Nick might have charisma, in *spades,* but he had no f.p.—father potential—and f.p. was the only thing that mattered anymore.

"Truth or dare," she said.

"After that last question, I think I'll choose dare. I'd rather eat coffee grounds than list all my past exploits."

Maggie tapped her lip. "Let me think." There were a lot of things she'd like to see Nick do—at this hour, having him take off his shirt sounded pretty appealing—but the fact that she'd even think of it told her she was getting punchy. "I dare you to sing me a song," she said at last.

He made a face. "Without music?"

"There's a radio here."

"What song?"

She smiled. "I'll let you choose."

He fiddled with the tuner and finally settled on a song by Savage Garden called "Truly Madly Deeply." His voice wasn't half-bad, but it was the way he looked at her as he sang, and the meaning behind the lyrics, that made an impact.

"Actually, I think that backfired," she admitted when he finished.

He raised his brows. "You liked it that much?"

"I liked it a little," she said grudgingly.

"Well, since I was such a good sport about embarrassing myself, maybe you'll trust me enough to choose dare this time."

"I won't sing," she said.

"I won't pick that."

Maggie hesitated a moment. "You promise you'll be kind?"

"We're friends now, aren't we?"

"That's a loaded question."

"Come on."

"Okay, dare." Maggie squeezed her eyes shut, knowing she wasn't going to like what was coming.

"I dare you to dance with me."

"Here?" she asked, staring around them. "We can't dance in the office. There's a security guard downstairs monitoring the closed-circuit televisions. He'd laugh his rear end off."

"I doubt old Ed's awake enough to even notice. We're the only ones here."

"There's at least half a dozen others—"

"—buried in the offices lining the perimeter. They won't see us."

"They could poke their heads out at any time."

"I don't think you're worried about that. I think you're scared of me. You have a problem with fear, you know that?"

Maggie did know that, but she wasn't about to admit it to Nick. "I work nights. I'm not afraid of anything."

"Then dance with me." He scanned radio stations until he found one playing a slow ballad and turned to her expectantly.

What would Darla say about this? Maggie wondered. For someone who'd decided to keep her distance from Nick Sorenson, she was getting awfully close.

"A slow dance?" she asked.

"Would you rather it be fast?"

Maggie considered her lack of experience in that area and shook her head. "No."

"Okay, then come on."

Standing, she took a deep breath. The police scanners and their accompanying static left a lot to be desired as far as atmosphere, but something told her she was going to like being in Nick's arms, regardless of what was happening around them.

Maybe she'd be less affected if she kept a foot or so of space between them, she thought, but Nick quickly dispensed with that possibility when his hands slipped around her waist and he pulled her close. Maggie caught her breath and tried not to notice the solid chest pressed against her, the thigh muscles flexing against her legs as they moved slowly to the music.

"Relax," he murmured, and the moment she did, he settled her even more closely. "See, this isn't so bad, is it?"

Maggie could only shake her head. Her heart was beating too hard to let her speak. The smell of clean cotton and warm male made her want to bury her nose in Nick's neck. Her fingers itched to find their way into his hair. How had he done this to her in the process of one night?

"I don't do casual sex," she suddenly announced.

He stopped abruptly, then said, "Good. Neither do I."

Maggie didn't know where to go with that. She'd expected him to tease her about her prudish stance, or to play the innocent and pretend he didn't know why she'd bring that up at this particular moment, but his answer seemed as honest and straightforward as her declaration had been. So she relaxed and simply let herself enjoy the dance.

As the song ended, he drew back to look into her face. "Truth or dare?" he asked.

His gaze slipped down to her lips before returning to her eyes, and Maggie knew better than to choose dare. She wasn't sure she wanted to choose truth, either. "I don't think it's your turn."

"Truth or dare?" he repeated.

Could she help it if her own eyes kept straying to his mouth? It was only inches away. If she tilted her head just right, he might bring his lips to hers and give her a sample of that raw masculinity Darla was always talking about. Maybe she could finally bury the pain of those years of rejection and take a page out of her best friend's book, act bold and confident with men...

"Truth," she whispered, hanging on to her last shred of self-control.

"What would you say if I asked you out again?"

"Yes" hovered on the tip of her tongue. It was what she *wanted* to say. But then she remembered Zach and the f.p. factor. No matter what Nick said, he wasn't the marrying type. She could feel it. "No," she said. "I'm sort of involved with someone else."

He immediately released her and stepped back. "You *are?*"

She nodded, feeling the loss of his body's warmth in the air-conditioned room.

"With who?" he asked.

Maggie knew she was stretching here. But she needed some excuse. She couldn't get involved with a guaranteed heartbreaker. "His name is John."

"John?" He blinked at her as though she'd suddenly grown two heads. "John who?"

"You don't know him," she said. "I met him on the Internet."

GREAT! NOW HE WAS competing against himself.

Nick sat at his desk, pretending to go over some paperwork, although in reality he was doing nothing more than wondering how he'd managed to strike out with Maggie again. The night had been going so well. Only minutes earlier, they'd been talking, laughing, dancing. He'd held her in his arms and felt the softness of her body molding perfectly to his. He'd easily recognized the signals she was sending—they told him he wasn't alone in his attraction to her. Yet, when he'd gone for the close, she'd shot him down. Because of "John."

And he couldn't even ask what "John" had that he didn't!

He heard Maggie on the phone in her small cubicle and realized she was checking in with the various police dispatchers. Just in case she missed something on the scanners, she made a series of calls every few hours.

He glanced at his watch. Five o'clock. In another half hour or so, she'd gather her stuff and leave, and he'd have to rely on the Internet to keep tabs on her.

Unless he created an opportunity for some "hands-on" protection.

Shoving away from his desk, Nick took the escalator to the lobby, where Ed, the security guard, was sitting, half-asleep, at his perch. "Heading out for the night Mr. Sorenson?" he called, rousing himself enough to wave.

"Just getting something from my truck," Nick responded.

Outside it was still dark. The streets were deserted. Maggie's silver Toyota Camry sat in the lot alone beneath a yellow pool of fluorescent light not far from Nick's truck. But even if the lot had been full, he'd have recognized it instantly.

She'd insisted they take her car to the drive-by shooting; he'd been with her when she parked.

He crossed the lot to his truck, just in case Ed had come to the glass doors to gaze after him. Then he curved around, keeping to the shadows until he was beside Maggie's car.

OH, NO! NOT TODAY. Not when she'd been up for twenty-one hours. Disheartened, Maggie stared at her lopsided car as she hurried across the lot, wondering at the extent of the damage. Located on the fringes of downtown, the *Trib*'s offices weren't far from some of the rougher neighborhoods in the Sacramento metropolitan area, but Maggie had never had a problem. Until now. Had her stereo been taken? Had they broken the steering column in an attempt to steal the car itself?

She peered around, wondering if perhaps she'd caught the perpetrator in the act, but she couldn't see any movement. And she didn't hear anything besides the occasional rumble of a passing car and the hum of the floodlights overhead. Still, she remembered Darla's many warnings about walking to her car alone at night—remembered the body found in the Dumpster—and would have been frightened except she was too tired for fear. All she wanted to do was go home and sleep. Was that too much to ask?

Evidently it was.

The doors to her car were locked, the windows unbroken. Everything looked fine inside. The only problem seemed to be that two of her tires were flat, but that was enough to mean she wouldn't be using it this morning.

She sighed and gazed around the parking lot. Too exhausted to last, she'd cut out a half hour early, so no one from the next shift had arrived yet. But Nick was still in the office. His black four-by-four was angled carelessly in a space not far away—and she couldn't help noticing there wasn't a thing wrong with any of his tires.

Of course it would have to be *her* car, she thought, retracing her steps to the building.

"I thought you were on your way home," Ed said, when he saw her.

She passed through the metal detector and started up the escalator that ran between the first and second floors. "Someone vandalized my car. You didn't see anyone suspicious hanging around tonight, did you?"

The grooves in Ed's lined face deepened. "Nope. You might ask Nick, though. He went out to his truck about a half hour ago."

Maybe that was why his truck hadn't been touched. Maybe he'd scared away whoever it was. "Thanks," Maggie said, and hopped off the escalator to find Nick at his desk going through some photos.

"Back already?" he asked when he heard her approach.

She frowned. "Someone let the air out of my tires. Can you believe it?"

"No, jeez, that's terrible. Did you happen to see if my truck's okay?"

"It's fine. Ed said you went out a while ago. I was hoping maybe you saw something."

"Not a thing. But then I wasn't really paying much attention."

"When I said goodbye a few minutes ago, you said you were planning to head home soon. Is that still the case?"

"Yeah." He slid the pictures back into a manila envelope and placed them in a drawer he locked. "Want a ride?"

"I'd really appreciate it," she said. "I don't live far from here."

A smile curved his lips. "No problem, but it's going to cost you."

Maggie raised one brow. "I'm not playing any more Truth or Dare."

"This is more like 'I scratch your back, you scratch mine.'"

Anything that physical had its pitfalls. "What's that supposed to mean?" she asked, now leery.

"I drive you home and you make me breakfast. I'll even come back later and get your car fixed up." He winked. "Now that's not a bad offer, eh?"

Nick seemed to be the perfect antidote for fatigue. Just the thought of taking him home gave Maggie an energy spike. "I guess I can live with that," she said.

# CHAPTER SIX

MAGGIE'S HOUSE WAS A CLASSIC—sort of a run-down classic, but a classic all the same. Constructed completely of wood, with the kind of enduring craftsmanship that marked home-building at the turn of the century, it had a narrow yard with a small detached garage, five steps leading to a wide front porch, and tall heavy-paned windows. Some of the neighboring homes had been remodeled and turned into offices for attorneys, engineers or the like. Others had been divided into apartments. Maggie's had probably escaped such a fate because it was a single story—not large enough for the apartment plan and not elaborate enough for someone with a lot of money to come in and restore, at least not with the idea of realizing a quick profit.

But Nick could see why Maggie liked it. A person could do a lot with this house.

He parked on the street and got out of his truck. Maggie came around the other side. The sun was just starting to gild the horizon with white-gold. Nothing moved, except for a few birds twittering in the trees overhead.

"What time does Zach wake up?" he asked as they passed through a short wire gate and made their way to Maggie's front door.

"He seems to have an internal clock that knows the moment I get home. I'm sure we'll be hearing from him soon."

The inside of Maggie's house was cozy, a nice blend of old and new. She'd softened the high ceilings and hardwood floors with drapes at the windows, plenty of throw rugs and brown wicker furniture tossed in among some mission-style antiques. Lap blankets and pillows added to the warm homey effect, along with a big plastic tub full of toys.

"This is nice," he said. "How long have you lived here?"

"Nearly two years now."

A woman who seemed to be about ninety sat at the kitchen table, reading the paper and drinking coffee. She wore a scarf wrapped around a head of rollers, a dated terry cloth robe and a pair of pink fuzzy slippers.

Nick thought she looked as though she'd just stepped off the cover of a Shoebox greeting card.

"Well, this is a good sign," she exclaimed, eyeing him through a pair of bifocals. "After that cyber thing, I was beginning to worry about Maggie."

Nick glanced at Maggie. Maggie shook her head. "Never mind. Nick, this is Mrs. Gruber, my neighbor. Mrs. Gruber watches Zach while I work and sleep."

"But I'm going home now," Mrs. Gruber piped up. "I wasn't born yesterday. I know three's a crowd." The old lady rocked twice before gaining enough impetus to stand. Then she headed toward the hallway leading to what Nick supposed were the bedrooms.

"You don't have to go," Maggie called after her. "This isn't what you think. Nick's a co-worker at the paper."

When Mrs. Gruber didn't change course, Maggie sighed and opened the refrigerator. "What did you have in mind for breakfast?"

Nick flipped through the paper, even though he'd read it hot off the press, at work. "What do you have?"

"Spaghetti."

For breakfast? She really *didn't* like to cook. "Sounds good," he said, sauntering around while he assessed the security of Maggie's house. Two routes of entry, front door

and back. Keyed dead bolts on each. Did Maggie use them?
Nick hoped so. No sense making things easy if Dr. Dan decided to take an interest.

The family room, dining area, kitchen and living room were
on the main floor. A half bath and laundry area were situated
in an enclosed porch at the back. There were quite a few
windows, but they were higher off the ground than most, had
sturdy frames and some were covered with metal bars. If the
doors and windows were locked, an intruder would have to
break the glass to get in. Unless there was an easier point of
entry Nick didn't know about—possibly in the bedrooms.

He stopped on the porch and gazed out over the backyard.
Low fences, plenty of foliage, not much light. If a man were
to stalk Maggie, he could easily hide out in the shrubbery at
night and watch her movements inside the house. Or he could
follow Maggie home from work and attack her on her way in.

"Where do you park your car?" he asked, returning to the
kitchen.

"What?" She'd put a frying pan on the stove and was
busy cracking eggs into it. Bacon was sizzling on another
burner. Lucky for him she'd been joking about the spaghetti.

"Do you park in the garage?"

"No, I park at the side of the house. Darla's using the
garage to store some of her things right now."

"Like what?"

"A bedroom set. A couch and chair. She inherited a bunch
of furniture when her mother passed away, but she lives in
a studio apartment and it's already furnished. Problem is, the
stuff's got too much sentimental value to sell."

"And what's in the shed? More of Darla's inheritance?"

"No. A lawn mower. Rake. A few tools. The usual."

Great. If Dr. Dan left his crowbar at home, he could always
borrow Maggie's.

She was watching him, frowning. "Why?"

"Just curious." It was general information, the kind of details he should know about her habits, her situation. But he was starting to wonder if he'd ever need it. As far as he knew, Maggie hadn't received any letters. Dr. Dan had been quiet lately. A little too quiet. Even the bureau hadn't heard anything since the announcement of his move from Washington.

The big question was why? Was Dr. Dan changing his M.O.? Serial killers rarely did. They tended to stick with whatever was working. But anything was possible. Maybe Nick was wasting his time with Maggie. Maybe he should be helping Mendez and Hurley question Sarah Ritter's friends, neighbors and family. An investigation like this could take an infinite number of hours, and he had only a finite number to give it.

Except now that he'd gotten inside Maggie's house, he didn't find himself particularly eager to leave.

"Who're you?" a child's voice demanded.

Nick turned to see a sleep-tousled, towheaded boy standing at the entrance to the kitchen, wearing superhero pajamas. "I'm Nick. You must be Zach."

"Hi, baby," Maggie said from the stove. "Come give Mommy a hug."

Zach kept his eyes trained on Nick as he crossed the floor. "Who's-s-s that?" he whispered loudly as she lifted him into her arms and kissed his cheek.

"Nick's a friend of mine. Can you tell him hello?"

"Hello," he repeated.

Nick smiled. Zach was a handsome boy, even more than his pictures suggested. Round head, blue eyes, cherub mouth. He was big, too. Other than the traces of baby in his face, he looked a good year older than his age. "Those are pretty cool pajamas, Zach. Where'd you get 'em?" he asked.

Zach fingered his cape. "Mrs-s-s. Goober gave 'em to me. I have a cape s-s-so I can fly."

"I see that."

The boy started squirming to escape his mother's embrace, and Maggie put him down to flip the eggs. "Where's-s-s Mrs-s-s. Goober?" he asked.

"Right here, dear." Now clad in a muumuu-style dress with a button-up sweater, knee-high nylons and white orthopedic shoes, Mrs. Gruber went to the dishwasher to retrieve an icebox container, which she thrust into one of the bags on her arm. "I'm going home now. Why don't you come with me, Zach? We can read some books while your mother and her new friend get to know each other."

"No, I want to stay with Mommy." Zach threw his arms around his mother's legs as though he feared he'd be carted off against his will.

"I'll walk him over after breakfast. He's too taken with the appearance of a strange man in the house to abandon me now," Maggie explained.

Mrs. Gruber adjusted her bags. "I don't blame him. It certainly isn't something that happens every day."

Maggie cleared her throat and quickly changed the subject. "Are you sure you don't want to stay for breakfast? You won't be intruding."

"Yeah, don't worry," Nick volunteered. "I'm not her type."

Maggie shot him a glance that said she didn't appreciate his interjection.

"Maybe she needs glasses," Mrs. Gruber muttered. She turned to face Maggie. "If I were thirty years younger, I wouldn't mind letting a man like him park his boots under my bed."

Nick laughed and Maggie blushed. "Then stay for breakfast," she told her neighbor.

Mrs. Gruber shook her head. "No, I have oatmeal and prunes every morning. Keeps me regular."

While Maggie walked Mrs. Gruber to the front door, Zach sidled closer to Nick. "Do you play bas-s-sketball?" he asked.

"Sometimes."

"I have a hoop. Want to s-s-see it?"

"Sure," he said, letting Zach lead him outside. Even though it was only six-thirty, he could tell the day was going to be another scorcher.

He played basketball with Zach for a few minutes, tried to help the boy improve his dribble, then went to his truck for his camera. He couldn't miss the opportunity to catch the frowns of concentration and the smiles of delight on Zach's face.

He was taking some shots when Maggie came out to tell him breakfast was ready. Her brows went up as she noticed his camera, but she didn't say anything about the pictures.

"You keep those scanners on all the time?" Nick asked, hearing the cop band as soon as he entered the house.

"When Mrs. Gruber's not here," Maggie answered. "The noise makes her nervous."

"Don't you ever get tired of it?"

She shrugged. "Not yet. I'm still pretty new at my job, and I realized before I ever got into this business that following the cop beat wasn't going to be a nine-to-five proposition."

*No kidding,* Nick thought. *Try being a cop.* He'd given the bureau twenty hours a day for ten years already. But he loved his job. Loved the thrill of the hunt, the sense of accomplishment that came with closing a case and putting another menace to society behind bars. Police work was in his blood. He didn't get discouraged by the amount of crime out there. He took it as a personal challenge, a chance to make a difference.

He studied the living room as he ate. The coloring books on the coffee table, picture books on the counter, the baby blanket on the couch. The domesticity of it all reminded him of Irene and the lifestyle she'd wanted—the lifestyle he couldn't give her.

"You're tired," he said, finishing his eggs and standing to rinse off his plate. "Why don't you get some sleep while I go back and fix your tire? I'll bring your car over here later."

"Aren't you tired? You were up all night, too."

"I caught a few winks yesterday afternoon. I'll be okay." He put his plate in the dishwasher.

"Well…" Maggie looked at her son, who smiled at her with his cheeks full of food. "I am pretty tired," she admitted. "Are you sure you don't mind going back alone?"

"Not at all." It was the least he could do after sabotaging her ride home in the first place.

"Thanks. I'll get Zach dressed while you finish your coffee, so he's ready to go to Mrs. Gruber's."

As Maggie disappeared down the hall with her son, Nick took the opportunity to look through a stack of mail on top of her refrigerator. He found a notice from the DMV—her registration was due. A utility bill. A statement from Dugan, Lawrence and Tate, attorneys, showing final payment on what was probably her divorce. Nothing exciting. Nothing from Dr. Dan. Nick had already checked her desk at work and would have a similar chance to look through her car, a chance he knew he'd take. But he was beginning to worry his hunch had been wrong. And much as he wanted to keep Maggie safe, the thought didn't please him. It meant Dr. Dan was probably busy with someone else, an unknown woman Nick had no way to protect.

It meant another murder.

"MAGGIE, WHAT'S GOING ON? I just went out for a bagel and saw Nick Sorenson in the parking lot with your car!"

Maggie rubbed her face, trying to come out of the fog that encompassed her brain. She squinted at the digital alarm on her nightstand. Ten o'clock in the morning. She'd only been asleep an hour. No wonder she was having a hard time waking up. Zach was with Mrs. G. and would be for several more hours. Why in the world had she answered the phone?

"Darla? That you?"

"Yeah, it's me. Did you hear what I said?"

Maggie stifled a groan and covered her head with her pillow. "I think so," she muttered. "It was about Nick, right?"

"Right. Only not just any Nick. I'm talking about the same Nick you said you didn't want to date. The same Nick you didn't like staring at you."

The same Nick she'd danced with last night. The same Nick she'd wanted to kiss... Not that she was going to volunteer *that* information to Darla.

"It's not what you think. How's my car, by the way? Is the tire fixed?"

"I don't know. I didn't stop to ask. I raced up here to call and tell you how full of you-know-what you are."

Maggie rolled onto her stomach and propped herself up on her elbows. "I wasn't blowing smoke when I said I wasn't interested in Nick. We went on a call together last night. That's all. Then someone vandalized my car, and he drove me home. End of story."

"The man is in the parking lot, taking care of *your* flat while you're home sleeping. That's hardly the end of the story."

"Okay, so it wasn't quite that simple. I fed him breakfast, *then* he offered to fix my car so I could sleep. What's the big deal?"

A pause, pregnant with skepticism. "What are you giving him for helping you out?" Darla asked, changing tactics.

"Nothing."

"And you're still trying to convince yourself this guy isn't nice?"

"I never said he wasn't nice. I'm sure he can be very nice

when he wants to be.'' So could a lot of men who wouldn't necessarily make good husbands.

"Jeez, you're a cynic."

"Not really. But I'm trying." Maggie hugged a pillow to her chest and kicked off the heavier blankets, keeping only the sheet. "Is Ben around?"

"Yeah, but I just heard him screaming at someone on the phone. You sure you want to talk to him now?"

Maggie considered her options. She wanted to know if her editor had been pleased with her follow-up story on the Sarah Ritter murder. She wanted to know if it was going in tomorrow's paper. But she didn't want to step into the line of fire if Ben was having a bad day. "Just give him a message to call me."

Hanging up, Maggie climbed out of bed to get a drink of water. She was still craving sleep but, thanks to Darla, the memories of last night with Nick Sorenson were coming between her and oblivion. She needed to get him out of her mind, so she stopped at her computer to check her e-mail for a message from John.

Nothing. Nada. Just more spam and another chain letter from Aunt Rita, threatening her with horrendous luck if she didn't burden fifteen other people with the same message. No distraction there. But that didn't mean she couldn't write John first.

She put her cursor on the pencil icon, clicked and tried to remember back, before last night, before Nick.

But it wasn't easy.

Hi, John—
Just wanted to thank you for an incredible date last night. You really know how to show a girl a good time. <G>

The cursor blinked, waiting for Maggie to continue, but she didn't know what else to say.

*I spent last night playing Truth or Dare with the sexiest man alive?*

No.

*He's coming back here today and it's all I can do not to rush into the bathroom and shave my legs?*

Absolutely not!

Maggie sighed. What good was pursuing a cyber-relationship with John if it wasn't going to save her from falling for the wrong guy? Words on a screen just couldn't compare with the physical reality of Nick Sorenson.

Unless she could get John to relent and send her a photo. That would make him more real, give her something to hang on to until they decided whether or not they wanted to meet.

I'm attaching some .jpg files with this message. I know looks don't matter, but I think a visual will help us get to know each other. So ready or not, here are some pictures of Zach and me.

She wondered if her hint that he should return the favor was broad enough. Considering she'd already asked him for a photo once, she thought it was.

I'd better get some sleep now. I had quite a time at work last night.

She didn't need to add that it wasn't *entirely* bad.

Write when you can.
Maggie

## CHAPTER SEVEN

NICK GAZED DOWN at the photographs Maggie had sent John as they came rolling out of his color printer. She was as photogenic as he'd expected. Thick auburn hair up, her smile wide and warm, she was holding Zach cheek to cheek—and looking more beautiful than any woman had a right to. He could see a birthday cake with three candles in the background. Obviously these pictures were taken at Zach's last birthday party.

Damn. He was going to have a tough time with this assignment. He could tell already.

Taping the pictures on the wall above his desk, he slouched back in his chair. Seeing him finally settled, his dog crossed the room to nudge his hand with a wet nose.

"What do you think, Rambo?" he asked, stroking the Rottweiler's head. "She's pretty, huh?"

Rambo yawned, then sat on the floor and scratched his side.

"Evidently you're not as impressed as I am." He sighed dramatically. "But I can't let things get out of hand."

Rambo raised his doggy brows as if to question that statement—or maybe Nick's interpretation of Rambo's response was influenced by self-doubt. In either case, when Nick spoke again, he injected a measure of conviction into his voice, hoping to convince himself, if no one else. "I've never had trouble resisting a woman before. I'm certainly not going to start now."

Giving his dog a final pat, Nick told himself to focus on the case and forget about Maggie.

The first thing he did was check his voice mail messages. The lab had called. As expected, the dirt under Sarah Ritter's nails had most closely matched the sample he'd sent from the American River.

He decided to rent a bike and take the bike path this afternoon, just to get a better feel for the lay of the land and to check ingress and egress at various points along the river. He'd been to the Nimbus Fish Hatchery off Hazel, and Bannister Park off Fair Oaks Boulevard, but he knew there were other parks, horse trails and more remote sites along the thirty-some miles of trail.

His second voice mail was from Detective Mendez.

"Yo, Sorenson. Thought you should know someone phoned in a lead early this morning. Hurley and I are checkin' it out. We'll be back in touch if it amounts to anything."

Nick noticed that Mendez didn't volunteer any specific information about the lead. The cocky young detective was too busy resenting the FBI's interference in a case he thought he and the local boys could handle themselves.

Using his cordless phone, Nick dialed Mendez's cell. "I got your message. What's up? Why didn't you page me?"

"I was just about to. I think we might have a possible crime scene for the Ritter murder."

That took him aback. "Where?"

"A cozy little spot on the American River just east of the old Fair Oaks Bridge. Seein' as how you're not from around here, you might not know that area...."

Nick set his jaw, determined to ignore the subtle taunt. It was intended to remind him that he might be in charge of this operation, but he was still an outsider. "I'm familiar with it. I collected soil samples not far from the bridge yesterday.

What makes you think Ritter might've been murdered there?''

"A man by the name of Bates came forward this morning. He works for Solid Security, the company hired by the parks and recreation district to lock up the public rest rooms. He normally starts at dusk. That's when the parks close. But ten days ago, he was running late on his rounds. He stopped for a Coke at the 7-Eleven on the corner of Fair Oaks and San Juan and ran into a friend from his church who'd just bought an old Corvette. They took a ride in it, shot the breeze for a while, then Bates got back to work. He was closing down the rest rooms on the Sunrise Bridge around ten-thirty when he saw a flicker of light in the trees upriver. He thought some clown was driving his truck down the bike path, so he headed over to see what was going on. When he got there, he found a Geo Metro parked at that small boat launch just beyond the old Fair Oaks Bridge.''

"Okay, so what's the significance of the Geo?''

"Bates couldn't find the owner. Even though he'd just seen the headlights, whoever had driven the car had disappeared.''

"Bates is a security guard. Doesn't he carry a flashlight?''

"Yeah, and he used it. He looked in the car. He looked in the brush and down by the water. He called out. Nothing.''

"I'm still waiting for the connection to Sarah Ritter.''

"He couldn't find any people, but he found something else.''

"What?''

"A tennis bracelet.''

"Where?''

"On the ground.''

Steve Ritter had given his wife an expensive diamond bracelet for her last birthday. He'd said she wore it all the time, never took it off. But it had been missing when her body was discovered in the Dumpster.

Nick's heart started to pound. Maybe, just maybe, he'd finally caught a break. He wanted to believe it, wanted to crack this case wide open. Then Maggie would be safe and he could abandon the lies he was perpetuating where she was concerned.

But Bates's story bothered him. "He found a diamond bracelet in the dirt and leaves and rocks when he was looking for the driver of the vehicle?"

"That's what he said. He met me and Hurley here at the river just a few minutes ago and showed me where. It was at the opening of a small footpath leading off into the trees."

"Did he get the plate number off the car?"

"No. Said he didn't think to check the plates."

He was a security guard and he didn't think to check the plates? "So when did this happen?"

"A week ago last Wednesday."

"What took him so long to come forward? The *Trib* ran a story about the murder the day after the body was found. It mentioned the missing bracelet. I know, because I made sure of it. And it was on all the news stations."

"Bates didn't see any of that. This guy doesn't read the paper or listen to the news. He's a real movie buff, apparently. Rents film after film. Anyway, when he couldn't find anyone at the river and nothing about the car seemed suspicious, he thought someone had simply lost the bracelet. So he pocketed it to give to his wife as an anniversary present. But she knew it was far more expensive than he could afford and questioned him about it."

Nick rubbed the stiff muscles in his neck. He'd been up too long and was starting to feel it. "So she's the one who made him call in?"

"Yeah."

They'd connected Sarah Ritter to a place by the river that was very likely where she died. He should be elated, Nick told himself. Now he could go in and comb the area for other evidence that might lead him to her murderer. But he was having a hard time believing that a security guard who'd come upon an empty car and was looking for its driver would instead find something as small as a bracelet lying on the ground. There were no lights along the river. At ten-thirty, it would be pitch-black, except for the small halo from his flashlight and any effect the moon might have had.

Nick decided to check the calendar and see what phase the moon was in that night, but even if it was full, he felt Bates's explanation of the evening's events a stretch. If the security guard had truly been looking for the driver of the car, he should've been shining his flashlight waist-high or higher, for his own safety, if for no other reason. He wouldn't want someone to come at him from the trees, unseen….

Mendez broke into Nick's thoughts. "What's wrong?"

"I don't know," Nick replied. "Having someone like Bates come forward is just too good to be true. And when something seems too good to be true, it usually is. How long did he say he's been on the job?"

"Seven years."

"Where is he now?"

"He met us at the park to show us where he found the bracelet, but then he had to go take care of his mother."

"He had to *what?*"

"Take care of his mother."

A sick feeling began in the pit of Nick's stomach. "What did you say this guy's name was?"

"Bates. Norman Bates."

Nick dropped his head into his hand. "Son of a bitch," he muttered.

"What's wrong?" Mendez demanded. "I have his address and phone number. You can contact him if you want."

"It would be a waste of time to even try. We won't be able to find him."

"Why? He lives right here in Fair Oaks. If the information he gave us is wrong, we'll put a trace on the call he made to the department—"

"Definitely give it a try, but I seriously doubt it'll do us any good. Haven't you ever seen *Psycho,* Mendez?"

"Are you talking about a damn movie? What's a horror flick got to do with—" Mendez's voice fell off and Nick knew he finally understood. "Shit. Norman Bates was the name of the slasher in that movie. Dr. Dan just played me for a chump."

*If the shoe fits...* Nick's hand tightened on the receiver as he struggled to swallow his irritation. Dammit! Mendez should've paged him, then Nick would have met Dr. Dan face to face, just like Mendez and Hurley had. It was a lot to forgive, but making enemies of these two detectives wouldn't help the investigation. He could only hope Mendez had been sufficiently humbled and would now be easier to work with. In any event, Nick had to make the most of what their killer had given them.

"Meet me at the bridge in twenty minutes," he said. "Maybe we won't walk away empty-handed, after all."


MAGGIE COULD SENSE Nick's presence before she opened her eyes. She could smell his masculine scent, feel him hovering over her.

"Nick?" she murmured, forcing her heavy lids to open. Her blinds were shut, but a harsh yellow sun filtered through the cracks at the edges, and the temperature in her room had edged up to eighty or more degrees. "What time is it? Is my car fixed?"

Nick's gaze slid over her face, but his tawny eyes were shuttered. He seemed different than he had during the night, more distant. "It's fixed, but I don't have time for you to drive me back to the paper to get my truck right now. I've got some things to do and I'm sort of in a hurry. Can I borrow your car for the next few hours, instead?"

Somehow, leaving Nick with a good excuse to return to her house later in the day wasn't as unappealing to Maggie as she would have preferred. She'd already made him breakfast, but her brain immediately started supplying her with a menu she could prepare him for dinner—steak with mushrooms, baked potato, salad, wine. And she didn't even like to cook.

"Sure. When will you be back?"

"I don't know yet. If you need something, just page me. I'll leave my number on the counter in the kitchen."

"Okay."

Maggie heard his brisk stride on the hardwood floor as he retreated down the hall. There was a brief silence, some more steps, and then the click of the front door. Finally her car engine roared to life.

She rolled over and called Mrs. Gruber to check on Zach, then got up to lower the thermostat on the air conditioner in her window. Opening her blind partway, she squinted at the brightness outside. She wondered why Ben hadn't called her. Hadn't he liked her story?

She picked up the phone and dialed the paper. After two short rings, her editor's gruff voice came on the line.

"Ben Cartland."

"Ben, Maggie. Did you see my piece?"

"Yeah. It's going in tonight. Lower right."

"Lower right of what?"

"Front page."

*Front page?* Her story was going on the *front page?* Maggie couldn't believe it. How many nights had she lain awake, dreaming of seeing an article of her own on the front page of a major newspaper? "So you like it?"

"It's just what I was looking for. But don't pat yourself on the back too soon. This story isn't over yet. You stay on top of the police and keep tabs on what's happening with this killer, you hear? Sacramento hasn't seen the likes of a story this big since the lady on F Street started killing her boarders and planting them in her backyard so she could collect their social security."

Maggie swallowed. It was *that* big. So big it frightened her. No more tabloids. No more blaming Tim for the reason she wasn't doing exactly what she wanted to do. She finally had a chance to prove herself, and she was terrified she'd blow it. Did she really have what it took to make it in this business? Her ex-husband didn't think so. He'd patronized her and pretended, at times, but when it came down to it, he didn't think she'd ever be more than she was right now—a minor player. Her mother didn't understand her aspirations, either. Rosalyn Anderson thought a woman's place was in the home and couldn't relate to a female whose ambitions extended beyond ironing. But Aunt Rita sympathized. Every time her mother called to talk Maggie into moving home and "settling down to find a man," Aunt Rita got on the extension to tell her not to buy into the guilt. Live your own life. Remain true to your dream, she'd say.

And that was exactly what Maggie planned to do. For her and for Zach. She only hoped her dream would remain true to her.

"Will you give me the exclusive on this, Ben?" she asked, clenching her fists and holding her breath until he answered.

"Jorge's had a lot more experience than you have," Ben replied. "I'm not sure I want to cut him out this early in—"

"But I'm the one who dug up the details of the other

murders. If not for me, we'd all still believe this was a one-shot deal.''

''That's true.'' Her editor paused, but when he spoke again his voice revealed his irritation. ''I'll think about it. For now, just concentrate on doing your job.''

He hung up and Maggie sighed. So much for the exclusive. Jorge could easily end up stealing her story—and her raise and the long-coveted satisfaction of success. By this time next year, she could be making pot roast in Iowa.

Maggie looked at her rumpled bed. It was barely noon, but after talking to Ben, she doubted she could relax enough to sleep again. She'd found it hard enough to drop off after Darla's call. Now she had Jorge and her job to worry about.

Turning up her police scanners, she scooped up the telephone to check her voice mail at work.

''Maggie, this is Ray from Sports. I've got to cover an Oakland A's game tomorrow afternoon. Want to come along? We could take the top off my Mustang and buzz down for a hot dog or two. Maybe I'll even get you a signed ball. Give me a jingle.''

Maggie raised her brows. Ray was asking her out? Jeez, just a few days ago, she was considering a dating service. Now she was juggling three guys at once. Granted, Ray wasn't going to take up much time. He couldn't pass a mirror without stopping to admire himself. She wasn't about to go out with a man like that, but there was John. He'd definitely piqued her interest. And Nick, of course. Nick piqued a lot more than her interest. He made her libido skyrocket. But she wasn't planning to let physical attraction replace genuine admiration. Or good sense.

She jotted down Ray's cell phone number and skipped to the next message, then froze when she realized it was from Dorothy Jones, one of the Sacramento Police Department's dispatchers. ''My shift is over and I'm just heading home,''

Dorothy said, "but something came in this morning just after you called that I thought might interest you. It was a tip on the Ritter case. Some guy's found the victim's diamond tennis bracelet just east of the Sunrise Bridge along the bike trail. Hope this helps. If it does, you owe me lunch."

Maggie smiled. Hallelujah! With any luck at all, she'd owe Dorothy a really nice lunch, something along the order of steak and lobster with champagne.

NICK GLANCED DOWN at his beeper and swore. He'd only left Maggie twenty minutes ago. What could she want already?

Tempted to ignore her page, he looked up at Detectives Mendez and Hurley. He'd just arrived at the Sunrise entrance to the river, and the detectives were walking up the short incline from the footbridge to meet him in the parking lot. Thin and wiry with brown eyes and blue-black hair that glistened in the sun, Mendez seemed small next to Hurley. His lithe build reminded Nick of a sleek, fast greyhound. But if Mendez was a greyhound, Hurley would be a mastiff. Almost six foot six, three-hundred-plus pounds and as white as a white man came, he made everyone else look small and considerably more cunning. Fortunately, Nick had spent enough time with him to know his mind was actually rather quick.

"I'm sorry about what happened," Mendez said. Hurley nodded but didn't speak. He wasn't one to waste words. His strong suits included watching and listening, which was a good thing considering that Mendez typically shot his mouth off enough for both of them.

"You wouldn't expect something like that. It's not every day a murderer contacts the police pretending to be a tipster," Nick said, deciding to be generous.

"You told me about the letters, but we haven't received any, and I never dreamed our perp would pull something like this."

"Well, now you know the kind of arrogance we're dealing with. Dr. Dan likes to feed his ego by making fools of us. He has a thing about law enforcement. He's obsessed with it, determined to prove he's faster and smarter than we are."

"Maybe he wanted to be a cop at one time and was turned down for some reason. Or maybe he really does work in security."

"That's certainly a possibility. Only he seems to be good at a lot of things. The way he wields a knife suggests other interests or vocations. But the next time you receive a tip like this, I want you to get hold of me even if you have to dial my number a hundred times." Nick stared pointedly from one detective to the other, his expression stony enough to let them know he wouldn't tolerate another breach in conduct.

"You got it, man," Mendez said, his voice resolute.

Hurley's nod was almost imperceptible, but Nick knew a promise had been made.

"At least we know what our man looks like," Mendez said. "Hurley and I both met him, so now we can work with an artist to get a sketch going."

Nick nodded. "A composite would really help at this point. Did you get some tape around the crime scene? I don't want any joggers or bikers in there until I've had a chance to search the area."

"Tape's in place. The other members of the task force just left," Mendez said.

"Good." Nick's beeper went off, and the detectives waited while he checked the number on his screen. Maggie again. She'd paged him twice in five minutes. She obviously needed something. Using the cellular phone he carried on his hip, he dialed her at home.

"You're supposed to be sleeping. What's up?" he asked.

"I need my car. And I need you."

"I was wondering when you'd come around. What about John?"

"I mean I need a good photographer," she clarified. "A friend of mine just tipped me off that the Ritter bracelet has been found."

Nick frowned. Already? Apparently Maggie had better contacts than he'd realized. The details she'd dug up about the other murders, despite his call to Atkinson, had been his first clue. This was his second. He'd have to be careful or they'd bump into each other and blow his cover. "What do you want to have photographed?" he asked her.

"Where the bracelet was discovered on the American River, near the Sunrise Bridge."

Damn. He hadn't even had a chance to go over the crime scene yet and Maggie was already landing in the middle of it. "I'm pretty busy. Is there any hurry?"

"Are you kidding? This kind of stuff doesn't wait. Right now I have the jump, but if I don't get my story in to Ben right away, we'll end up seeing it on Channel 10 News or somewhere else. Reporting is very time-sensitive. And first place is always better than second—or last."

"What about Zach?"

"Mrs. Gruber's still got him. He'll be fine with her."

"I'll tell you what," Nick said, swallowing a sigh. "Take a taxi to the Sunrise access, and I'll meet you there."

"That's going to cost me time and money," Maggie complained.

"I'll make it up to you."

"How?"

"Dinner. A massage. Free baby-sitting. You choose."

Mendez raised his brows and looked at Hurley. Hurley shrugged.

"I'm leaning toward the baby-sitting."

"You might want to think about it. I'm not so good at baby-sitting."

"Yeah, something tells me you're better at massage."

Nick lowered his voice. "You can find out."

"Uh…I think I'll go for door number three and take the dinner."

"That comes as no surprise."

"What's that supposed to mean?"

"You always play it safe."

"Not always."

"You're scared."

"No, I'm not."

"I'm just about ready to make you prove that."

"How?"

"I'll think of something. See you in about thirty minutes."

He ended the call and looked at Mendez and Hurley, who were regarding him quizzically. "You got a girl already?" Mendez asked.

"Some parts of this job are better than others," Nick said. "Now, show me where Dr. Dan told you he found the bracelet, then head downtown and get started on that composite. I want the details of this creep's face while they're still fresh in your mind."

"I'm not likely to forget the bastard now," Mendez grumbled.

Nick couldn't help chuckling. "We'll get him," he promised. "Because we won't rest until we do."

# CHAPTER EIGHT

MAGGIE FOUND NICK sitting in a shady spot on the riverbank, staring out over the water, deep in concentration. At three o'clock, the sun was still high in the sky, the weather sticky-hot. Maggie's cotton top and shorts clung to her from the taxi ride. The car's air conditioner hadn't quite made it to the back seat. But the meter ran like a dream.

Orange crime-scene tape roped off a section of a dirt boat-launch and some surrounding trees not far from where Nick sat. Everything smelled green and woodsy and a little like licorice, because of the anise growing next to the bridge.

"What are you thinking about?" she asked, coming up on him from the side.

He took a deep breath, glanced over at the crime scene area, then shook his head. "Just wondering what was keeping you. It's been more than an hour."

"Sorry. I've been trying to get hold of the guy who found the bracelet—Mr. Bates—but he doesn't answer his phone. A little old lady lives at his address. She said the police came by, too, but she's never heard of him. I knocked on every apartment in the complex. And there had to be sixty."

A sardonic smile curved Nick's generous mouth.

"What?" Maggie demanded.

"Nothing."

"That smile means something."

"Did you pay the cab to wait while you did all that door knocking?"

"Of course."

"Then it means I owe you more than just dinner. How 'bout a night on the town?"

"Tonight?" Maggie frowned at the fatigue showing in Nick's eyes. "You're exhausted. I think you should go home and get some sleep."

He nodded. "That would probably be best. What do you want me to shoot? I've been looking at the crime scene over there. Nothing makes it any different from the rest of the riverbank."

Maggie checked for herself. The boat launch sank into the water just twenty feet below the paved bike trail. A small clearing on the other side boasted a gravel lot with two trucks, one trailer and a green Porta Potti. The launch wasn't designed for anything bigger than kayaks and fishing boats.

"Let's get a few shots of the trees over there." She indicated a stand of oak next to a small footpath leading into denser foliage. "I want to show the police tape blocking off this section, with the river beyond. I need something to give the impression that an incident of importance happened here, right in our communal backyard."

"Okay." He stood and took several pictures of the crime scene, then turned his camera on her.

"What are you doing?" Maggie asked, embarrassed. She waved him away, but his shutter clicked again and again. "Stop! The *Trib*'s not going to like owning an extra twenty pictures of me."

"Which is why I'll process them myself," he said.

"And do what with them?"

"Keep them to remember you by."

That took Maggie by surprise. "Are you planning on leaving?"

He shrugged. "Not right away."

"But eventually?"

"We all move on eventually."

Which was exactly the type of answer Maggie should have expected from a man like Nick, but it bothered her all the same. "I don't think I want to have dinner with you," she said.

"Tonight?"

"Ever. Let's go."

He didn't say anything as he followed her to her car. When she reached out for the keys, he handed them over without argument. Then he climbed in the passenger side and lowered the seat into a reclining position.

"Where do you live?" she asked.

"Just take me to the office. I have some things to do there, and my truck's in the lot anyway.

"I thought you were going to get some sleep."

"I am. I'm going to grab a twenty-minute nap right now."

If he wanted to kill himself from overwork, it wasn't up to Maggie to stop him. She bit her tongue so she wouldn't sound like her mother or Mrs. Gruber and started the car. Nick was capable of making his own decisions. He'd be fine, she told herself, but she glanced over at him every few minutes, just to be sure. Now that his eyes were closed, she could study him with an abandon she'd never allowed herself before. The broad forehead, square-cut jaw, blunt chin and contours of cheek and lip, combined with the recent memory of his taunting grin and the devilish glint that entered his eyes every now and then, created a package so perfect she should have been content just to look.

But since when was looking enough for anyone?

Her gaze lowered to the muscular definition of the tanned arms crossed over his chest, the flat stomach beneath and finally the snug fit of his jeans....

Maggie jerked her attention back to the road. She'd never

had a truly passionate affair, even with her husband. But that wasn't what she needed now. She wanted to get married again, and married life was more than passion. A good relationship required selfless love and true dedication. A good relationship required commitment strong enough to pull a couple through the bad times as well as the good. All of which spoke of permanence.

Nothing about Nick said forever. Live for the moment, maybe. *Que sera, sera.* But definitely not "till death do us part."

*Wrong guy,* she told herself. But she couldn't stop thinking about the woman Nick had admitted making love to sometime during the past three years. What had she been like? Tall and fair? Short, dark and busty? Either way, she obviously hadn't managed to capture Nick's heart. But that wouldn't be an easy feat for any woman.

"Poor thing," Maggie muttered.

"NICK, WE'RE HERE." Maggie let her Camry idle in the *Trib*'s parking lot behind Nick's truck and gently shook his shoulder.

He didn't wake immediately. When he did, he shifted in the seat and mumbled something about taking him home. Maggie was glad to see he'd decided to get some real sleep. Only problem was she didn't know where he lived.

"What's your address?" she asked.

He didn't respond.

"Nick." She put a hand on the warm flesh of his forearm and pretended, without success, that it felt like any other man's—her brother's, her ex-husband's, Ray from Sports, who'd hung up on her when she'd called him back to tell him she couldn't go to the game with him. "Are you going to wake up?"

This earned her an irritated grunt and another change in

position but not full consciousness. Only a moment later, Nick's breathing evened out and his chest once again rose and fell in a steady rhythm.

What now? Maggie wondered. She had a two-hundred-pound man in her car and didn't know how to get rid of him. Worse, it was Nick Sorenson, and they were sitting in front of the office. If Darla or any of the other women who worked in the newsroom happened to see them, Maggie would never hear the end of it.

Glancing at the front doors of the building, which had a stream of people coming and going, as usual, she shifted into drive and exited the lot.

They reached her place ten minutes later. She pulled along-side the house, halfway between her detached garage and the narrow tree-lined street out front and cut the engine.

Still Nick didn't move.

Maggie went around the car, opened his door and leaned in. "Nick? We're here. Wake up long enough to help me get you inside, okay?"

His eyelids cracked open and a slice of honey-gold iris showed through. "Give me fifteen minutes," he muttered, and his eyes slid shut again.

"It's too hot to leave you out here. Come on, let's go inside."

Nothing.

"Nick? There's an air conditioner in my bedroom window. It's cooler in there."

His lids lifted again. "You're going to let me sleep in your bed?"

Maggie tried not to smile. "I doubt you'd fit in Zach's toddler bed, and Mrs. Gruber's room smells like a medicine cabinet. She plasters her nose and chest with some kind of ointment before bedtime." Of course, there was always the couch, but wicker wasn't the most comfortable thing in the world, and Nick needed several hours of deep sleep. He was more likely to manage that in her room, away from the heat that permeated the rest of the house and the noise Zach would make when he came home, if he and Mrs. Gruber weren't there already.

"Are you going to lie down with me?" he asked. "You need sleep, too."

"I don't need it that badly."

The corner of his mouth lifted in a lopsided grin. "What's it gonna take for you to trust me?"

"I wouldn't trust you if you were a eunuch."

"Eunuch." He grimaced. "Few words are less appealing to a man."

She laughed and tugged on his arm. He finally launched himself up and out of the car while she went ahead to unlock the house.

Inside, everything was completely still except for the steady hum of the air conditioner in her bedroom, the whir of the fan in Zach's room, and the cough and rattle of the old fridge in the kitchen. Evidently, Zach and Mrs. Gruber had decided to spend the day next door, where the whole place was air-conditioned.

Maggie showed Nick down the hall to her room, then closed the door behind him and hurried to the kitchen to call Mrs. Gruber.

"I'm home. I'll be over to grab Zach as soon as I can get a cold drink."

"I bought a wading pool and Eric's bringing Rusty over. I think Zach would like to stay a little longer so he can swim."

Eric was Mrs. Gruber's married son, a resident of Elk Grove, thirty minutes away. Rusty was her grandson and Zach's only friend. Of course Zach would want to see Rusty.

"That's fine. Just call me when they're done swimming."

"Okay. Zach's asking to talk to you."

Maggie spoke to her son and confirmed that he had his heart set on staying, then hung up. Zach would be occupied for a couple more hours, which would've been great. Except today she had Nick Sorenson in her bed and nothing to distract her. She couldn't even log on to the Internet to see if John had written because the computer was in her room...with Nick.

She crossed the kitchen to stare inside the freezer, wondering whether or not she should make the steak dinner she'd thought about earlier, when a quick knock sounded at the front door and Darla breezed into the house. "Maggie, time to wake up," she called.

*Oh no!* Maggie dashed around the corner in time to see her friend turn down the hall to her bedroom. "Hey, I wasn't expecting you," she said before Darla could reach the door. "What's up?"

Darla glanced at the closed bedroom as though surprised to see Maggie coming from the opposite direction but allowed herself to be drawn back to the living room. "Just got off work and thought I'd stop by to see whether you're rested up for the day. I figured maybe you, me and Zach could go out for pizza."

"Mrs. Gruber's grandson is coming over. Zach wants to stay there for a little longer so he can play."

"Just you and me, then."

Now was probably a good time to mention that Nick was sleeping in her bed. But Maggie didn't want Darla to say or do anything that would embarrass her while he was close enough to hear if he woke.

"I don't think so, thanks. Not tonight," she said.

"Why not? You want to get something besides pizza, then?"

Maggie considered the invitation, chagrined by her own

reluctance to accept it. Nick had been in her house for fifteen minutes and already she wanted to throw over a night out with a friend for a night spent in his presence.

She'd known he was trouble from the start.

Probably it was smarter to override the stay-home-with-Nick instinct, get out of the house and forget about the man in her bed. Otherwise, she might make him dinner...and momentarily forget her high ideals.

"Okay. Let me get my purse and call Mrs. Gruber to tell her I'm going," she said.

A few minutes later, she followed Darla through the door and down the path to the sidewalk, rounded a blue Geo Metro someone had parked in front of her house, and climbed into Darla's Toyota 4Runner.

NICK WOKE to the smell of Maggie. Fresh and clean and completely feminine, her scent was everywhere. On the pillow, on the sheets, in the air. He took a deep breath, remembering where he was and savoring the feel of being in her personal space. Then he forced his eyes open. What time was it? He hadn't meant to sleep more than a few hours. He needed to get his truck and go back to his apartment. He needed to call Mendez and check on the progress of that composite. He needed to get a copy of the tire tracks at the river and send the trace evidence to the lab and—

The darkness beyond the window finally penetrated his brain, and he shot upright. It was late. Far later than he'd thought. Where was Maggie? Had she left for work? Why didn't she wake him?

Running a hand through his sleep-tousled hair, he skirted the bed and headed for the hall. Zach was asleep in the room next to Maggie's. From where he paused in the doorway, Nick could easily see the child's silhouette in the moonlight filtering through his open window.

*Open* was the operative word. Zach's window had bars on it, but there were plenty of others in the house that didn't. Were they open, too? That worried him. If Dr. Dan ever came to call, he'd only have to cut the screen and slip inside—

*Forget it.* It wasn't going to happen. Not to Maggie or Zach. Dr. Dan hadn't even contacted her. He was too busy playing other games, like the one today at the river.

The floor creaked as Nick walked to Mrs. Gruber's room. He expected to find the old lady snoring softly beneath a heavy quilt, despite the warm night, but her bed was perfectly made and perfectly empty. Where, then, was Maggie?

Retracing his steps down the hall, Nick turned left and entered the living room to find the back door open to the screened-in porch. It allowed a cool breeze to circulate through the house, but for Maggie's safety, Nick wanted to shut the door and bolt the lock. He'd have to warn her somehow. He couldn't let her continue taking these risks.

*If it wasn't too late already.* No one was sleeping on the couch. No one was rummaging through the refrigerator for a midnight snack. Maggie wasn't anywhere in the house.

Nick's heart started to pound and his fingers craved the gun he'd left at his apartment. He glanced outside to find her car where she'd parked it earlier, a dim shadow, along with all the other dim shadows in the night. He didn't think it had been moved since she'd brought him home.

Slipping outside through the back, he checked the yard. Nothing. No sign of her. The hood of her car was cool. No lights blazed in Mrs. Gruber's house next door. He was just about to go inside to try calling Maggie at work, hoping Darla or someone else had given her a ride, when he saw a feminine form sleeping in the lawn chair on the porch.

It was Maggie. He could see her pretty face in the same moonlight that illuminated Zach's room. A pale-colored sheet was drawn to her waist, covering her legs. He let his breath out in a rush. God, she'd scared him.

Bending over her, he wrapped a silky lock of auburn hair around one finger while he waited for his blood pressure to settle down. She was alive, fine, asleep. His imagination, fueled by the gruesome images of the murder victims he'd seen over and over again, had run away with him. That was all. "Maggie?"

He ran a finger from temple to chin, and her eyes fluttered open, widening when she recognized him. "Nick?"

"Why are you sleeping out here?" he asked.

A faint smile touched her lips. "Because the last time I looked, there was a strange man in my bed."

"You should have kicked me out."

"You were sleeping so soundly I didn't want to disturb you. And it's much cooler out here than in the living room. I can't sleep when it's so hot."

"You need central air."

"I need two thousand dollars." She adjusted the back of her chair into a sitting position, and Nick stepped away to sink into the wicker loveseat across from her. Dressed in a spaghetti strap T-shirt, and what he guessed was a pair of boxers under the sheet, Maggie wasn't wearing a bra. Most women didn't sleep in one, but his body's immediate and powerful reaction to the gentle sway of her breasts surprised him.

For a moment, he feared he was getting pulled too far into his cover. When all was said and done, he had to be able to walk away. It went with the job.

"Why aren't you at the office?" he asked.

"Because I worked most of the day. Before I came out here, I wrote a short piece about the diamond bracelet being found and faxed it to Ben, but I knew I'd never make it through another night on three hours of sleep. So I called someone to take my place." She smiled. "I let them know not to expect you, either. I told them you'd been working with me all day and went home dog-tired."

He *had* been tired, but Nick could find no trace of that exhaustion now. Awareness of Maggie zipped through every nerve; he had to make a conscious effort not to reach for her. He wanted to see if he could get her to respond to him. He wanted to draw her out in a passionate kiss. He wanted to teach her what good lovemaking could feel like....

"Do you always leave your doors and windows open?" he asked.

"In the summer."

"Do you think that's smart?"

She yawned. "Probably not. But we couldn't survive the heat any other way." Still filled with sleep, her voice was deeper than usual. More sultry. Downright sexy. Nick didn't know if it was the late hour, the creamy cleavage her shirt revealed or the way he could still smell her on his clothes and body after sleeping in her bed, but he had to take a quick breath and slide his chair farther away. Otherwise, the temptation to run a finger along her collarbone and down the swell of one breast until he cupped it in his palm would be too difficult to refuse.

He was doing his job. It wasn't real, he reminded himself. He couldn't take advantage of the involvement his cover gave him in other people's lives.

But the knowledge of how wrong it would be to touch Maggie the way he wanted to did little to ease the tightness in his body. Rubbing the day's growth of whiskers on his chin, he cleared his throat and tried to think of something else. "What if I lent you the money for the air conditioner?"

"You can't be serious." She yanked the sheet up under her arms and studied him. "Why would you even say that?

Two thousand dollars is a lot of money. You don't know me well enough to take that kind of risk."

He knew her well enough to know he didn't want to see her dead. Money was nothing compared to her life. "Will you keep your doors and windows locked?"

"This serial killer really has you spooked."

"After what you wrote last night about the other murders, he should have you spooked, too. Wasn't one of the women he killed a journalist?"

"Yeah. She worked for the *Seattle Independent*. And I *have* been a little nervous," she admitted. "The Dumpster where Sarah Ritter's body was found is only a few blocks from here. Normally I wouldn't sleep outside, but tonight I felt safe." She gave a little shrug. "You were here."

"I can't protect you if I'm fast asleep in the other part of the house. You need to stay closer to me."

"Just knowing someone else is around helps."

"It's not enough. This guy is…this guy is beyond sick. He's confident and he's bold and he's extremely dangerous." Nick forced himself to leave it at that before the passion he felt about capturing Dr. Dan gave him away. What he'd already said was enough to make Maggie shiver.

"Let's not talk about him. You're scaring me," she said, but then she quirked one eyebrow. "Or is that what you're trying to do?"

"It is what I'm trying to do. But not for the reason you think." Resting his elbows on his knees, Nick leaned forward and set the flirting and teasing aside. This was serious. They were talking about life and death. Maybe hers. And if he kept going along the same track he had been with Maggie, he'd cross lines he had no right to cross. It was time to level with her—as much as he could.

"I want you, Maggie," he said softly. "I think you know that. I've wanted you from almost the first moment I laid eyes on you. But I won't act on that desire. I know it wouldn't be good for you in the long run. I don't plan to be around for more than a few months. I've got job opportunities opening up elsewhere, and you deserve more than a temporary fling."

Her chest lifted as though he'd just dealt her a stinging blow, but if she was feeling any emotion, she didn't reveal it. She kept her face passive. After a moment, she even smiled. "Is that little confession supposed to make me trust you?"

"I was hoping it would. I want to be friends. I want us to agree that's all our relationship will ever be. And I want you to know I won't act beyond the boundaries that go with friendship."

"Right. Friends. I understand. It's not like I was expecting anything more."

"You act as though I'm proving you right about something."

She tilted her chin. "You are."

"I guess that's good," he said, even though it didn't feel very good. After Irene, some small part of him wanted to see if he was capable of a deep, fulfilling relationship, one in which the thought of marriage didn't leave him in a cold sweat. But another part warned what it would cost Maggie—and himself—when the time came to leave. "I'm going to take a taxi home now. In the morning, I'll get a good HVAC company out here and—"

"No." Maggie shook her head, adamant. "I'm not going to let you pay for my air-conditioning. That's a little much to accept from a friend, especially one as new as you are."

"You can pay me back when you get the money."

"I need all of my paycheck just to take care of my monthly bills. I'm not going to borrow an amount that could take me years to repay."

"Maggie, there's a crazy man out there running around, raping and stabbing women. I want your doors and windows locked, at least the ones without bars."

"What are the chances he'll set his sights on me?" she demanded.

Nick couldn't answer that without giving himself away. But he knew her chances were better than most.

"I'm a big girl," she went on. "I can take care of myself."

Nick wondered if Sarah Ritter had thought the same thing.

# *CHAPTER NINE*

WHEN MAGGIE'S ALARM went off at five-thirty the next morning, her first thought was that she wasn't going to dwell on what had happened with Nick. She'd known from the beginning that he wasn't husband material, so last night's revelations shouldn't have come as any surprise. Of course, he was a little more honest than she'd expected, which made him more admirable, too. But honest didn't change the bottom line. So why the nagging disappointment? Especially today, when her article would be on the front page of the paper?

Remembering the reason she'd set her alarm, Maggie untangled herself from the sheet and padded barefoot to the door. She poked her head outside, glanced up and down the dark street to be sure she could venture forth in her sleepwear, and dashed down the walk to retrieve her paper. Then she set herself up in the kitchen for the big moment.

Birds chirped in the trees outside as Maggie stared down at the rolled newspaper for several seconds before ripping off the rubber band and flattening the paper out in front of her.

Finally, there it was:

RITTER MURDER—LATEST OF SEVEN?

By *Tribune* Reporter Maggie Russell

SACRAMENTO—At first glance Sarah Ritter, Sophie Johnson, Helen Swanson, Lola Fillmore, Jeanie Savoy, Winnie Hartman and Tasha Thomas would seem to have little in common. They didn't know each other. For the most part they lived in different states, had different jobs, different backgrounds, different marital status. Yet they were all murdered in the past year by what authorities believe to be the same man...

Those were her words, the result of her research. Because of her, Sacramento was better informed about the threat posed by Sarah Ritter's murderer. The women in California's capital would now know that he might strike again. They could take precautions and not leave themselves vulnerable. They could keep an eye out, stay in groups whenever possible and lock their doors and windows at night.

She looked up at the window above her sink and amended her last thought to include *if they have central air,* which brought her full circle to Nick. But she refused to let what he'd said last night darken her mood—either the rambling man routine or the frightening admonishments. She was on the front page of the paper! This was a special day. Although it was a little lonely being the only one to celebrate... Who could she tell? Darla would kill her if she woke her this early, and Mrs. Gruber didn't get up until eight. Nick would probably be awake—he'd left her house only a few hours earlier and Maggie doubted it was to go back to bed—but despite the new classification he'd given their relationship, he hardly felt like that kind of friend. So she called her mother and Aunt Rita in Iowa.

"What is it? Is something wrong?" her mother asked as soon as she heard the pitch of Maggie's voice.

"No. I'm fine. Zach's fine. I just wanted to tell you that my article's on the front page of the paper today. The front page! For the first time."

"Your article?"

"One I wrote."

"That's nice, dear. What is it about?"

"A mass murderer."

"Oh." Silence. "I guess that's good, if you like that sort of thing."

"I don't 'like' mass murderers, Mom. I report on them. Don't you think it's important for the public to know if there's a killer in their midst?"

"So they won't feel safe at night? What use is that?"

"It puts pressure on the police to solve these crimes, for one thing. It keeps the public aware of the state of our society, too, so good people can make positive changes. And it warns potential victims to be careful."

"There's not much crime out here. No one in Cedar Rapids has been murdered. When are you going to settle down and forget this terrible fascination with crime?" her mother asked. "It's unnatural. And it's not like they're paying you a lot for what you do. You barely get by. What you need is a man."

After the way she'd paced the floor last night—agonizing over whether or not to wake Nick, wondering whether he'd leave if she did, not knowing if she actually *wanted* him to stay—Maggie was beginning to believe she needed a man, all right. But not for the reasons her mother thought. "It just hasn't been in the cards."

"You're too busy running around writing about sickos."

"It's what I do. It's what I'm good at, I hope."

"What about that nice young man from around here who was moving to California? Ralph Peters?"

"The Ralph who has seven kids by five different women?"

"Poor man. He just can't seem to find a decent wife."

In Maggie's opinion, Ralph was the common denominator, not his ex-wives, but she wasn't about to throw her hat in the ring on that one.

"I gave him your number," her mother was saying. "Did you ever hear from him?"

"No." *Thank God.*

"Well, Bertha has a cousin who lives out in California. I wonder if she has any sons who are available. Or there's always Luke Wordelly. His boys are all plumbers. I think one of them lives in Auburn, which isn't far from—"

"Whoa, that's okay, Mom," Maggie interrupted. "You've set me up enough times already. There's no need to do it again. I've met someone I sort of like, anyway."

"Really? How wonderful." Rosalyn's voice warmed considerably. "What's his name?"

"Nick—I mean John." Maggie felt a blush warm her cheeks even though no one was around to witness her embarrassment. "His name's John," she said to reinforce it to her own mind as much as her mother's. "I'll be sure and let you know how things progress. We've only gone out once so far—" she decided to save herself a lot of grief and not mention the cyber thing "—but I like him. Is Aunt Rita there?"

After grilling her for another ten minutes about John, Rosalyn passed the phone to Aunt Rita, and Maggie finally got the joy of sharing her accomplishment with someone who seemed genuinely excited for her. She was still smiling when she hung up and Zach wandered into the room.

Proudly, Maggie presented the newspaper to him. "See this, Zachy? Mommy wrote this. This is my story."

He blinked at it, obviously unimpressed.

"It's on the *front* page," she pointed out.

He switched his focus to her. "I'm hungry."

Evidently lack of enthusiasm ran in the family. Maggie sighed, pulled out a box of cereal and poured him a bowl, adding milk. "There you go, kiddo. Maybe by the time I win the Pulitzer, you'll be old enough to understand."

Zach shoved a spoonful of cornflakes into his mouth and

smiled at her as he chewed. Maggie smiled back—at him and the paper. John would probably appreciate the significance of her big day, she decided.

She got some juice and grapes to go with Zach's cereal, put the whole thing on a breakfast tray, and helped him carry it into her bedroom so he wouldn't have to eat alone. Then she signed on to the Internet. She was dying to hear if John had received her pictures. What did he think of her red hair? Did the reality of seeing her with her son frighten him at all? Did he mind that she had a child?

Maggie raised her brows as she watched her screen. She could always ask him. According to her buddy list, he was online, too. But he'd sent her an e-mail, and she wanted to see what that said before contacting him via instant message.

She clicked on the small envelope icon, expecting a few paragraphs, at least, but soon saw that he'd sent only one word: *Beautiful.*

No signature. No attachments. No promise to send pictures soon. Nothing. Just "beautiful." Maggie frowned at it. "Cheater," she muttered irritably. Maybe she'd been wrong about John. He'd seemed so nice on their cyber-date, but anyone could seem nice online. Men could be serial killers and describe themselves as the kindest, most generous beings on the face of the earth. They could also say they looked like Mel Gibson when they really looked like Ralph from Cedar Rapids.

Probably her request for pictures had scared him. Maybe he wasn't really six two, one hundred and ninety-five pounds. Maybe he was closer to sixty and bald, with a hairy back.

**Mntnbiker: Hi, Maggie.**

Evidently she was on John's buddy list, too, because he was contacting her instead of the other way around.

Mntnbiker: What are you doing up so early?

Zachman: Wondering if you have a hairy back.

Mntnbiker: Was there a typo in that last response?

Zachman: No.

Mntnbiker: Hmmm. No back hair. Want to check out my dental records?

Zachman: Maybe. There must be some reason you won't send me a picture.

Mntnbiker: I told you. I don't have a scanner. And I've been really busy lately.

Zachman: I assumed that from your one-word e-mail.

Mntnbiker: Hey, it might have been short but it was sweet. I don't tell every woman I meet that she's beautiful.

Zachman: You didn't say *I* was beautiful. You said "beautiful." That could mean you think Zach's a beautiful child, that the pictures came through beautifully, that my coloring is a beautiful example of red hair without many freckles...

Mntnbiker: Don't pout, Maggie. It means your pictures are all over my walls right now. Sometimes I look at them and imagine pulling you into my arms and kissing you. But I didn't want you to think I was some kind of pervert, so I left that part out, okay?

Maggie took a deep breath. So he *had* liked the pictures. Perhaps she'd overreacted just a bit, but she couldn't very well explain that her preoccupation with Nick Sorenson was making her desperate to establish a relationship with someone safer, could she?

Before she responded, John sent her another line of text.

Mntnbiker: I bought you something at a virtual reality

store, by the way. They'll be notifying you by e-mail so you can tell them where to ship it.

Zachman: I think I'm feeling better already.

Mntnbiker: LOL. Glad I could help. How's work going? Anything new on that serial killer?

Zachman: An article I wrote about him is on the front page of the paper today.

Mntnbiker: Congratulations! How'd you get the story?

Maggie explained what had happened with the coroner's wife and her own subsequent research. Then she told about her tip from Dorothy Jones and the diamond bracelet find.

Mntnbiker: Great work. Sounds like you're better at investigation than some of the detectives on the case. Or are they feeding you information, too?

Zachman: They're pretty stingy. I don't think their mothers taught them to play nice with others. What did you buy me?

Mntnbiker: It's a surprise.

Zachman: What kind of surprise? An edible surprise? A photo surprise? Something else?

Mntnbiker: Yes.

Zachman: Yes, what?

Mntnbiker: It's something else.

Zachman: Like?

Mntnbiker: I'm not going to give it away. Want to meet me online again tonight? We can drink a glass of champagne to toast your journalistic success.

Zachman: Together?

Mntnbiker: At the same time.

Zachman: Ooo, same time, huh? That really gets me excited.

Mntnbiker: I'm getting the feeling you're not crazy about long-distance relationships.

How could a long-distance relationship satisfy her when Nick Sorenson was so real, vital—and close? When her mother was threatening to set her up with one of the Wordelly brothers? Maybe she should've gone out with Ray from Sports....

Nah, she wasn't that desperate.

Zachman: Just tell me that eventually, if we get to know each other and like each other, you'll want to meet me in person.

There was a long pause.

Mntnbiker: It's a little early to worry about that, isn't it? Let's just take it one day at a time and see where things go, okay?

A dodge. He was dodging her. Maggie had asked enough questions in her lifetime to know. But why?

Zachman: Now you've scared me again. I'm thinking you might be some reclusive freak who weighs eight hundred pounds, eats sixty cheeseburgers, fifty orders of fries and a dozen shakes at each meal and won't leave his bedroom.
Mntnbiker: Don't beat around the bush, Maggie. Tell me what you really think. LOL

Another dodge?

Zachman: Well?
Mntnbiker: I'm normal. Would you relax?
Zachman: Normal can be a very broad term. It can include all kinds of phobias and maladies. For instance, some men think fear of commitment is normal.

Mntnbiker: It's not?

Zachman: Very funny.

Mntnbiker: Okay. I don't think I'm particularly afraid of commitment, just really involved in my work.

Zachman: My ex-husband was really involved in his work.

Mntnbiker: Holy cow, are you having a bad day?

Maggie stared at the screen and sighed. Why was she grilling John? What was she hoping to achieve? Obviously some of her own insecurities and phobias were taking over.

Zachman: I'm sorry. I just talked to my mother. She's afraid I'm never going to get married again. She's going through her list of friends and calling in favors. She tried to set me up with a man who already has five ex-wives!

Mntnbiker: What did she say about your article?

Zachman: She wasn't excited.

Mntnbiker: And you're disappointed.

Tears brimmed in Maggie's eyes at the simple statement. She missed her father, she regretted that she and her brother had never been close and didn't keep in touch aside from a yearly Christmas card, even though that would probably never change, and she wished she and her mother could connect with each other. But she was also grateful to Aunt Rita for being the tether that held her to the family and her roots. Sometimes she thought that if Aunt Rita ever let her go, she'd just drift away.

Zachman: Maybe. Since my father died, I occasionally feel a little lost. Do you ever wonder where you belong in this big world?

Mntnbiker: Sometimes. But then I see something beauti-

ful, something that moves me, like courage in the face of
loss or despair or the incredible sacrifices a parent makes
for a child, and I know I'm where I want to be—part of it
all, trying to make a difference, slugging it out like everybody else.

John's answer eased the ache of Maggie's loneliness. She
was part of it all, too. Her work was making a difference in
other people's lives. And what she was doing at home, rais-
ing Zach, promised to make a difference, as well. For the
second time, John had managed to soothe an ache inside her
no one else could reach.

Suddenly, her attraction to the handsome and charismatic
Nick Sorenson no longer seemed so frightening because she
knew she wanted what she was establishing with John—a
mature, cerebral, nurturing relationship.

Zachman: You know what?
Mntnbiker: What?
Zachman: Don't worry about sending me a photo. I don't
need one.
Mntnbiker: Why the change of heart?
Zachman: I like you just the way you are.

FOR A FEW SECONDS after signing off with Maggie, Nick sat
staring at the text of their conversation. *I like you just the
way you are,* she'd said. Unfortunately, he returned that sen-
timent much more intensely than he wanted to. She was vulnerable yet strong, direct, spunky, tenderhearted.

But Dr. Dan was still out there somewhere. He had to be
caught, and Nick was the one who had to do it. He needed
to step up his search, move faster, work smarter. He had to
use the information he'd gleaned from the murder scene to

bring Dan down, and he hoped the composite Mendez and Hurley were working on would help.

He clicked on the pencil icon and sent Tony an e-mail at the lab, informing him of the new evidence he was mailing. Before Maggie had arrived at the river, he'd had a chance to scour the crime scene and felt certain it was indeed where Sarah Ritter had been murdered. Why Dr. Dan would be so bold as to give up the true site of her death, he didn't know. But he wasn't unhappy with the results. He'd found a few strands of blond hair on a broken tree branch at the mouth of a narrow path. He guessed they belonged to the victim. He'd also discovered another size-twelve shoe imprint that matched the one outside the Ritters' window and had since gone back to make a plaster mold of it and of all the tire tracks he'd found in the damp earth. Unfortunately, Dr. Dan had killed Sarah Ritter at the launch almost two weeks ago, so his tires weren't the only ones pressed into the river-bank—but neither were there as many as would be, say, out at the lake, where recreationists launched scores of ski boats on any given day.

Nick had also collected bags full of leaves and twigs, hoping the lab would find a drop of blood or a strand of the killer's hair or something else in it. But the bracelet hadn't yielded anything. Dr. Dan had handed it to Mendez and Hurley in a plastic bag, already wiped clean of prints.

At least, they'd have their composite soon. Mendez and Hurley had spent hours with the police artist yesterday, and were meeting with her again this morning to put on the finishing touches. They'd circulate Dr. Dan's face as soon as it was finished and hope for some leads from the general public.

The big question now was whether or not Dr. Dan was really driving a Geo Metro. Nick suspected he was. He was having the lab check into the possibility that the fibers they'd gleaned so far were compatible with the carpeting in that type of vehicle. But he was still puzzling over why Dr. Dan had killed Sarah at the river, then hauled her body all the way to the Midtown Dumpster. Had someone surprised him?

He pinched his lips, picturing the scene by the river and going over the story "Bates" had fed Mendez and Hurley. Maybe, just maybe, someone had interrupted Dr. Dan that night and caused him to panic and flee. If so, that person could very possibly be the real security guard, or maybe a biker or jogger.

Picking up the telephone, Nick called Mendez at the station. "Did you get in touch with the security company that locks the bathrooms?"

He heard Mendez draw a bolstering breath, as though the answer to this question was painful for him. "Yeah. It's like you thought. They've never heard of Bates."

"Did you trace the phone number he gave us?"

"It goes to a prepaid cell phone. Dr. Dan bought it at a kiosk in the mall by giving them the same fake name and address he gave us. They didn't even ask him for I.D."

Just as Nick had suspected. "They wouldn't need that information if he bought the phone outright and paid for his minutes upfront. The whole package would cost about a hundred bucks total, which isn't out of most people's price range. Dr. Dan probably pitched the phone in the river after he left you, but if we can find it, we might get some prints. Do you know who has the route Dr. Dan claimed to have for Solid Security?"

"Name's Steele. He's been with the company two years."

"Was he working the night Sarah Ritter was murdered?"

"The person I spoke to on the phone wasn't sure. Rather than wait for her to look it up, I told her I'd come down and take a peek at the records myself. She's expecting me anytime."

"Get me Steele's number while you're there. I want to talk to him."

"Okay. I sent Hurley over to your place with a copy of the composite. He should be arriving any minute."

"How'd it come out?"

"The artist did a great job. Looks just like him."

"Good. Call Maggie Russell at the *Trib* and get her a copy. Contact the smaller papers, as well. I want this loser's mug circulating as soon as possible."

"Right. Did you see her article in the paper today, by the way?"

"Yeah."

"That chick's incredible. She calls me night and day, pumping me for information. I tell her as little as possible, but somehow she's getting the facts, anyway."

"I told you. She's getting her facts from the dispatchers."

"And I put a lid on that. Which is why she's hounding me again and it's driving me crazy."

Maggie was driving Nick crazy, too, but for entirely different reasons. After their last conversation on the Internet, he was beginning to wonder how long he could keep her at arm's length. Worse, he sometimes forgot why he wanted to.

It was a bad sign.

"She's just doing her job," he told Mendez.

"Wow, I never expected you to defend the press."

"I wasn't defending her." Fortunately, the doorbell rang at that moment and Rambo started barking, saving Nick from having to voice any more hollow denials. "I gotta go, Hurley's here."

"Get ready for your first glimpse of Dr. Dan," Mendez said.

Nick knew he was more than ready.

## CHAPTER TEN

"I CAN'T BELIEVE you didn't tell me about John." Darla sat on the couch eating ice cream out of the container and scowling at Maggie. It was Monday, one of her days off, and she was spending the afternoon with Maggie and Zach.

Maggie glanced up from the living room floor where she was helping Zach put together a puzzle. They'd just had a lunch of veggie burgers and apple slices. Zach had finished off his meal with a frozen juice treat, traces of which were still evident on his face. Maggie was eyeing Darla's ice cream with interest, thinking that this might be a good time to splurge. "I didn't imagine it would amount to anything," she said. "I'm still not sure. We're just trading e-mails."

"And going on cyber-dates."

"Tonight's only our second."

"But you like him?"

"Look, Mama. I did it," Zach interrupted.

Maggie admired her son's completed puzzle, then pulled him onto her lap and rested her chin on his head before responding to Darla. "Yeah. John's easy to talk to. He's thoughtful. He seems intelligent."

"And he's sending you a present. That always helps."

Maggie smiled. "I don't expect gifts, but I have to admit I'm dying to find out what it is."

"Do I get one, Mama? Do I get a pres-s-sent, too?" Zach demanded.

"We'll see, babe."

"Where does John live?"

"Somewhere in Utah. We haven't exchanged that kind of detail yet. It's crazy. On the one hand I've revealed some things about myself I don't tell anyone. On the other hand, I haven't even told him where I live."

Darla propped her feet up on the coffee table. "Better safe than sorry. It won't hurt to know him a little better first. There's no rush, right?"

Maggie agreed—but she wanted to chuckle at the fact that it was Darla who offered this advice. Especially since she'd let Reese, the guy who'd stuck her with the long-distance telephone bills, move back in last night. "I actually think this is a great way to get to know someone. You say things on e-mail you wouldn't say otherwise. It seems to me people play fewer games when you're communicating online."

"I think that depends on the people. I'm sure Reese would manage a few games no matter what the forum."

"If you think that, why'd you let him back in?"

"I'm hoping he'll pay the damn phone bill."

Maggie laughed. "Well, John seems sincere."

"What about the other part of getting to know someone?" Darla asked. "The touching, the kissing. Won't you miss not having that?"

When she was around Nick Sorenson she missed it. But Maggie wasn't going to let herself think about that.

She offered Zach his crayons and settled him in front of a coloring book featuring animals and their babies, then slanted a grin at Darla. "That's probably the *real* reason you let Reese move back in, isn't it?"

A contented smile curved Darla's lips. "He's better at some things than others."

"I hope you're protecting your pocketbook this time."

"I disconnected my long-distance service. If I have to make a long-distance call, I just use my cell phone, which I keep with me. He can't hurt me on that bill. All I have to worry about now is the dozen or so movies he rents at one time on my video store card.''

Maggie shook her head. ''The more I listen to you, the more convinced I become that there are benefits to an online relationship.''

''Only if you think saving a few bucks is better than having a warm body in your bed at night. It's all a matter of priorities.''

''That warm body stuff will happen later, if it ever comes to a commitment. For now, I think we'll continue as we are. Where is Reese by the way?''

''He's at the gym where he works.''

''Last I heard he didn't work.''

''That was one of the stipulations of getting back together.'' Darla took a big spoonful and let it melt in her mouth. ''Just think, if you and John end up married and with a dozen kids, you'll owe it all to me,'' she said. ''I'm the one who dragged you to that chat room.''

''Cows say *mooo*. Pigs say *oink oink*,'' Zach announced.

Darla gave him a reproving look. ''No oinks, kid, I'm eating ice cream here.''

Used to Darla's sense of humor, Zach ignored her and kept talking happily to himself.

''What if John becomes my next ex? What if he kills me in my sleep?'' Maggie teased.

Darla grimaced. ''Don't mention murder. That article of yours in the paper today is pretty gruesome stuff. It's hard to believe anyone could be so sick. Cutting out his victims' tongues? Where did you learn he did that?''

Maggie checked Zach's face to make sure Darla's words had flown over his head. Sure enough, he was completely absorbed in coloring a zebra. ''Not from the police, that's for sure. I think they're really worried about this guy, probably because they're having such a hard time catching him. I have another article going in the paper tomorrow, about the tennis bracelet that was found. One of my dispatcher friends came through on that one. Looks like Sarah Ritter was murdered near Sunrise at the American River.''

"Oh, good news," Darla responded. "He didn't kill anyone down the street from you. He just dumped the body there. Gives you a whole new sense of security, doesn't it?''

"Not if you're sleeping with your windows open," Maggie said, ignoring her sarcasm.

"Maybe you and Zach should move in with me until he's caught.''

"Are you kidding? You have a studio apartment, three cats and Reese is back. We'd all hate each other in less than a week.''

"At least you'd be alive for Reese and me to hate.''

Maggie shook her head. "No. That would make my babysitting arrangements more difficult, too. We're all set up here, living next to Mrs. Gruber. Besides, this creep moves around a lot. He might have gone to Texas or somewhere else by now.''

"And he might not have.''

"Come on, Darla. Think positive. We can't give in to fear. We have lives to lead, jobs to do." Maggie got up from the floor. "Speaking of which, I should check my voice mail at the office. I didn't make it in to work last night. For all I know, another body's been discovered.''

"Wouldn't want to miss that," Darla muttered.

"Eighteen messages," Maggie said when her voice mail informed her of the status of her mailbox. She took the cordless phone with her to the kitchen counter so she could jot down names and numbers, quickly skipping from one to the next out of long habit. But then a man's voice came on the line, a husky, raspy voice that made the hair on the back of Maggie's neck stand on end.

"Maaagggiiee…Maaagggiiee…where are you Maggie? This is Dr. Dan. If you don't know me yet, you will. I liked your article, by the way. Front page. Nice job. We're both there in the limelight, aren't we, Maggie? There's something so arousing about that." A pause. "Well, we'll be there together again, you and I, provided you're not like Lola Fillmore. If you are, you might not like losing your tongue any more than she did."

The voice faded away and the computer informed Maggie that she could save, delete or repeat the message by pushing the appropriate keys on the number pad.

More than anything, Maggie wanted to erase it, from her mailbox and from her memory. Knowing the killer's name, hearing his voice, made him so much more *real*. She wished she could make him disappear as easily as his message. But she couldn't destroy it. The police might need to use it as evidence.

Her hand shaking, she saved it.

"What is it?" Darla asked, getting off the couch to come toward her. "You look a little pale."

Maggie swallowed. Goose bumps tingled all down her arms and legs. She felt as though she was going to be sick. Lola Fillmore had worked for the *Seattle Independent.* Lola Fillmore was dead.

"I just got a message from the man who killed Sarah Ritter."

Darla's hand flew to her mouth. "Oh God, Maggie, what did he say?"

Maggie couldn't bring herself to repeat Dr. Dan's message. Not yet. All she could say was, "It doesn't sound like he's leaving town any time soon."

NICK STARED at the composite drawing Hurley handed him. Dr. Dan appeared to be an everyday sort of man, not particularly handsome, but not particularly fiendish-looking, either. Hurley described his coloring as dark, his build as average, and his size as about five feet eleven inches tall, two hundred pounds. The artist's rendition revealed the rest—eyes that bulged slightly beneath a prominent brow, hollowed-out cheeks, a neatly trimmed goatee and fine, straight brown hair combed across a sloping forehead. Wong, the FBI's profiler, had guessed he was Caucasian because serial killers rarely kill outside their own race, and she was right. But Dr. Dan was older than expected, closer to his late thirties than his twenties. With Dr. Dan's presumed education, Nick had expected someone who looked more...refined.

"What was his demeanor?" Nick asked.

Hurley jammed his hands in his pockets and nodded at Rambo. "Dog doesn't bite, does it?"

Nick raised an eyebrow. A lot of people were afraid of dogs, but he wouldn't have pegged Hurley as one of them. "Only if I tell him to."

"Then I'm glad we're on the same side. He looks like he could wrestle a bear and win."

"What was Dr. Dan's demeanor?" Nick repeated.

Hurley gave Rambo one last nervous look before he answered. "Seemed awed by our jobs. Kept asking questions about how we got on the force. Typical cop wanna-be, I thought at the time."

"And now?"

"Now I think it was an act. I think he was pandering to our egos."

See? Hurley wasn't as dumb as he looked, Nick told himself. "You think he was trying to alter his appearance with the goatee?"

"Didn't pay much attention to his face, to be honest. I was

more interested in what we might find at the crime scene." He glanced around, apparently noticing Maggie's pictures for the first time. "Isn't that the *Trib* reporter who's been following this case?" he asked.

Nick considered explaining, then decided against it. There wasn't any reason the photos were still up, except that he liked looking at them. To claim otherwise would only make him seem defensive. "Yeah, that's her," he said and went back to the composite. "This guy's got a pretty generic face, no moles, no scars. Was there anything else that might help identify him? Any birthmarks? Tattoos? What was he wearing?"

"He was wearing a long-sleeved blue button-up shirt and a pair of jeans. So if he's got tattoos, I couldn't see 'em. But maybe that's why he was dressed so warmly in hundred-degree weather."

Somehow Nick didn't picture Dr. Dan as the type to get a tattoo. "Maybe one of his victims scratched him or bit him, and he didn't want you to see it," he said.

Hurley shrugged. "No way to know."

"Anything else you can remember about him? Anything distinguishing about his speech, like an accent?"

The detective took a moment to ponder this question but finally shook his head. "No accent. Talked a lot, though. On and on. Once we got the facts, I tuned him out. Now I wish I hadn't."

So did Nick. "All right. Let's get this composite circulating. Dr. Dan will be feeling pretty full of himself after what he pulled off at the river. He'll be looking for more prey, if he hasn't targeted someone already."

Nick's cell phone rang. He dug it out from beneath the case files on his desk and hit the talk button.

"Nick Sorenson."

"Nick, it's Mendez. I just got a call from Maggie Russell. Sounds like Dr. Dan has contacted her."

Nick's heart skipped a beat. "He sent Maggie a letter?"

"He left a message on her voice mail."

*That bold sonovabitch.* The validation that Nick's hunch had been right was small consolation in the face of the risk to Maggie. "Have you heard it?"

"No. I'm on my way over there right now. I wanted to let you know first."

The mutilated bodies of the seven victims flashed across Nick's mind, and the temptation to drop everything and drive straight to Maggie's house was almost irresistible. But he couldn't afford to blow his cover. Especially now that Dr. Dan was contacting the paper. For the sake of the investigation, he had to sit this one out. "Get me a copy of that message as soon as you can, and get her permission to put a tap on her phone, at home and at work, just in case he calls again."

"You think the *Trib* will give us their phone records so we can trace the call?"

"No way. You know how it is with papers. Because of the privacy issues involved, the owners would never agree. We'd have to get a warrant, and there isn't a judge out there who'd give us one, not for a newspaper's phone records. But Maggie's office phone has a direct line. They might let us tap it—if she will."

"I'll see what I can do."

"Hurley will meet you at Maggie's."

Nick disconnected and glanced up at Hurley.

"What's up?" the other man asked expectantly.

Taking a breath to ease the stranglehold of fear clutching his stomach, Nick focused on the photograph of Maggie and Zach hanging over his desk. "Dr. Dan may have found his next target."

"The reporter?"

"Yeah."

"Good thing we know who it is."

"Yeah, now all we have to do is catch him," Nick muttered. But it was difficult to feel very excited with Maggie's life hanging in the balance.

MAGGIE COULDN'T pull her eyes away from the composite drawing Detectives Mendez and Hurley had left with her. Long after they were gone, she sat on the couch, holding the picture in front of her and memorizing every contour of Dr. Dan's face.

This was the man who'd stalked and killed seven women. This was the man who'd just left her a telephone message promising future contact.

How could such a terrible monster live inside such a plain, average-looking face? It didn't seem fair that there was nothing to mark him, nothing that warned of the evil within....

"So that's him?"

Maggie turned around to see Darla standing behind her, gazing over her shoulder. Her friend had played with Zach in the backyard while Maggie met with the detectives, but now Zach was down for his nap and, for the moment, she and Darla were alone.

"What's amazing is that this guy probably has friends and family somewhere who'd be shocked to find out what he's done," Maggie said.

Darla shoved her hands in her pockets and scowled. "That's pretty creepy, Mag. Makes me feel like I can't trust anyone."

"I know." Maggie was seeing threats everywhere. Though Dr. Dan had obviously altered his voice, the intimacy of his half-whispered syllables stayed with her like a song she hated but couldn't get out of her head. And now she had the image of his face to haunt her, as well....

"The police want to tap my phone," she said, putting the composite on the coffee table.

Darla crossed the room and sank into the opposite chair. "But the message was on your voice mail at work, not your home phone."

"I know. They want to tap my office line, too."

"So what do you think? Are you going to do it?"

Maggie shook her head. "I can't. The people who call me, especially at work, have a right to privacy. I'd feel completely dishonest accepting a tip from someone who doesn't know the police are listening in, that his or her call might be traced. Besides, I'd have to get permission from the paper, and I doubt they'd give me that—for the same reason I'm not going to ask."

The worried look on Darla's face intensified. "But what about you? What if this guy comes after you?"

Maggie shivered. "The fact that he's calling the paper and not the house tells me he doesn't have my personal information and—"

"Or he's too smart to use it. Maybe he doesn't want to show his hand just yet."

What Darla said was possible, but it was a possibility Maggie didn't want to consider. She was already spooked enough. "I'm unlisted," she said.

"That doesn't matter. You have phone service, don't you? And electricity? He could find you if he really wanted to. Let's face it, it wouldn't be that hard."

"Thanks for making me feel so safe and secure."

"I think you should come home with me tonight."

Maggie tucked her hair behind her ears and went to stand at the window, staring out at the shimmering heat. "That might be a little hasty," she said. "I really don't think Dr.

Dan knows where I live. Besides, the police are going to be watching the house.''

Darla made a sound of irritation. ''Come on. Don't be like those stupid bimbos in scary movies who always walk into the forest alone. I'm really not difficult to put up with.''

Maggie bit her lip. ''Reese won't be happy about it, and I don't want to come between you two.''

''Don't worry. The phone bill will probably do that.''

Maggie chuckled in spite of herself. ''You're wonderful to offer,'' she said. ''And I'll keep it in mind, but Mrs. Gruber and I agree that Zach should spend his nights at her place until Dr. Dan's caught, and I feel pretty safe here during the day. I doubt anyone who does what Dr. Dan does to his victims would attack me in broad daylight, especially with the police periodically driving by the house.''

Darla shook her head. ''I wouldn't take anything for granted with this guy, Maggie,'' she said.

Maggie crossed her arms and resumed staring out at the empty yard. If she thought staying with Darla would keep her safe, she would've moved immediately. But she knew that if Dr. Dan wanted to find her badly enough, he could find her at Darla's as easily as he could find her at home. All he had to do was talk to someone who knew them. It came down to whether he wanted her badly enough—and whether the police were good enough to stop him.

## CHAPTER ELEVEN

NICK STOOD AT THE EDGE of the bike trail with Rambo on his leash, surrounded by trees that blotted out what little light the night's sliver of moon managed to shed. A cool breeze kicked up off the river, rustling leaves on every side and making him wonder if he should have brought a lightweight jacket. Evidently the delta breezes he'd heard so much about since coming to Sacramento had finally deigned to appear, and they made a big difference in the stifling heat.

But he wasn't out to enjoy the evening. He was looking for a witness. Joggers and cyclists were creatures of habit. It was a long shot, he knew, but he was hoping he'd come across someone who'd seen something at the boat launch the night Sarah Ritter was murdered. The only way to do that was to spend some time at the trail in order to see who used it at night. He needed someone to verify the blue Geo Metro, for one, especially since he hadn't been able to talk to the security guard, Steele. Solid Security said Steele had taken his family to a reunion in New Mexico and the man's neighbors had confirmed it. Nick wouldn't be able to reach him until next week.

A squirrel scrambled up the closest tree as cicadas chirped a chorus in the surrounding vegetation, but the area seemed empty of people. Nick had passed a crusty old fisherman when he'd crossed the footbridge at nine-thirty, but he hadn't seen anyone since, and that was half an hour ago.

Using his flashlight, he watched the wide, shallow river on

its journey to the sea, then went over the crime scene a third time. He spotted nothing of interest until a light glimmered several hundred feet up the trail. A cyclist was coming, riding fast as he pumped his way west.

Nick stepped into his path, Rambo at his side, and called out, giving the cyclist plenty of time to stop. He didn't want to frighten anyone. He only wanted answers.

The man slowed, obviously unsure whether or not to get off his bike, especially when he saw Rambo.

"I'm a police officer," Nick called. "Don't mind the dog. He won't hurt you. I just have a few questions I'd like to ask." He shined his flashlight on his ID, and the cyclist finally came close enough for Nick to make out the shape of a tall, gangly man.

A high school teacher in Folsom, he told Nick he rode the trail fairly often, but hadn't been on it much in the past few weeks; he'd been home the night of Sarah Ritter's murder. Nick thanked him and let him move on, then questioned another cyclist who rounded a bend, coming from the other direction. The second one told Nick he generally rode in the mornings. Tonight was an exception.

Another dead end.

Nick let the guy go, turned off his flashlight and tied Rambo's leash to a sturdy branch, allowing him to poke through the woods while Nick sat on a fallen log. Earlier he'd called to make sure Maggie had made it safely to work. She was surrounded at the paper now, by the *Trib*'s security, but he hated the thought of Dr. Dan lying in wait somewhere, stalking her. He had to find the sonovabitch…had to put him away for good. Which would be easier if he wasn't so exhausted. Fatigue, along with the cool, quiet night and its noises, lulled him toward sleep. His head nodded several times, then bumped his chest, and a brief period of oblivion fell before he was awakened by Rambo's bark and the rumble of a car's engine close by. At least it sounded close. It was difficult to tell with the quiet ripple of the river at his back and the steady *warp, warp, warp* of tires running over the car bridge overhead.

Pulling himself out of sleep, Nick took Rambo's leash and jogged with him to the parking area, where he found the same two empty cars he'd seen on his way in. Nothing had changed there. But he'd been right about hearing an engine. It was coming from across the river. Headlights appeared, reflected off the water, then dipped as what looked to be a Jeep Cherokee crossed the footbridge.

Nick checked his watch. The security company had locked the bathrooms on both sides of the bridge more than an hour earlier. So who was this and why was he driving his vehicle on the bike trail? Certainly, Dr. Dan wouldn't be stupid enough to return to the same spot....

Nick gently tugged Rambo into the cover of the nearby trees to watch. But when the SUV came even with him he saw the writing and emblem on the door—it was a park ranger.

Snapping on his flashlight, Nick flagged him down.

"Evening," the ranger said through his open window. He was a white-haired man of fifty or so, and although his voice was amiable enough, his eyes held suspicion. "Park closes at dusk, I'm afraid. You need to walk your dog before that, young man."

Young man? Nick hadn't been called that in a while. He showed his identification. "I'm not exactly walking my dog. I'm investigating a murder."

The older man blinked, then squinted as if wanting to get a better look at him. "FBI, huh? This have somethin' to do with that crime scene up the trail a ways? The Ritter murder?"

"It does."

"Read about it in the paper, and I saw the taped-off area, of course. Name's Davis, Larry Davis."

"It's nice to meet you." Nick offered his hand, and the older man clasped it in a firm shake. "How often do you make the rounds down here?"

"Every night."

"What time?"

"Varies. I try not to be too predictable."

"What part of the trail were you on at ten-thirty on May 16th?"

Davis hesitated. "I'm not sure I can say with any accuracy. That was two weeks ago."

"It was a Friday night," Nick said, hoping to nudge his memory.

"Hmmm. Let's see." He rubbed his chin. "I think I was down by Watt Avenue at ten-thirty."

"Which means you'd already been past here?"

"No, I was coming upriver."

"Did you see anything strange when you reached the Fair Oaks Bridge?"

The instruments in the ranger's Jeep glowed green and Davis's radio crackled. He turned it down. "Can't say I did. If it's the night I'm thinking of, I stopped to use the Porta Potti, but I didn't see anyone around. The lot had a single car parked in it, though."

"Do you remember the make or model?"

"It was one of those small trucks, maybe a Nissan or a Toyota."

So no Geo Metro. "At any point on your rounds did you see Solid Security?"

"No, but we miss each other a lot. They lock up at dusk."

"Doesn't their man ever run late?"

"Sometimes."

"Do you know Weston Steele?"

"Not well. We say a few words when we happen to cross paths. That's about it."

Disappointed that he hadn't found the witness he'd been hoping for, Nick nodded. "You haven't found a blue blanket discarded anywhere, have you? A cellular phone, a knife, duct tape…" *Body parts?*

"No. The past two weeks I've found the same kind of trash I always do—food wrappers, beer and soda cans, forgotten shirts and lost sunglasses."

"I'd appreciate it if you'd keep an eye out and contact me if you come across anything." Nick handed him a card that listed his cell phone number.

"Sure thing." Davis gave the Jeep some gas and started to pull away, but Nick hailed him again.

"Mr. Davis?"

Brake lights flashed. "Yes?"

"Where do you put the sunglasses and T-shirts you find?"

Davis hitched a thumb toward the back of his vehicle. "I throw 'em in a box in the back of the Jeep here, then turn 'em over to the Lost and Found at the Parks and Rec office."

"When was the last time you emptied that box?"

Davis shrugged. "A few weeks ago, I guess."

"Mind if I take a look?"

"Not at all." Davis parked the Jeep in the lot a few feet away and opened the back. Nick used his flashlight to go through a large box containing bathing suits, T-shirts, bottles of suntan lotion, water guns, a snorkeling mask—and a dressy white blouse with ruffles around a wide neck. He paused when his fingers encountered the silky material because it was so inconsistent with the other items in the box, and because Sarah Ritter's husband had described her as wearing something similar when she disappeared.

"Do you remember where you found this?" Nick asked, pulling the blouse out from beneath the articles on top of it.

The ranger slid his hands into his pockets and rattled his loose change. "Steele gave it to me a week or so ago. Said he found it in one of the bathrooms."

Nick took a closer look at the garment. It was obviously expensive, which was probably why the security guard hadn't simply thrown it away. But the buttons had been ripped off and two drops of a brownish substance marred one sleeve— a substance Nick guessed to be blood.

"WHAT A NIGHT," Maggie muttered, unlocking her front door at five in the morning. She'd spent more than eight hours at work and had managed, through close attention to her scanners, to catch the tail end of a drug bust going down in one of the seedy motels of Sacramento's red-light district. But despite the mad rush to reach the scene in time, despite the adrenaline that had coursed through her as she'd watched the DEA agents in action and the effort involved in writing her article, she hadn't been able to escape the haunting fear Dr. Dan's message had left with her. For the first time in her life, she heard steps behind her, glanced repeatedly over her shoulder and shrank from entering her own house.

"Hello?" she called, sticking her head inside the living room. Her voice seemed to echo back at her. The shadowy interior was dark, hot and quiet. When she'd headed out, she'd locked everything up tight and hoped it remained that way.

Fortunately, she'd asked Mrs. Gruber to watch Zach until mid-morning so she could catch up on her sleep; it was a relief to know they were both safe next door. Maggie considered joining them instead of braving the empty house alone. The composite sketch published in today's paper made Dr. Dan feel that much more menacing. Every time she closed her eyes, she could see him staring at her with his dark, close-set eyes. Maybe he was already following her, stalking her...

No, fear was playing tricks on her. The police were keeping an eye on the house. And she didn't want to wake Zach and Mrs. Gruber at this hour.

Slipping inside the front hall, Maggie closed and locked the door, then quickly turned on every light in the house, checking to make sure nothing had been disturbed.

No open windows. No overturned furniture. No filthy words spray-painted on her walls—sometimes she hated her imagination.

Her heels clicked hollowly on the hardwood floor as she opened the windows that had bars. Then she returned to her bedroom where she stripped off her clothes and shoes, cranked up her air conditioner and climbed into bed. John had stood her up last night, but she didn't want to think about that. Maybe something had come up. Maybe he forgot. There could be a thousand good excuses....

But she'd been frightened and had wanted to talk to him and he hadn't been there. She'd spent her night staring at the face of a murderer as she'd written her piece about Dr. Dan, a man who'd called her and used her name with terrifying familiarity.

Sleep, Maggie ordered herself. The longer she stayed awake, the more noises she'd hear and the more frightened she'd become. If she didn't drift into unconsciousness soon, she ran the risk of dwelling on Lola Fillmore again. When Maggie first got to work, she'd used the Internet to dig up a few more details about the other woman's murder. She'd read every article Lola had written, poring over the ones about Dr. Dan; she'd even e-mailed Lola's editor.

His response had arrived just before she left the office, and it had been particularly disturbing....

*Don't! That was her, not me. It's not going to happen! The police will catch him before—*

The front porch creaked beneath a footfall.

Maggie froze, her heart beating loud in her chest. Had she imagined it?

No. There was a muffled bump, another creak, then nothing for several seconds. Finally the sound of movement beyond her window sent chills racing up her spine. A twig snapped. Grass rustled. Whoever had been on the porch was now moving to the back of the house. Checking the windows? Looking for a good point of entry?

Fortunately, the back door was locked. But what if Dr. Dan simply broke a window? Would Mrs. Gruber hear? Would anyone hear?

Maggie grabbed the phone by her bed and heard the reassurance of a dial tone. She was just about to dial 9-1-1 when there was a loud knock. Surprisingly enough, it came from the front door.

"Maggie? Are you home? It's Nick."

*Nick?* Maggie hauled in a deep breath, letting relief settle over her like a warm quilt, and hung up the phone. Nick hadn't been at the paper last night, and she'd wondered about him, but as long as reporters or photographers remained productive and did quality work, they enjoyed flexible hours. She'd assumed he was catching up on his sleep—until she pulled on a robe and opened the door. Then she saw how exhausted he looked. He had dark circles beneath his eyes, a wrinkled shirt on his back and three suitcases at his feet.

Her jaw dropped. "You have luggage," she said.

He smiled sheepishly. "Yeah, uh, I was going to talk to you about that."

"It's after five in the morning!"

"Exactly the reason I didn't call first."

"You nearly scared me to death."

He stabbed a hand through his hair. "Sorry. I just walked around the house to be sure everything was okay."

Maggie flipped back her sleep-tousled hair, wishing she'd gathered it into a ponytail before going to bed. She was hot enough without the weight of it on her neck. "The house is locked up tighter than a drum. The fact that I'm melting is proof of it."

"There are worse things than melting," he said.

"Being scared out of your wits is one of them. You haven't mentioned why you're here."

He glanced down at his feet. "My girlfriend kicked me out."

"Your *what?*"

"My girlfriend. We've been on the rocks a long time, and tonight things just kind of came to a head."

Maggie tried to ignore the quick burst of jealousy that shot through her. She hadn't known about any girlfriend. But she'd never asked, either, and the fact that Nick had been living with someone would certainly explain his tame love life over the past three years. "You tried to date me," she said indignantly.

"Like I said, things have been over between Shelley and me for a long time. We had hopes at the beginning. She moved out here from Connecticut and talked me into following her, but after the first few weeks, we knew the relationship wasn't going to work. Since then, we've basically been cohabiting, but she's found someone else, and our arrangement's come to an end. She brought him home with her last night." He hooked his hands on the doorjamb above them and leaned forward, his gaze settling on her mouth. "Besides, if I remember right, you turned me down every time I asked you out. I've never so much as kissed you."

Maggie thought the dance they'd shared was pretty sensual—the way he was looking at her now reminded her of the desire it had stirred low in her belly—but she supposed that was proof of her naiveté. He'd probably felt nothing. "No harm done, is that it?"

"No, it's simpler than that. I just need a friend."

"Why me?" she asked.

"I've lived in Sacramento less than four months. Shelley's about the only other person I know."

"Is that why you were talking about leaving when we were down by the river?"

"Yeah, I was considering moving back to—" he paused "—Connecticut."

"And now?"

He shrugged. "I still might. In either case, I'd only need to stay with you a couple of weeks, just until I decide. Then I'll get my own place or head back."

Maggie glanced at the biceps that bulged beneath the short sleeves of his T-shirt and the golden skin she could see wherever his clothes didn't cover, and took a deep breath. She wasn't opposed to helping a friend, especially for such a short time, but calling Nick Sorenson *friend* felt a lot like dressing a wolf in sheep's clothing. He'd drive her crazy with that crooked smile and those perfect buns and—

"Where will you sleep?" she asked.

"You've got a couch, haven't you?"

"Yeah, but that wouldn't be very comfortable. I guess you could sleep in Mrs. Gruber's room until this thing with Dr. Dan is over. She's keeping Zach at her place at night until then. But what about the bathroom? I only have one shower."

"I guess we'll have to share."

"Take turns, you mean?"

His smile gained meaning. "Right. That's what I meant, take turns."

"It'll be a tight fit." Surely they'd brush past each other, wearing nothing but a towel now and then....

"Think of the positive side," he said. "Now you won't be alone when you get home from work."

With Dr. Dan on the loose, that point held considerable merit. *Let's face it*, Maggie thought. *Some things are more important than emotional well-being.* Preserving life and limb was one of them.

"I'll pay this month's rent," Nick was saying, "and my half of the other bills, of course. And I'll be happy to baby-sit Zach sometimes if I'm available. I'll do my own laundry and pick up my own stuff and..." He hesitated for a moment. "I'll provide dinner three or four nights a week, but I can't promise I'll cook it. Good enough?"

Maggie raised her brows. He'd had her the second she saw his suitcases. She could never turn away someone who had nowhere else to go, but he was right: there were some definite advantages. He was offering monetary compensation, the re-assurance of his physical presence and baby-sitting for Zach. The only negatives Maggie could foresee included telling Darla, having her mother assume she was living in sin—and the possibility that at some point she'd succumb and actually would be.

"You'll have to sleep on the couch until I talk to Mrs. Gruber and get her room cleaned out for you," she said, "but that should happen later today." She stepped out of his way and motioned him in. "Welcome home."

"OH, MY GOSH!"

Maggie woke to the sound of those words spoken on a screech. She realized almost immediately that one of the neg-atives she'd anticipated when she let Nick move in three hours earlier had already been accomplished. Darla was in her living room. And she'd just discovered Nick.

*Click, click, click.* High heels tapped down the hallway, coming at double speed. Then Darla flung the door open and stood there, eyebrows cocked, hands on her hips. When she saw that Maggie was awake, she stepped inside and shut the door, and for the first time Maggie regretted giving her a house key.

"I guess you don't tell me anything anymore, is that it?"

Maggie struggled to wake up enough to speak without slurring her words. "Darla, what are you doing here? It's eight o'clock in the morning. Why aren't you on your way to work?"

"After that message you received yesterday, I was worried about my best friend, so I decided to drop in, that's why. Because I thought we *were* best friends. But that was back when we told each what was going on in our lives."

Covering a yawn, Maggie struggled into a sitting position. "You wanted me to wake you up at five o'clock this morning to tell you Nick Sorenson was standing on my porch with his suitcases?"

"That's how it happened?"

"Cross my heart."

"But why? What's he doing here?"

Maggie related the story Nick had given her, and Darla rubbed her hands. "Hot damn! He's available. And he's here, sleeping on your couch!"

"Shh. He can probably hear you," Maggie admonished. Then, in a softer voice, "Nick and I are just friends, Darla. That's all we're ever going to be."

"Only because you won't give him a chance. I keep telling you, you're crazy—"

"The friends part was actually his idea. He's thinking about moving back to Connecticut and just needs a place to stay for a few weeks, that's all."

"And you're making him sleep on the *couch?*"

Maggie tucked her hair behind her ears in hopes of straightening out the wild mess. "I'm not making him sleep anywhere. We have an arrangement."

"I think I could negotiate a better deal. Want my help?"

"No." Maggie laughed. "I have Zach to think about. And Mrs. Gruber. Because of Dr. Dan, she'll be glad to know there's a man in the house, but I need this arrangement to be on the up-and-up. How are things with Reese?"

"So far, so good. We watched *Gladiator* together last night. How was your cyber-date with John?"

"He didn't show." Hearing the disappointment in her own voice, Maggie injected a positive note. "But maybe there was a good reason."

Darla's face showed sympathy. "Yeah, maybe he was in a car accident or something, Mags. You never know."

"Jeez, are you still mad at me about Nick? A car accident—is that supposed to make me feel better?"

"It would make me feel better if I was the one he stood up," she said, shrugging. "What about work? How'd that go? You haven't received any more threatening messages, have you?"

"Not last I checked." Maggie didn't add that she hadn't checked since the police left yesterday afternoon. If by any chance Dr. Dan had called her back, she didn't want to hear.

"Okay, well, I have to go. I'm going to be late as it is." Darla flashed Maggie a wide smile. "Don't do anything I wouldn't do."

In the aftermath of Darla's whirlwind visit, Maggie sat on her bed in a daze. Sleep. She needed more sleep. Working nights, she never seemed to get enough. But now that she was awake and daylight was glimmering cheerily around her blinds, she remembered the e-mail Lola Fillmore's editor had sent—and felt the need to dig a little deeper.

Stumbling out of bed, she signed on to the Internet, deter-

mined to get right to work and not take time to search for a
message from John. But her resolve lasted all of two seconds.
Her computer informed her she had mail, and she immediately skimmed through the list of senders, stopping only
when she saw his screen name near the bottom.

Maggie—
I'm so sorry about our date. I got caught up at work.
Please forgive me. I'll make it up to you.
Love,
John

How should she respond? *Should* she respond?

"What was up with Darla?"

Startled, Maggie turned and saw Nick. Wearing nothing
but a pair of faded blue jeans, he leaned against her door,
arms folded across a bare chest. Dark blond hair, the same
color as that on his head, swirled above his pectorals, then
darkened as it thinned and trailed down toward his navel. His
hair was mussed, his jaw shadowed with stubble, but all in
all, he made a pretty good picture.

Steeling herself against the sudden flutter in her stomach,
Maggie said, "Nothing."

"Are you kidding?" he asked. "She gaped at me as
though she'd never seen a man sleeping on a couch before."

"Well, in her defense, she's never seen a man sleeping on
*my* couch."

Nick gave her a skeptical look. "From what I've heard her
say, she's never seen a man sleeping on hers, either, not if
she can put him to better use."

Maggie laughed in spite of herself. "Darla's a free spirit.
She doesn't let much get in the way of what she wants, but
she's not as easy as you might think."

"Why are you up so early? Can't you go back to sleep?"

"I'd like to, but I've got work I should be doing."

"Is everything okay?"

"Yeah."

"Then why the frown?"

Maggie sighed. "I was just checking my e-mail. I had a date last night with a guy who stood me up. He's written to say he's sorry, but I can't help thinking that if he really cared about me, he would've found the time to send me a quick message saying he needed to reschedule." She rested her chin on one fist and gazed up at him. "What do you think? Are guys usually sincere with this kind of thing? Or should I forget about him?"

"Anybody can make a mistake," he said. "I wouldn't automatically say you should forget about him." He cleared his throat. "What does his message say?"

Maggie read John's message aloud.

"This is the John you told me about? The one you met online?"

"Yeah."

"Well, he seems like a decent guy. I'd definitely believe him."

Considering, Maggie chewed on her lower lip.

"How well do you like him?" he asked.

"Sometimes I like him a lot."

He grinned. "Better than me?"

"I'm not going to answer that. The two of you are nothing alike."

Nick coughed into his hand. "Really? How are we different?"

"You just are."

"I take it I wouldn't compare favorably."

"He's just more my type."

"Oh, we're back to types, huh? Maybe it's time we talked about *stereo*types."

Maggie stood to face him. "I'm not stereotyping you."

"Then what do you have against me? I've done nothing wrong."

"I know. We're friends."

"You don't think I meant what I said that night on the porch. You don't think I'll respect my boundaries, is that it?"

How could she when his eyes said one thing and his mouth said another? "I think you'll respect the boundaries as long as I make you."

"You're wrong."

"Want me to prove it?"

"Give it your best shot."

Stepping closer, Maggie pressed her palms flat against his bare chest. He felt every bit as good as she'd imagined—no, even better. She let her hands slide up and around his broad shoulders to lock behind his neck. His hair tickled her knuckles, and the look on his face grew shuttered, unfathomable, but when he didn't react, Maggie almost lost her nerve. Deep down, she was still the tortured, shy girl she'd been in high school, wasn't she? She had no business doing this. Except that her marriage, her divorce, her profession had taught her to confront her fears. And she'd seen the desire in Nick's eyes. He'd confessed to wanting her....

Standing on tiptoe, she brought her lips to his and he...did nothing.

"Satisfied?" he asked when she pulled away.

*Satisfied* probably wasn't the word Maggie would have chosen, but she finally believed him. He was serious about the boundaries he'd drawn.

"I guess," she said, finding it difficult to look him in the eye. She'd felt a pull when she touched him and had to admit, at least to herself, that she'd never so badly wanted a man to make some sort of move. But evidently she'd been wrong about the desire in his eyes, wrong about his sincerity a few nights ago when he'd said he wanted her. He'd obviously felt nothing when she'd kissed him, which meant, as far as her new roommate was concerned, that she had nothing to worry about.

Which was *good* news, right?

## *CHAPTER TWELVE*

STEPPING OUTSIDE Maggie's bedroom, Nick closed his eyes, curled his hands into fists and took a steadying breath. The feel of Maggie's lips against his mouth was still with him, along with the softness of her breasts brushing his bare chest through the thin fabric of her tank top. Two strides, only two strides, and he could pull her back into his arms. Except this time he'd crush her to him and let his hands delve beneath her shirt to massage the soft skin he knew he'd find there—

No! Nick shoved the resolve-weakening image from his mind and, by the slimmest of margins, held on to his self-control. Remembering Irene helped. Irene crying, surrounded by the gifts they'd received for their wedding... He still felt terrible for putting her through such hurt and humiliation. Especially because he didn't entirely understand why he'd backed away from her. He'd thought he was committed. He'd thought he could marry her. He should have been happy to have her as his wife. She was an intelligent, lovely woman, and she'd waited nearly two years for his proposal. But for some reason, when it came right down to it, he simply couldn't walk up to the altar and promise her the rest of his life.

At least he knew his limitations now. He wouldn't leave Maggie crying.

Heading back to the living room, Nick yanked on his T-shirt and gathered his beeper and cell phone. It was mid-morning. He worried less about Dr. Dan hurting Maggie during the day than when she was coming home in the dark predawn. Now that he'd be staying at her place and could protect her during those hours, he felt calmer about the whole situation, but he'd continue to have a squad car drive past the house a few times per hour to keep an eye on her so he could get back to work. Steve Ritter had given him a list of his wife's associates, and he'd spoken to most of them, but a few had been out of town or were otherwise unavailable. He hoped they could provide a clue—something she said or did in the days before her death—that might bring him a step closer to her killer. He also wanted to listen one more time to the recording Mendez had made of Dr. Dan's message to Maggie, just in case he'd missed a subtle hint or inflection that might spin the investigation in a new direction. Now that Dr. Dan's face was in the paper, he hoped the tips would come rolling in....

His beeper chirped and Nick glanced at the number on its screen. Mendez. Maybe one of those tips had already revealed something important.

Glancing down the hall to make sure Maggie was still in her room, he dialed the detective on his cell phone, holding it against his ear with his shoulder while he scooped up his wallet and change from the coffee table and thrust them back in his pockets.

"Sorenson here."

"Glad I caught you," Mendez said.

"What's up?"

"Me an' Hurley are at Discovery Park. I think you'd better get down here."

Nick had been expecting good news, but the gravity in the detective's voice caused his stomach to clench with the wrong kind of anticipation. "Why?"

"I think you need to see this."

MINUTES LATER, Maggie heard the front door close and the engine of Nick's truck turn over. He was out of the house and on his way to God knew where. She could breathe easier and try to forget her uncharacteristically forward display, at least until he returned. Then the humiliation and embarrassment would come tumbling back. It wasn't as though she could avoid him forever now that they were living in the same house—but she hoped that, by the time she saw him again, she'd have it all in perspective. Or maybe she'd be at work and he'd take another night off....

*Luck is never that much in my corner.* How had she come to let Nick move in with her, anyway? Only a few weeks ago, she'd been determined to keep her distance. Yet he'd slipped easily and quickly past her defenses, and *she'd* ended up kissing *him.* She'd actually crossed the room, run her hands over his incredible bare chest, slid her arms around his neck and lifted her mouth to his—

Flushing, Maggie wound her hair into a knot and fanned herself with one hand. Darla must be having an effect on her psyche. With Tim, she'd been reserved and unassertive, afraid to say or do anything that might make him turn on her. Now...well, her behavior didn't bear thinking about. That kiss had been more than the challenge it appeared to be and she knew it, but she was determined to forget about the whole incident. She had work to do.

Clicking on her "Old Mail" file, she decided to let her response to John wait and pulled up the message she'd received from Lola Fillmore's editor.

Dear Ms. Russell—
Your message has me very concerned. Lola's murder was a difficult thing for all of us here at the *Independent.* We're anxiously awaiting the time the police catch her killer so we can come to some sort of resolution, but if Dr. Dan is

now contacting you, as he was contacting Lola, I want to stress how important it is that you work closely with the police. Because Lola was my friend, as well as my employee, I wouldn't admit this to just anyone, but Lola's ambition sometimes came between her and good judgment. Don't make the same mistake.

Mr. Dale Henderson, Editor

Maggie twirled a lock of hair around her finger, pondering the words on her screen. Dr. Dan had been contacting Lola, and now Lola was dead. The connection certainly hadn't escaped her. But there were other things in Henderson's letter that raised her curiosity and her interest. *Lola's ambition sometimes came between her and good judgment.* What did Henderson mean? He couldn't be intimating that Lola had used her connection to Dr. Dan to build her career instead of helping the police...or was he? And, if so, how had her actions played a part in her murder?

The telephone sat on the corner of the desk. Maggie's eyes darted to it, and she hesitated only a moment before lifting the receiver to dial information. Based on her own relationship with her editor and how closely he was involved in her work, she sensed that Dale Henderson knew more than he was saying. He might even know more than he'd told the police. Maybe Lola had done something that wouldn't reflect well on her or the paper. In any case, Maggie needed more than a dire warning to be careful. She needed to know exactly what had happened between Lola Fillmore and Dr. Dan.

After getting the number, she called the *Independent* and the receptionist came on the line.

"I'm sorry, Mr. Henderson is unavailable at the moment, but I could transfer you to his voice mail."

Maggie agreed, left him a message, then called back. If the *Independent* was anything like the *Tribune*, there'd be

others working at the paper who knew something about Lola
and the stories she'd been writing on Dr. Dan. Maybe she
had a friend like Darla or worked with one particular photographer. Or maybe she collaborated with another cop reporter. Maggie knew that if she talked to enough people,
she'd find *someone* who could tell her about Lola and Dr.
Dan. There'd been a growing familiarity between them that
was apparent in the articles Lola had written. If only Maggie
could find out how he'd first approached her, what had drawn
him to her—and what Lola had done in response. That information could very possibly save her life.

IT WAS ANOTHER VICTIM.

A knot formed in Nick's stomach as he viewed the female
corpse found only hours earlier in the shrubbery of the park.
A petite brunette, she'd once been an attractive woman. Now
she was dead. And like the rest of Dr. Dan's victims, she'd
died a violent death.

The guy who'd stumbled upon her body as he was coming
back from a morning jog was sitting on a park bench, still
looking like he might be sick. When Nick arrived, the jogger
had been shaky and desperately wanted to go home to assure
himself of his family's safety. Only after Mendez had let him
use his cell phone to call his wife, had he calmed down
enough to answer a few questions.

Hurley was with him now, but as soon as the coroner arrived, Nick joined them. He'd been listening to their conversation with half an ear already and was intrigued by the jogger's sighting of a man who'd apparently been crossing the
park when he first got there.

"—have you seen him here before?" Hurley was asking.

The jogger, who'd given his name as Mike Flynn, shook
his head. "No, I don't think so, but I don't always pay a lot

of attention. This park draws all kinds. I just go about my business—''

''But this was early. There couldn't have been a lot of people in the park at 6:00 a.m.?''

''Not a lot, but some.''

''Mostly joggers, cyclists, that sort of thing?''

''And people walking their dogs.''

''Was the guy you saw out walking his dog?''

''No, he didn't have a dog.''

''And he wasn't dressed like a jogger.''

''He was wearing dark pants and a jacket of some sort.''

''It's the end of June. Didn't the jacket strike you as odd?''

''Not really. It's pretty cool here in the mornings. I mean, I wouldn't wear one, but this guy looked kind of wrinkled, like he might've been sleeping in his clothes. Or maybe he spent the night drinking or something.''

''So he looked homeless?''

Mike Flynn ran a hand over the top of his short Afro. ''Maybe that's why he seemed a little furtive. I don't know, man. By the time I saw him, he was walkin' away from me and seemed to have some purpose. But like I said, I didn't look at him real close. He was just some middle-aged white guy wearing street clothes.''

''Have you seen the paper this morning?''

''No. I only take it on weekends.''

Hurley slid the composite of Dr. Dan in front of him. ''Could this be the man you saw?''

Nick crossed his arms and leaned against the picnic table, carefully watching Flynn's reaction for any flicker of recognition. What he saw was confusion.

''I don't know. The guy didn't have a beard or a mustache and his hair wasn't so dark. It was bleached on the ends, you know? And spiked up. I noticed because it was sort of a young style for a man his age.''

"Can you remember anything about the way he walked? Did he look at you or speak?"

"No. He had his head down and was moving pretty fast."

"Did you notice any cars in the lot?" Nick asked, entering the conversation for the first time.

Flynn shot him a glance but spoke to Hurley. "Just the one this guy unlocked and seemed to be getting into. I was starting my run then, so my attention was on the bike trail, not the parking lot."

"Do you know the make and model of the car you saw?" Nick persisted.

Flynn stood, looked nervously at the coroner, who was overseeing the removal of the body, and began to edge away. "Did I hear him right? Did he just say that woman had her tongue cut out?"

Hurley nodded. "I'm afraid so."

"I just want to go home. It's not every day I stumble on a dead person, especially one who's been...mutilated. I feel bad about what happened to that poor woman, but I really didn't see anything that could—"

Nick identified himself and showed his I.D. "Mr. Flynn, sometimes the smallest details are the ones that help the most. I know what you saw wasn't a pretty sight, but it's our job to make sure this type of thing doesn't happen again, and we need to ask you these questions while the answers are still fresh in your mind. Now, can you remember anything about the car?"

Flynn sighed and turned so he could no longer see the body. "It was a late-model Geo."

"What color?"

"Blue."

"Are you sure?"

"That's the only thing I *am* sure of. Can I please go now? I just want to be with my wife."

"Just one more question. Did you happen to see if it had local plates?"

"No, man. I didn't even look."

Nick thanked him, and Hurley jotted down his personal information so they could reach him again if needed, then let him go.

As Nick watched, he headed up the hill to the street that dead-ended into the park. Flynn hadn't been able to give them much, but at least he'd been able to confirm the Geo Metro. Without any information on the plates, it wasn't enough to take to the DMV. But they could leak it to the press. Sightings of the Geo could generate more leads. So far, the composite hadn't netted them anything. On the other hand, Dr. Dan would learn that they knew what he was driving and might simply park the Geo in a garage somewhere and buy, steal or borrow a new vehicle. Then the investigation would be no better off than before.

Suddenly, Nick realized that Hurley was shifting uncomfortably and acting as though he had something to say but didn't want to say it.

"What is it?" he asked.

Mendez finished with the coroner just then and joined them, and Hurley shot his partner a meaningful glance. "Tell him," he said.

Mendez shook his head ruefully and cursed. "We got something in the mail today."

Nick raised his brows. "You gonna tell me what?"

"It's a letter. From Dr. Dan."

"What does he have to say this time? Anything new?"

"Not a lot," Hurley said.

Mendez cleared his throat. "He gloats for three pages."

"About what happened at the river?"

The smaller detective scowled. "Yep. He even signed the letter Norman Bates."

"Asshole," Hurley added.

If a woman hadn't just been killed, Nick would have laughed. Mendez and Hurley had earned Dr. Dan's derision. Dr. Dan had dangled himself right in front of them and had still managed to slip through their fingers.

But not for long.

Checking his watch to make sure it was late enough, Nick called Oliver Steele from Solid Security. According to the company's secretary, he was supposed to be back at work today at two o'clock, which meant he was probably in town.

"Hello?"

"Mr. Steele? This is Special Agent Sorenson with the Federal Bureau of Investigation. I'd like to come over and talk with you. It's important. Do you have a few minutes this morning?"

"Actually, I'm glad you called, Agent Sorenson. Lucy, the gal at work, left a message on my answering machine telling me what happened to that poor woman, and I wanted to tell you what I saw the night she was killed. I didn't think much of it at the time, but now I think it might be significant."

"What's that, Mr. Steele?"

"Well, when I was locking the bathrooms at Sunrise Boulevard, I saw the flicker of headlights coming down the bike trail on the other side of the river and went to investigate."

Already the story sounded familiar. Evidently Dr. Dan didn't have much of an imagination. "And?"

"I found a man and a woman in a blue Geo Metro."

"Did you speak to them?"

"I didn't have much to say. I'd realized by then that they hadn't been driving down the bike trail, like I'd thought. They'd entered via the parking lot across from the boat launch, so I simply told them the park closed at dusk. The man thanked me, but the woman said nothing. It was pretty dark, but I could see that she was kind of slumped against the car, propped up by the man. When I didn't leave right away, he helped her back into the car and took off.''

"Why didn't you contact the police?''

"The man held her like he was her husband or boyfriend. I assumed the woman was drunk. But when I heard about the murder, well, I knew I was wrong.''

So that was why Dr. Dan had hauled Sarah Ritter out; he'd been interrupted. With Steele right there, he couldn't float her down the river the way he'd planned. "Sit tight, Mr. Steele. I'm going to bring over a composite sketch of the murder suspect. I'd like to see if it's the same man you saw that night.''

"There's no need,'' Steele told him. "I'm looking at it right now.''

"And?''

"That's the man.''

"No! NO WAY! No dog!'' Barefoot, Maggie stood with her hands on her hips as she confronted Nick in the entryway, wearing a pair of shin-length jeans and a T-shirt that hugged her breasts and was just short enough to show a tantalizing slice of midsection. Her hair was up in some sort of clip and was sticking out all over, and she wore no makeup, but she looked better to Nick than ever before. Of course, he'd been staying at his apartment, buried by the investigation and hadn't seen her for twenty-four hours, which probably had something to do with the power of his response.

Ignoring the impulse to slide his hands over that strip of soft, bare midriff, he focused on her face and tried not to laugh at her abhorrence as she stared at his dog.

"First you show up with your luggage and ask to move in. I enlist Mrs. Gruber's support and clean her room. Then you disappear for a day and a night. And now you show up with a *dog,*'' she complained.

"Does that mean you missed me?" he asked hopefully.

She gave Rambo a baleful glance. "Not enough to let you bring home a dog."

"Come on, Maggie. Rambo's a great pet."

"Maybe he is, but big dogs scare me, and I don't want to worry about my shoes being chewed up while I'm at work or—"

"He doesn't chew. And look at Zach."

Zach had come to stand by Rambo and was giggling as the dog licked his face. Nick could tell the sight had an effect on Maggie, but he wasn't sure it would be enough to convince her to let Rambo stay.

"Come on, Maggie. We'll only be here for a few weeks," he coaxed.

She bit her lip, continuing to watch as her son hugged his dog. "The house could be destroyed by then."

"Rambo's well-trained, and he's completely safe around Zach," Nick argued. "I've had to take a second job as a wedding photographer to pay off some old debts, so I'll be gone more than I expected. Rambo will be here when I'm not, guarding you and Zach. Don't you like the idea of that?"

"With my luck, the only person he'll protect is you," she grumbled. "You'll walk out that door and two seconds later he'll take a chunk out of Zach's arm."

"No, he won't. Look how gentle he is. And he won't hurt you, either. Come here." Nick took Maggie's hand and slid their entwined fingers beneath the dog's nose. "See? He'll associate our scents and know you're my friend. He'll never harm you."

Rambo sniffed their hands, then returned his attention to Zach. Nick told himself to let go of Maggie, but his fingers refused to obey. Instead, they trailed up her arm, and he couldn't help lowering his head to breathe in the smell of her hair. After two days with no more than a few hours' sleep, she seemed like heaven. He barely managed to stop himself from kissing her neck.

As if she could sense the change in him, she stiffened and moved away. "You're saying this dog will protect us?"

"He doesn't like intruders."

"And he'd never harm Zach?"

"Never." Nick studied her. "You trust me, don't you, Maggie?"

She hesitated.

"Come on," Nick said. "How could you *not* trust me after Tuesday morning?" If she knew the self-control refusing her kiss had required, she'd consider him a saint. She'd never doubt another word he said. She'd trust him with her life—and if she knew what was good for her, she'd never tempt him like that again.

"If Zach was older, I probably wouldn't mind," she said, "but..." She let her words trail off as Zach tried to ride Rambo and ended up hugging him again, instead.

"I do worry about Zach getting lonely," she admitted, frowning. "There aren't any little kids to play with on this street, just Mrs. Gruber's grandson when he comes to visit."

"And it's not like Zach has any siblings," Nick added.

Maggie rolled her eyes. "Don't overdo it, buddy, or I'll change my mind. First you show up on my porch with luggage. Now you bring a dog. What next?"

Nick gave her an endearing grin and ambled into the kitchen. "I was kind of hoping for dinner. Is it by any chance your night to cook?"

MAGGIE COULD HEAR Nick banging around in the kitchen and was almost afraid to see what he was doing. In the past week, she'd acquired a roommate, a dog and a psychopathic killer who was now sending her threatening letters as well as voice-mail messages. How much more exciting could life get? She wondered what would've happened if she'd joined the dating service.

"In the morning I'll go to the grocery store," Nick called out.

Maggie smiled at her son and his efforts to drag Rambo to his bedroom. Zach had hold of his collar, but the dog was far stronger and apparently not sure he was going to allow it.

"Why go shopping?" Maggie asked, leaving her son to play with the dog and joining Nick in the kitchen. "We may as well share the groceries I have and split the bill. You probably eat as much as Zach and me put together, so that should be fair. Otherwise, it'll be too difficult to keep everything separate. And the good news is we're all set." She opened the cupboards to show him her neat rows of wheat bread, wheat crackers, bran cereal, cans of Healthy Request soups, natural peanut butter, honey and raisins. "I had Mrs. Gruber get me some groceries when she went the other day. We're stocked up on just about everything."

Nick made a disapproving face at her display. "Not to be critical or anything," he said, "but we could use a few more items."

"Like what?"

"You know, the essentials of life—brownies, chocolate milk, condoms."

*"What?"*

He cracked a devilish smile. "Just making sure you were paying attention."

The telephone rang and the doorbell sounded at the same time, saving Maggie from having to respond and sending Rambo into a barking frenzy that started in the hall and lasted all the way to the front door.

"Tell me he didn't just say condoms," she muttered to herself and reached for the phone, leaving the door to Nick.

It was Darla calling. "Did you hear?" she asked without preamble.

"Hear what?" Maggie pulled the telephone cord taut as she strained to see around the corner. She wanted to enjoy the view of Nick from behind as much as she wanted to determine who was at her door, but the wall blocked her line of vision. She could only hear the murmur of voices, no words.

"There's been another victim. A thirty-one-year-old state worker named Marge Brown was stabbed to death and found in Discovery Park yesterday morning. I heard Jorge talking about it with Ben."

"You're kidding." Maggie instantly forgot about condoms. And, suddenly, she didn't care who was at the door. Her knees felt weak. Searching behind her for a chair, she sank into the first one her hands encountered. After all her diligence with the police scanners, how had she missed Dr. Dan's next strike? The fact that she'd been so blissfully unaware made her feel out of touch and vulnerable, in more ways than one. She'd been busy worrying about Nick, wondering about this sudden disappearance and trying to decide whether or not to forgive John. And all the while, Dr. Dan had been out stabbing another woman. Knowing it might have been her went a long way toward putting her problems in perspective.

The whispery recording on her voice mail came back to her, as did the composite in the paper and the letter she'd received yesterday, and Maggie shivered. Jumping to her feet because she couldn't sit still any longer, she went to the kitchen window to gaze out over the backyard. He could be anywhere. He could be watching her right now....

"When did the call come in?" she asked.

"I guess the dispatchers must've been warned to keep things hush-hush. It didn't go out over the scanners. The detectives were called privately as soon as the guy who found the body phoned in, but I can't tell you any more than that. You'll have to talk to Ben.''

Ben. There'd been another murder and he hadn't called her. He was letting Jorge write the story.

''Maggie? Are you still there?'' Darla asked.

''Yeah.''

''You okay?''

''I will be when the police catch up with this creep, which I hope is sooner rather than later. But I'd better go. I've got to get into the office to see if I can straighten things out with Ben. This is my story, and he knows it. Dr. Dan sent me a letter just yesterday, and I've been on the phone most of the day. I dug up some great stuff on the Lola Fillmore murder. It's going to make a good article.''

''He sent a letter? To your home address?'' Darla sounded as horrified as Maggie felt.

''No, he sent it to the paper.''

''What did it say?''

''Basically more of the same. Listen, I gotta go.''

''Okay, I'll see you soon. By the way, what's all the noise over there?''

Maggie glanced over her shoulder, remembering that she had a visitor. ''Someone's at the door.''

''Sounds like a dog,'' Darla said.

Maggie sighed. ''You don't want to know.''

# CHAPTER THIRTEEN

"WHO WAS IT?" Maggie asked, coming from the kitchen, still upset by Darla's news.

Nick kept a firm hold on his dog as he closed the front door. "Your neighbor, Milly Something."

"It's not Milly S-s-something, s-s-silly. It's Milly S-s-sims-s," Zach informed him.

Nick smiled. "Okay, Milly Sims."

"She owns the dry cleaner's down the street," Maggie said. "What did she want?"

Nick kept his voice neutral but Maggie could tell by the look in his eyes that something was wrong. "She saw someone lurking around the house while you were at work last night. But don't worry. I'll check the yard and the garage. And I'll be here when you get home in the morning."

"Milly's always seeing something," Maggie said. "She jumps at her own shadow." But her words rang hollow, even to her. She looked at her son, then at Rambo, whom she suddenly saw in a whole new way. Nick was right. Rambo would provide her with some peace of mind. Dogs made noise. They sensed things long before humans did. She figured she could abide him in the house, at least until Dr. Dan was caught, just in case Milly wasn't imagining things this time.

"What about Zach? Do you think he and Mrs. Gruber are safe at her place?" she asked.

"Just to be sure, let's have them take Rambo tonight."

"Good idea. I'm going to get ready for work. I have to go in early today."

"I'll go to the office with you," Nick said.

The telephone rang again, catching Maggie just as she was on her way to change. What now? she wondered, half hoping it was Ben. She raced to her room and snatched the handset off its cradle, but the voice that came across the line wasn't her editor's.

"Maggie? This is Brian Wordelly."

"Brian who?"

"Wordelly. I live in Auburn, but my family's from Iowa. Your mother contacted me last night."

"Oh, God, she didn't."

"What?"

"Nothing. I'm sorry. How are you?"

"Good. Fine. Listen, your mother suggested we get together. I thought I'd call and see if you were interested in having dinner this weekend. I'm relatively new in town and I don't know a lot of people...."

Maggie opened her mouth to refuse, then remembered that Nick had mentioned another job. If he started doing weddings, she was going to be alone a lot. She needed a social life. She needed to meet new people, make a change. What did it matter whether her mother set her up with someone or a dating service did?

"I work nights as a journalist, but I'm off on Sunday," she heard herself say.

"Great," Brian replied. "Why don't I pick you up at seven?"

"Sounds good." Maggie gave him directions to her house, then hung up, wearing a bittersweet smile. She might have accepted Brian's offer of a date, but she certainly wasn't excited about it.

FOR SOME REASON, the noise level at the paper seemed higher than normal. Probably because Maggie's ears were still ringing from the last fifteen minutes with Ben. For the first time since she'd started at the paper, she'd marched into his office and stood up for herself. She'd demanded the exclusive she deserved. When he yelled, she yelled. When he'd tried to put her off, she'd insisted on an answer. And, amazingly enough, when the emotional maelstrom had passed, she'd won. Maggie could hardly believe it had been *her* in that room—and from the stares of those around her when she walked out of Ben's office, neither could anyone else.

But it had worked. She'd gotten the exclusive. Now she had to perform.

A daunting thought…but Maggie refused to let the old doubts get the better of her. Not this soon, anyway. She was feeling good about herself, strangely empowered, less inhibited. It was an intoxicating experience, so intoxicating that when Nick looked at her from his desk down the hall, she met his gaze without flinching—thrilling at the way he made her breath catch and her heart pound.

A slow, sensual smile curved his lips, and Maggie smiled right back. She wasn't sure she was any more of a match for Nick Sorenson now than she'd been six weeks ago, but it didn't do any harm to flirt with him.

"You going to forgive John?"

Maggie glanced up to see Darla standing at her cubicle, carrying her purse and a water bottle. It was five o'clock. From the looks of it, she was heading home.

"Who?" Maggie asked absently, still preoccupied with her recent success, as well as the story she had yet to write…and Nick. Unfortunately, Nick usurped more than his share of her thoughts, but she seemed to have little control over that.

"John," Darla repeated.

Of course. Maggie had nearly forgotten him. Now that Nick was back, he seemed to absorb all the surrounding energy. But what about poor John? What had happened to "I like you just the way you are"? And "No need to send a picture"?

"Probably," she said. "I just haven't had time to e-mail him yet."

Darla studied her. "You've been pretty busy."

"Yeah."

"What do you think he's going to say when you tell him you have a man living in the house?"

"I'm not going to tell him. Nick's not a 'man,' he's a roommate."

"Try selling that 'Nick's not a man' stuff to any woman you meet."

"Come on, Darla. Forget about Nick. Anyway, I have a date with someone else this Sunday."

"Who?"

"A guy my mother set me up with."

"Yikes! I'm glad I'm not the one who's going. On another topic…any more messages or letters from Dr. Dan?"

Maggie shook her head. She hadn't wanted to sift through her mail or check her messages, but she knew she couldn't simply ignore the possibility. She'd summoned up the courage to do both as soon as she arrived at work and had been pleasantly surprised to find nothing from any mass murderers. "Not so far, thank goodness. Did you hear I had it out with Ben?"

"Are you kidding? Everyone knows you had it out with Ben. Even Ben's proud of you."

Maggie couldn't resist a smile. "I got the exclusive."

"Good for you. You have the inside track on this story. You deserve the chance to run with it."

"That's what I told him. Thanks for the heads-up call, by the way."

"You'd do the same for me. Hey, when you're finished here, why don't you come over and we'll celebrate your good fortune?"

"Reese won't want me showing up in the middle of the night."

Darla frowned. "Reese's gone."

Maggie reached up to squeeze her friend's hand. Darla acted as though she didn't really care about Reese, but Maggie knew she did. "What went wrong this time?"

"He quit his job. I just can't respect a man who won't work."

"I'm sorry, Darla. I'll finish the article I promised Ben, then I'll stop by the store and buy some goodies on my way over to your apartment. We'll eat until we forget all our troubles. I should be there before midnight."

"Are you sure Ben won't mind you taking off so early?"

Maggie grinned. "I won't be taking off early. I'll bring my scanners with me and monitor them from your place."

Darla looked heartened. "Okay. If I can't have a man, I guess chocolate's the next best thing, right?"

*BROWNIES...BROWNIES...BROWNIES. Frosted or plain? Walnuts or no?* Maggie frowned as she considered the selection in Safeway's bakery. She liked frosting and Darla liked nuts. Why not go for the double whammy?

Putting eight good-sized, thick-frosted walnut brownies in her cart, she moved on to see what else she and Darla might want. Tortilla chips were a must, along with some good salsa. But what about yogurt-covered raisins? A bag of microwave popcorn?

Might as well go for the works, Maggie decided. At this

point, health was a secondary issue. Darla had seemed pretty upset.

Her cart squeaked as she wheeled it around the perimeter of the store, taking her time, enjoying the air-conditioning and the quiet, empty spaces. Safeway wasn't a particularly popular place to be at eleven o'clock at night, but she had some company—a man reading in the magazine aisle, a tired-looking woman buying children's Tylenol, a couple of men in their mid-twenties happily loading their cart with cases of beer.

Maggie skirted the man whose nose was buried in a magazine and made her way to the dairy section, where she spotted the chocolate milk. Remembering Nick and his list of life's necessities—brownies, chocolate milk, condoms—she paused. If she got the chocolate milk, she'd only be missing the condoms.

Feeling daring and a little shy, Maggie added the milk to her cart, then glanced around to make sure she wasn't being observed before heading to the Feminine Hygiene aisle. Sure enough, birth control was right there, next to the pregnancy tests. And other than a few passersby at either end, the aisle was deserted—a good thing considering she'd never bought anything like condoms before and would've kept going if anyone had noticed her.

Finally comfortable that no one was paying any particular attention, Maggie read a few labels. Tim had insisted she stay on the pill until he'd agreed to have a baby, so they'd never used any over-the-counter stuff. She didn't even know what was available. Not that it was difficult to learn—lubricated, ribbed, sheepskin, neon colors.

Maggie bit the insides of her cheeks to keep from smiling as she thought about these choices in connection with Nick Sorenson. What would he buy? He didn't look like a neon kind of man. Ribbed maybe. Real sheepskin definitely—

*Not* that she was planning to sleep with him. She was just checking things out. A girl never knew what she might encounter. Or whom...

"Finding everything okay?"

Maggie jumped and turned to see a woman wearing a Safeway smock and knee pads standing behind her. Evidently she'd come around the corner while Maggie was busy imagining Nick in nothing but a neon orange condom. "Yes, fine. Everything's—" she cleared her throat "—right here. Thanks."

"No problem. I stock these shelves, so if you need anything, just let me know." The woman knelt down and started straightening packages in the section behind Maggie and, for a fleeting moment, Maggie considered asking her if she'd ever tried any of these products. Instead, she decided to make her own decision, and that was when she noticed the different sizes—regular and large. Who would ever have guessed there'd be so many choices involved in buying a box of condoms?

When Maggie didn't move on right away, the store clerk turned to look at her again, and Maggie decided it was definitely time to go. Grabbing the first thing that came to hand—a six-pack of large, ribbed condoms—she shoved it into the cart next to the brownies and started off.

"Have a good night," the woman called after her.

Maggie felt a warm blush rise to her face. "Thank you," she mumbled and hurried out of sight.

SHE'D DONE IT. She'd actually bought her first box of condoms. Not that Maggie knew what she was going to do with them. It was all part of her new, liberated self. She fought with her editor. She lived with a male roommate. She bought condoms. How much more modern could a woman be?

Still, she didn't want Darla to see them. Slipping the package into her purse the minute she unlocked her car, she situated the groceries in the back seat, got behind the wheel and started her engine. If she didn't hurry, Darla might fall asleep. Then she'd have to return to her own house, or to work, if Nick's truck wasn't in her driveway yet. She'd promised him she wouldn't go anywhere she'd be alone, and she meant to keep that promise. The condom purchase had distracted her for a moment, but now she felt the same uneasiness she'd experienced when she left the office, a lingering sense of being watched or followed. But other than a blue Geo Metro parked several spaces away, the lot was empty.

## MURDER VICTIM FIRST BECOMES CONFIDANTE OF KILLER

By *Tribune* Reporter Maggie Russell

SACRAMENTO—According to an unidentified source, the late Lola Fillmore, crime reporter for the *Seattle Independent,* received several letters from the man who subsequently murdered her and recently struck down two victims in the Sacramento area. The first letter from the self-dubbed Dr. Dan arrived in March. It was a response to the article Ms. Fillmore had written on the woman he'd stabbed only days before in Seattle, and it reprimanded her for not including certain information on the crime—"obvious" clues the detectives couldn't, or shouldn't, have missed, he said. In the letter he censured police and seemed angry that Ms. Fillmore hadn't reported their ineptitude with greater accuracy. He demanded she set the record straight. She subsequently wrote an article blasting the task force's inability to apprehend such a violent criminal. Dr. Dan continued to contact her over the next five weeks, feeding her information about his victims and his crimes, but only after the fourth letter, when the killer's tone became personally threatening, did Ms. Fillmore turn to the police.

Amazed, Nick sat at Maggie's desk, staring at the article she'd written before she left work. It went on to say that Dr. Dan was now writing her at the *Trib,* but Maggie had already turned the letter over to Mendez, who'd given him a copy. What surprised Nick was the number of letters she claimed Lola had received. How the hell had she come up with this? Nothing in the files from the Seattle Police Department mentioned anything about the *Independent*'s reporter receiving more than the two letters he'd seen with his own eyes, letters that were as condescending and distinctly combative as the ones received by police. And none of the statements taken from Lola's friends and associates mentioned an ongoing relationship between the reporter and her killer. Yet Maggie's article intimated that Lola had cooperated with Dr. Dan, to a degree. Could her "unidentified source" be wrong? If not, how had the Seattle police missed such an important piece of the puzzle?

Nick snapped his cell phone off his belt and dialed information. He didn't care how late it was, he intended to track down James Jenson, the detective who'd been working the case in Seattle. Jenson was the one who'd established the connection between the murders out east and the two in Colorado and contacted the FBI. He probably knew more about Dr. Dan and his victims than anyone else; he'd been extremely helpful when Nick first took the case and was trying to orient himself.

Less than five minutes later, he had a disgruntled Jenson on the line. "*Who* is this?" the detective asked, for the second time.

"Special Agent Sorenson. I'm here in Sacramento, and I've run across something I'm hoping you can help me with."

"Now? Don't you ever sleep, Sorenson?"

Nick leaned back in his chair, crossed his legs and stared at Maggie's pictures of Zach. "We lost another one the other day," he said quietly. "Attractive, mother of two. Only thirty-one years old."

Silence. Then, "Damn that bastard."

"My sentiments exactly."

"What can I do?"

Nick explained about Maggie's article and the missing letters. "Do you know anything about this?"

"No, and like I told you a few weeks ago, I spoke with Lola Fillmore a number of times. She claimed the first letter didn't arrive until the *end* of March, not the beginning. You've probably seen it. It's dated, and it's in the file. I sent copies of everything to the Ogden office, just as I was instructed to do."

Nick sighed. It wasn't easy coming into the middle of a case. He'd inherited boxes and boxes of reports and statements from each department that had investigated one of Dr. Dan's murders. He'd read every slip of paper more than once. But he had no guarantee that the detectives who had assembled the information had done all their homework. And he didn't have the time or manpower to redo it for them. He had to take the quality of their work on faith, and go from there. "I've seen the two that are in the file," he said.

"Why wouldn't Lola come forward with any others once he started threatening her?" Jenson asked.

"Maybe a personal friend or someone at the paper told her not to. Or maybe she realized it would raise some very legitimate questions about her motivation and her delay in contacting the police."

"She was certainly driven, I'll give her that. If she was using Dr. Dan to build her career, though, she paid a high price."

"I don't want anyone else to pay that same price. See what you can do about finding those letters, okay? They may contain something that can help us."

"I take it you're in a hurry for this information."

"Exactly."

"Is there any chance you can tell me where to start? I interviewed everyone even remotely associated with Lola Fillmore when I was working the case and no one said anything about more letters. It's gonna take a while to contact those people again."

Nick pinched the bridge of his nose, regretting the fact that Maggie hadn't let the police tap her work phone. As a result, she was the only one who knew which sources to contact, and getting that information from her would require more lies, more manipulation. When she found out who he really was, she was going to hate him.

"This reporter would never knowingly give up her source," he said, "but in the interests of time, I'll see what I can do."

# CHAPTER FOURTEEN

THE FLOODLIGHTS AT Darla's apartment complex lit the parking lot brightly enough, but the less powerful pole lights left much of the grounds in shadow.

Maggie squinted to see between the buildings, which circled a pool and play area, noting the dark nooks, corners, patios, trees and shrubs that were everywhere. If Dr. Dan wanted to attack her, he'd have plenty of places to hide. But unless he was following her, he'd have no way of knowing where she was, and there hadn't been any cars on the road behind or in front of her for the past ten minutes. She was perfectly safe.

Finally locating a parking space, Maggie shut off the engine, then craned her neck to see all the way around, wanting to be sure there was no one nearby before she unlocked her doors. Darla's place was tiny, just a studio really, but she lived in a complex of over three hundred units, and her apartment was on the far side. Maggie didn't really want to leave the safety of her car to traipse through the dark grounds, but Darla was expecting her.

Slinging her purse over her shoulder, she gathered the groceries and her cell phone and considered her police scanners. Her arms were full. She'd have to come back for them, she decided reluctantly, and hurried to the sidewalk that circled the complex just as a small blue car entered the lot. Maggie could hear the whine of its engine, see its headlights cutting in and out as it passed the buildings on the far side and came around, but she didn't wait to discover who the driver was. She was afraid she'd see the face that matched the composite.

Running the rest of the way, she banged on Darla's door as soon as she reached it. "Darla, I'm here!" she called, but no one answered.

Footsteps were scuffing against the pavement somewhere behind her. Maggie didn't know if they belonged to the car's driver or someone else, but whoever it was didn't seem to be in any hurry. He—*was* it a man?—didn't move with purpose. He sort of…crept along.

Darla's door was on ground level behind a flight of stairs that climbed to the apartments above, which created an alcove of sorts. Maggie could easily imagine Dr. Dan catching up with her and trapping her here, killing her while Darla slept only fifteen feet away. "Darla, wake up!" she cried, banging again.

Several seconds passed and the footsteps drew nearer, then stopped.

Still Darla didn't come.

Maggie dropped her groceries and began to dig through her purse. She and Darla had given each other house keys, but Darla usually came to Maggie's place, so Maggie rarely used hers. Would she be able to find it now that she needed it?

She peered around the stairs to see if she could locate the person who went with the footsteps but couldn't make out anything besides shadowy buildings, black trees and softly glowing pole lights.

It was just someone coming home late, she told herself. The complex was a large one. Lots of people worked nights or stayed out with friends—

Dammit! She couldn't find the key. Ducking out from beneath the stairs so she could see better, she turned her purse upside down and let everything fall out. Darla's key pinged against the cement amid the clatter of everything else, and she snatched it up just as someone or something rustled the bushes about ten feet away.

Maggie felt her knees go weak. She had to get inside!

Heart pounding, hands shaking, she scooped up the contents of her purse, grabbed her groceries and let herself in. Then she locked the door behind her and leaned against it, taking deep breaths as she waited for...what?

"Maggie, is that you making all the noise? What's wrong? You have a key." Darla yawned and stretched on the couch where she'd plainly been sleeping. The television droned in front of her.

No one tried the door. No one approached the apartment.

"Go back to sleep," Maggie said. "Everything's okay."

"But what about the food?"

"We'll save it for tomorrow."

"You sure?"

"Yeah."

Darla turned over and was out again in a matter of seconds.

Slowly Maggie's breathing returned to normal. She'd over-reacted. She had no proof that whoever was out there meant her any harm. Lola Fillmore's murder and the whole Dr. Dan case had her in a frenzy. But that didn't mean she was going to push her luck by returning to her car for her police scanners.

Darla's three Siamese cats welcomed her by rubbing against her legs. Maggie gave them a scratch, then propelled herself away from the door to unload the groceries. So much for the party. Not that Maggie *wanted* to eat a brownie after her recent terror. She was more in favor of piling all the furniture against the door, boarding up the windows and sitting in the middle of the floor with a weapon.

Maybe she was still a little tense.

After putting the groceries away in the kitchen, Maggie

settled herself in the corner that contained Darla's computer and signed on to the Internet. She knew she couldn't sleep. She had no interest in television. And she'd already decided that she wasn't about to make the trek back to her car until daylight.

Her mailbox was beginning to fill up. She had messages from her mother and Aunt Rita and tons of spam, along with some legitimate messages from business associates. Those she needed to return, but for now, she was more interested in the message waiting for her from John. She clicked on the envelope icon just as her cell phone rang.

"Where are you?"

Nick. "I'm at Darla's," she whispered, keeping her voice low so she didn't wake Darla again.

"Why didn't you call me? You said you'd call as soon as you got there."

"I just walked through the door."

"It's not that long a drive. Where have you been?"

"I stopped at the store," she told him, skipping over her condom purchase and the scarier parts of her experience.

"When are you coming home?"

Home? She wished she was home now. Home sounded wonderful and incredibly safe, as long as Nick was there with her. But Mrs. Gruber was keeping Zach until midmorning again; she and Nick would be alone for hours. And she had condoms.

Not a good combination.

"Are you there now?" she asked.

"I will be in ten minutes. I'm getting gas. Want me to come pick you up?"

"Um…" The condoms in her purse seemed to scream out a resounding *yes,* but she ignored them and took the safe route. "I think I'll stay here."

"Darla okay?"

"She's asleep, but I've got her cats to keep me company."

"You're playing with her cats?"

"I'm online."

"You sure you don't want to come home?"

"Shut up," she told the condoms.

"What?" he asked, obviously surprised.

"I wasn't talking to you."

"So you're going to stay there?"

"Yeah, I need to answer John. I haven't gotten back to him since he stood me up."

"Right. John. Hey, I saw the piece you wrote for tomorrow's paper, by the way."

Maggie frowned. "How? Didn't I leave that on my desk?"

"Yeah. I walked past to get a drink and happened to see it lying there. I didn't think you'd mind my taking a look, since it's going in tomorrow's paper, anyway."

Maggie wasn't sure she was completely comfortable with Nick helping himself to the things on her desk, but he had a point about the article appearing in tomorrow's paper. "So what did you think?" she asked.

"I think it's a good article. Where did you come up with all that info about Lola?"

One of Darla's cats jumped into Maggie's lap and nudged her hand, and she petted him while she talked. "I just did a little research."

"You mean you talked to one of her friends or something?"

"Or something. I can't really say."

Silence. "Don't you trust me?"

"It's not a matter of trusting you," she said. "It's the fact that my source has already trusted me. I promised anonymity."

"What if lives are at risk?"

"You can't qualify anonymity. You either grant it or you

don't. If journalists revealed their sources because it's for a 'good reason,' everything becomes a judgement call. And who can depend on that?''

"I see." He sighed. "Okay, so are you going to call me when you leave Darla's?''

"If I leave before the sun comes up.''

"Do me a favor and call anyway, okay?''

Evidently Nick was taking the protection part of their arrangement very seriously. "Okay.''

He hung up, and Maggie scooted Darla's cat off her lap so she could turn her attention to John's e-mail, but it wasn't easy to forget Nick now that she knew he was on his way to her house—and that he'd be alone when he got there.

She pictured him as he'd looked when she kissed him, wearing only a pair of faded blue jeans. Darla would think she was crazy to miss out on such an incredible opportunity. Heck, *Maggie* thought she was crazy. But Nick was only temporary and Zach needed a good father. Besides, Nick had put certain boundaries on their relationship, and Maggie didn't plan to cross them again. She'd felt foolish enough the first time.

John's message was another sweet apology. Smiling, Maggie sent him a nice reply, then returned her other messages.

The sun was coming up when she finished. She was about to sign off when John sent her an instant message.

Mntnbiker: What are you doing up so early, beautiful?
Zachman: Returning my mail. Did you get my message?
Mntnbiker: Yes. Do you really forgive me?
Zachman: I think so, but it would help if that present you promised me would arrive. <G>
Mntnbiker: You'll have it in a day or two.
Zachman: How? You don't have my address.
Mntnbiker: Right. The online store was supposed to han-

dle that through e-mail, but I'll just take care of it myself. Why don't I send it to your office?

Zachman: That would work, but I was just kidding about the present.

Mntnbiker: No woman kids when it comes to a present.

Zachman: Okay, you found me out.

She gave him the paper's address, then asked what he was sending her.

Mntnbiker: You'll see.

Zachman: I'm excited.

Mntnbiker: I'm just glad you decided to forgive me. I was afraid I'd lost you.

Zachman: Truly?

Mntnbiker: Half the time I can't sleep for thinking of you.

Half the time Maggie couldn't sleep for thinking of Nick, but she wasn't about to write that.

Zachman: That's a nice thing to say. I would've written sooner, but I've been busy.

Mntnbiker: Doing what?

Zachman: Working and taking care of Zach.

She explained about Lola Fillmore and the missing letters.

Mntnbiker: Another front-page article?

Zachman: Ben hasn't said, but I think so.

Mntnbiker: That's great. Where'd you get the details?

Zachman: I made a few calls and tracked down someone who knew more than she wanted to tell the police.

Mntnbiker: She didn't mind telling you?

Zachman: I'm not the police.

Mntnbiker: Who was it?

Zachman: Just someone Lola worked with.

Mntnbiker: So she told you there'd been more letters. Did she actually see them?

Zachman: That's what she claims.

Mntnbiker: Do the police know about them?

Zachman: If not, they'll know tomorrow when the paper hits. The scary thing is that Dr. Dan is now contacting me.

John asked her some questions about Dr. Dan and his message and letter; Maggie explained the whole thing.

Mntnbiker: That worries me. Are you going to be okay, babe?

*Babe?* Babe was taking their relationship to a whole new level. It ranked right up there with ''I was afraid I'd lost you'' and ''Half the time I can't sleep for thinking of you.'' Were she and John now involved? If so, this was probably a good time to mention the man who'd just moved in with her. After all, it was only fair to be honest.

Zachman: I'm being careful. Actually, a friend moved in with me this week so I don't have to come home to an empty house.

Mntnbiker: That was nice of her.

Maggie took a deep breath and plunged on.

Zachman: Actually, it's a man.

His answer came quickly.

Mntnbiker: A man? What kind of man?

Maggie stared at her screen, feeling instant remorse. What was she doing? She was risking her whole relationship with John over a temporary roommate. So what if she'd bought condoms? Nick wasn't husband material. He had no f.p., remember? As long as the condoms stayed in her purse, John need never know how badly she'd been tempted. And neither did Nick...

She bit her lip, trying to think of a way to retract her words.

Half a second later, it occurred to her.

Zachman: Don't worry about him. I think he's gay.

This time there was a long pause.

Mntnbiker: What makes you think that?
Zachman: I live with him now, remember? Believe me, I could stroll in front of him naked and he wouldn't even notice. He's definitely not interested in women.
Mntnbiker: Maggie?
Zachman: Yeah?
Mntnbiker: I wouldn't try the naked thing, if I were you.

SO NOW HE WAS GAY? He didn't respond to that one kiss, and now he was *gay?*

Nick unplugged his laptop and put it in its carrying case, then stretched out on Maggie's bed, staring at the wallpaper that had been partially stripped from the wall. She'd said she could run around stark-naked and he wouldn't notice.

He'd like to see her try that. It would certainly be a quick way to learn what his appetites and preferences really were.

Except then he'd feel terrible when he left her for Utah. Even worse than he did now, what with his e-mail deception.

Who would've thought, when he took this assignment, that protecting a female journalist would be so difficult? Why did Maggie have to be different from every other woman he knew? She couldn't even cooperate with him enough to provide the information he needed on the Fillmore letters. He'd tried asking her as Nick; he'd tried as John. And he'd gotten very little either way.

He didn't like her, he decided. He was eager to get back home.

But that didn't make him feel any better. Probably because he knew, deep down, that if he didn't like her it was only because he liked her too much. As for wanting to go home, it was only because he was afraid that if he *didn't* leave soon, he never would.

"Damn," he said, angry at anything and everything without really knowing why. Picking up his cell phone, he dialed Mendez.

"What now?" the detective demanded when he finally answered.

Nick ignored him. "You getting any leads from the composite?"

"None that are panning out. And none that I haven't already told you about. You woke me up to ask me that?"

"No. There's an article coming out in the paper tomorrow. I want you to read it, then call Maggie Russell and see what you can get out of her."

"Oh, sure. I've been so helpful to her. She'll probably tell me everything."

Nick smiled grudgingly at the sarcasm because it fit his mood so well. "That was before. Now you're going to tell her lots of things—like the fact that we believe the murderer is driving a blue Geo Metro. You're going to confirm the connection between the murders and you're going to send her a copy of the coroner's report on Marge Brown. Then you're going to persuade her to tell you where you can get hold of the Fillmore letters.''

"And if I can't get these…what did you call them? Fillmore letters?''

"You will. If she won't reveal her source—it's a woman who works at the *Independent*, by the way—see if she can convince her to come forward. I think Maggie will do what she can. Just get me those letters.''

Mendez sighed in obvious frustration. "I'm completely lost.''

"You won't be in the morning,'' Nick said and hung up.

"MAAAGGGIIIE…Maaagggiiee…where are you Maggie? This is Dr. Dan. You remember me, don't you? I saw you at the grocery store last night. When you were buying some condoms to go with your brownies. Nice mix, by the way. Did you put it all to good use?''

Another message! Maggie stood in her kitchen gripping the phone so hard it hurt. Dr. Dan had been following her last night. He'd been there the whole time. He even knew what she'd bought!

She took a deep breath and bent over so she wouldn't be sick as the rest of his message played in her ear. "I could help you out with the party, you know. I could satisfy you permanently, and I'm tempted, believe me. Especially after that article you wrote today. You made it sound like I was *trying* to make the police look bad. But they don't need my help, Maggie. I think you're getting your facts confused, just like Lola did. Our police system is filled with a bunch of bumbling idiots, and it's time the public knows. I've sent you another letter, stating the facts. You'll probably get it tomorrow. I suggest you print it. Otherwise, I might take offense.''

Oh, God. This pervert, this homicidal maniac, had fixated on her, just like he had on Lola Fillmore. Only he was leaving her messages *and* sending her letters, which was worse. Somehow messages seemed far more intimate....

Straightening, Maggie pulled her robe tighter as her eyes flicked from window to window. Her voice mail system was asking her to save or delete Dr. Dan's message, but she couldn't move. She wasn't even sure she'd heard all of it. Was he out there right now? Watching her?

Maybe he'd seen her step onto the porch to retrieve the paper a few minutes ago. She'd wanted to see her article and had found it on the front page. But then she'd made the mistake of checking her voice mail, and Dr. Dan's most recent message had stolen all her joy. What was she going to do? What would happen to Zach if the police didn't catch Dr. Dan before he got her?

Suddenly Maggie wanted to see Zach more than she'd ever wanted to see anyone before. She wanted to hug him close and know that she'd be there to take care of him until he was a man and could take care of himself.

Nick came around the corner, dressed in a pair of long cargo shorts and a T-shirt, his hair still wet from a recent shower. When Maggie had gotten home, she'd found him asleep in her bed. ''What is it, Maggie?'' he asked now. Obviously, the look on her face had given her away.

Maggie opened her mouth to tell him about the message, then remembered what it said. She didn't want Nick to know she was buying condoms. She didn't want anyone to know.

Her finger hovered over the delete button. Surely there wasn't anything in this new message that could help the police. Dr. Dan had used the same false, raspy voice. He'd said similar things.

But if she deleted his message, she'd be doing what Lola Fillmore had done. She'd be keeping evidence from the police because it made her look bad. And they needed everything they could get on this guy....

With a grimace, she saved the message and hung up. Then she forced a smile for Nick. "I want to see Zach," she said. "I'm going over to Mrs. Gruber's to get him."

Nick watched her for a moment without saying anything. Finally he nodded. "Okay. I was just about to mow the lawn. Mower's in the shed, right?"

Maggie glanced through the window overlooking the backyard, wondering if Dr. Dan had ever attacked a man. He could hit Nick over the head when Nick least expected it, or stab him from behind....

"Yeah, but be careful," she said.

"Be careful?" he repeated.

"Just keep your eyes open."

"Maggie, you're not making any sense." He reached toward her to do something—Maggie wasn't sure what; clasp her hands?—but that simple motion was all the invitation she needed to melt into him. She buried her face in his shoulder, breathing in the wonderful clean scent that was Nick, and felt his arms go around her.

"Something's upset you," he said in her ear. "Tell me what it is."

Maggie shook her head. She didn't want to talk about it. She just wanted to feel safe.

"Please don't let go," she whispered. "Give me a minute."

"Maggie?"

She didn't answer. His hands were on her back, massaging their way slowly up her spine and pressing her against him.

"Maggie," he said again, only this time her name sounded more like a groan. And the next thing she knew, he was kissing her. She wasn't sure if she'd put her mouth to his or if he'd initiated the contact; more likely they'd come together at the same time. In any case, they were both active participants, which probably wasn't a good thing. Hadn't she just told John Nick was gay?

Ah, but a kiss had never felt so good. One of Nick's hands was clutching her hair, the other cupped her bottom, making her unavoidably aware of his complete arousal. Someone was even moaning. God, was that her?

Nick lifted his head and smiled. "Let's see what's under here," he said, tugging on the belt of her robe.

While Maggie was still trying to decide whether or not to let this go any further, the robe parted, revealing the only piece of lingerie she owned. A short bone-colored nightie with thin straps, it had small triangles of fabric that covered her nipples while leaving the rest of her breasts exposed to his view.

"Wow, where did you get this little number?" he asked with frank appreciation.

"Darla gave it to me for Christmas. It was one of her broad hints that I need to spice up my life." Maggie *wanted* him to touch her. She thought she might go crazy while she waited, feared she'd shrivel up and die if he never did.

His breath whistled through his teeth. "Definitely works for me," he said and slipped a hand underneath her nightie. Starting at her thigh, he moved slowly upward until he reached her panties, then slipped inside them, too, and stroked her bottom.

If such a simple touch could make her feel breathless, Maggie wondered what it would be like to hold Nick naked and sliding against her, the springy hair on his chest rubbing her breasts. The mental image brought a flood of heat—and a twinge of guilt. What about John?

"I thought we were just friends. I thought you'd set certain boundaries on our relationship that we weren't going to cross," she said, but she wasn't able to infuse her voice with any censure.

"I did," he responded. "For instance, I'd never do this." His hand relinquished her bottom and moved along the indentation at her waist and up over her ribs toward her breasts, where he cupped the fullness of each one before gently teasing her nipples. "Or this," he added, lowering his head to take one, then the other into his mouth over the thin fabric of her nightie.

A spurt of pleasure shot through Maggie, the likes of which she'd never experienced before, heightening her need. She wanted far more from Nick Sorenson than a little bit of touching and kissing, and she knew it. She was afraid he knew it, too.

"It's a good thing," she replied, "because I wouldn't let you." Then she threaded her fingers into his hair and dragged him back for another mind-numbing kiss.

"See?" he said against her mouth several seconds later. "We're on the same page here."

"Right." Breathless and giddy and far beyond the point of refusal as his hands roved possessively over her, she closed her eyes and let him sweep her away. She'd think about the consequences later, afterward... After he'd stopped the dull ache that was beginning to throb inside her.

"I'm glad we're not doing anything we agreed we wouldn't," she said.

Pushing her robe off her shoulders, he kissed along her collarbone and then nipped her neck. "I can't get close enough to you," he whispered, more serious now than she'd ever seen him. "Let me make love to you, Maggie."

She murmured something. It might have been assent. It certainly wasn't a denial. She was afraid the entire world would stop spinning if he let her go now. In any case, she was the one who dropped her robe to the ground, freeing her hands so she could slide them under his shirt and rake her nails along his back. "You feel so incredibly good," she admitted. "*This* feels so good."

"It gets better," he promised. "I want to show you, Maggie. I want to hear you gasp and moan with pleasure and beg me for more, and I want to give it to you over and over and over...."

Oh, boy! Darla was right. Nick *was* good at this, far better than Maggie had ever imagined. He made her feel as though she was the only woman in the world, made her heart pound so hard she feared it would leap out of her chest.

His eyes intent on what he was about to reveal, he started working the straps of her nightie off her shoulders when the front door banged open and a child's voice sang out, "Mommy! I picked s-s-some flowers-s-s for you!"

Zach! Panic gripped Maggie. She bent and grabbed her robe, and Nick hurried to help her cover herself before her son, followed closely by a tongue-lolling Rambo, charged into the kitchen.

"Mommy, Mommy, look! I picked you s-s-some flowers-s-s." Zach handed her several dandelions and smiled proudly, completely unaware of what had been happening only seconds earlier. But Mrs. Gruber, who came in behind the dog, wasn't so easily fooled.

"Must be hotter in here than I thought," she said, giving them both the once-over. "You're all sweaty."

Nick's eye caught Maggie's for a brief second. "Not as sweaty as we wanted to be," he grumbled and headed out the back door.

# CHAPTER FIFTEEN

"IF I LET YOU LISTEN to Dr. Dan's new message, will you promise me the contents will not be revealed? To *anyone*?" Maggie asked, staring intently at Detective Mendez, who was sitting on the couch across from her. Nick had finished his work in the yard an hour or so earlier. He'd come in long enough for them to have a brief, whispered discussion in the hallway—Mrs. Gruber was still in the house, cleaning the fridge—about the mistake they'd nearly made, how fortunate they were that Zach had arrived when he did, and how they wouldn't let the same thing happen again. Then he'd left the house to run some errands. Maggied prayed he'd be gone a good long while. After the incident in the kitchen, and their awkward conversation afterward, she didn't particularly want to spend the day in Nick's company. More importantly, she didn't want him showing up while Mendez was around, asking uncomfortable questions. The condoms were her business. She planned to keep it that way, which was why she'd puposely waited to contact the police until Mrs. Gruber had gone home, and why she'd hurried Darla away when she'd come over to apologize for falling asleep the night before.

Mendez hesitated. "I don't understand. Now that I know about the tape, you can't really keep it from me. It's evidence. I can subpoena—"

"I know. There's no need to become adversarial. I'm just asking for a little bit of human kindness and compassion here, okay?"

His brows drew together. "Why?"

"You'll see," she said, hoping Rambo and the modeling clay she'd given Zach to play with in his room would keep him busy for the duration of the detective's visit. "Dr. Dan says something that…well, that's sort of embarrassing, and I want to be sure you're going to handle it in a mature way, despite the fact that we've never been very good friends."

Mendez blinked in surprise, an appropriate reaction, Maggie thought, but he also seemed a little relieved, which was a reaction she hadn't expected. "Let me get this right. You're asking me for a favor?"

Why did he seem to like the idea of that so much? "I'm asking you to be discreet."

"You got it. I'll be as discreet as you want me to be, provided you understand that I'll have to share whatever's on that tape with Hurley and some of the other members of the force."

Everyone down at the station was probably going to have a great laugh at her expense, Maggie realized, but there was an investigation in progress. Mendez couldn't promise her any more than what he had, and she knew it. Still she held out some hope that… "The other members of the force you just mentioned—that doesn't include dispatchers, does it? Or anyone who might leak the information to…other reporters?"

"Reporters?" He smiled and shook his head. "Especially if you can see your way clear to doing me a favor in return."

A feeling of unease crept over Maggie. Mendez needed something from her, and she'd just given him the leverage he needed. That was why he seemed so happy. "What kind of favor?" she asked.

"Those letters you wrote about in the paper today? The ones Dr. Dan sent to Lola Fillmore? I need to get a copy of the first three."

"And you think I can give them to you?"

"I think you can *get* them."

"I can't reveal my source."

"Then talk your source into coming forward. Now let me hear that message, because afterward you'll want to start making some notes. Now that we're cooperating with each other, I've got a few things you might be interested in hearling for your next article on Dr. Dan."

NICK SAT IN HIS APARTMENT, irritated and grumpy and rubbing his temples to get rid of the headache that had plagued him ever since he'd left Maggie's house. The laser copies of the pictures she'd sent John were all around him, and drew his eye again and again, constant reminders of the intimacy they'd nearly shared only hours ago. Her smiling face added to his longing, increased his frustration. Yet he couldn't bring himself to take the pictures down. He wanted them exactly where they were because he wanted Maggie, which didn't exactly build his confidence that he'd be able to behave more professionally in the future than he had in the past.

Dammit! He was an FBI agent working on a life-and-death assignment, and all he could think about was getting his hands up Maggie's shirt. What was wrong with him? How had he lost his focus? Where was his self-discipline?

*Concentrate,* he ordered himself. He had to read through Mendez's report on the leads that had been generated by the composite they'd circulated in the papers. Mendez had checked them out and claimed they were all dead ends, but Nick wanted to go over them again, just to be sure. And he needed to comb through the sworn statements Mendez and Hurley had collected on Marge Brown. The quicker he assimilated the information they'd gathered, the quicker he could put a stop to Dr. Dan. Nick was angry now, angry that Dr. Dan thought he could kill at will, that he thought he could terrorize Maggie… Nick wasn't going to let him get away with it. He would catch Dr. Dan if it was the last thing he did, and he would do it soon. For Maggie and all the other women who might be at risk. And for the families and friends of those who'd been killed so they could receive the closure they deserved. Especially Marge Brown's husband, Jeff. Evidently, he and Marge had argued the night of her murder. She'd stormed out of the house and never returned, and he'd been too proud to go after her. Now he was devastated that they'd never have the chance to reconcile, and Nick felt for him.

Still, as a cop, he'd had to initially consider the possibility that Jeff had killed her himself and made it look like Dr. Dan's work. But that hadn't lasted long. The forensics team found some of the same blue fibers on Marge Brown that they'd found on the other victims. And the location of the murder fit Dr. Dan's profile. Though Discovery Park was twenty-five miles away from the Sunrise Bridge, it was right off the American River.

Nick flipped to a statement given to Hurley by one of the Browns' neighbors.

Q. Did you see or hear anything coming from the Smith home on the night of June 26th?

A. I heard some shouting but couldn't tell what it was about. I assumed Jeff and Marge were having some sort of disagreement, which seemed to be the case when the front door opened, then slammed and Marge got in her car and peeled away.

Q. Is this the first time you've ever heard the Browns argue?

A. It's summer, so the windows are open a lot at night. I've heard them fight occasionally, but not often. Usually over money. And nothing that ever escalates into violence.

Nick's cell phone rang. He answered it, "Sorenson," then skipped down the report and continued reading while he waited for whoever it was to speak.

> Q. Did you see anything unusual in the neighborhood that night, like a stranger lurking around? Or an unfamiliar car parked on the street?
>
> A. No, nothing, or I wouldn't have let my children play outside.

"Hello? Are you there?" Mendez's voice demanded in his ear, for the second time.

Nick pulled himself away from the report long enough to respond. "Yeah, I'm here. What's up?"

"I just left Maggie Russell's place."

Again? Mendez had been at Maggie's again? That could only mean one thing— "Dr. Dan called," he said, tensing.

"You got it. Contact number two."

"What did he say?"

Mendez paused. "Why don't I just let you hear it?"

After a moment, the same voice Nick recognized from the first recording came over the line. "Maaagggiiie… Maaagggiiee…where are you Maggie? This is Dr. Dan. You remember me, don't you? I saw you at the grocery store last night. When you were buying some condoms to go with your brownies. Nice mix, by the way. Did you…"

Stunned, Nick sat on the other end of the line, trying to absorb what Dr. Dan had said. He'd been following Maggie last night? And he'd seen her buy *condoms?* Maggie had no love life. She'd admitted as much. So why the box of rubbers?

"What do you think?" Mendez asked.

Nick didn't know what to think. He was torn between concern that Dr. Dan had come close enough to see the items Maggie had purchased last night and a definite preoccupation with what those items were.

"Maybe they were for her friend. Did she say why she bought them?" he asked.

Mendez chuckled. "Granted, I was asking her questions that are definitely secondary in importance—you know, police stuff like whether or not she saw anyone following her—but she didn't volunteer what she planned to do with the condoms."

Suddenly Nick remembered making some offhand comment about brownies and condoms. She couldn't have been reacting to that, he thought. She wouldn't have bought condoms for *him,* for *them.* Today when they'd talked, she'd agreed she wanted to keep their relationship strictly platonic. She regretted what had almost happened in her kitchen, didn't she?

If not, he was in trouble. Just the idea of her wanting what he wanted aroused him. Now that he knew about the condoms, he'd be lucky to pass the next few days without putting the entire box to good use.

"Do you think she'll print something to try and placate him?" Mendez asked.

"Like Lola did? No. The *Trib*'s not going to play those kinds of games," he said. "But I'm not taking any more chances. There's no question now that Dr. Dan knows Maggie's face. He knows what she drives and where she lives, which means I want someone watching her and her house twenty-four hours a day."

"Even when you're there?" Mendez asked.

"No." Nick definitely didn't want anyone watching too closely then, just in case he caved in the way he feared he would. Or maybe he was *planning* to cave...

Mendez laughed again. "Sounds like someone needs to protect her from you."

Nick was afraid he was right.

MAGGIE STRETCHED and sat up almost as soon as her alarm went off, interrupting her nap. Brian Wordelly had called a few hours earlier to see if they could get together tonight instead of Sunday, and to take her mind off Nick and Dr. Dan and Detective Mendez and the whole mess, she'd agreed. The intensity of her emotions over the past few weeks had left her exhausted. She was looking forward to taking a vacation from her life for a night, even if it was only with one of her mother's blind dates. *Especially* because it was with one of her mother's blind dates. A plumber from Auburn suddenly sounded appealingly simple and safe and boring enough to balance all the extremes she'd experienced of late.

Fortunately, everything was going to work out so she could go. She'd made a quick call to Jorge, who'd agreed to trade shifts, and she was planning on having Mrs. Gruber watch Zach—provided her neighbor returned from JCPenney's in time. All Maggie had to do was get ready, and she had an hour and a half to do it.

Being careful not to disturb Zach, who was sleeping next to her, and Rambo, who lay at her feet, eyes now open and watching her, she slipped off the bed. Was Nick back? She paused to listen for sounds of someone else in the house, but the silence, and the fact that Rambo hadn't deserted her and Zach in favor of his master, indicated that they were still alone. She hadn't heard from Nick since their little "talk" in the hallway. Where was he and why had he been gone so long? And why did she miss him so badly?

Stop! She took firm charge of her thoughts. It was Friday night, and she was going out on the town. She was going to be treated to dinner and some small talk, and she was going to forget that Dr. Dan had been following her last night in his little blue Geo. More than anything else, she had every intention of forgetting all about the raging hormones she'd experienced in her kitchen with the handsome—and incredibly talented—Nick Sorenson.

So what to wear? She stood gazing into her closet, wondering which outfit would suit her best. She doubted Brian Wordelly would dress up, but she wanted to wear something that made her feel sleek and elegant and attractive...

The black silk sheath dress, she decided, with her new strappy sandals. She'd paint her toenails, wear pearls at her ears and throat and look her absolute best. The outfit would probably be overkill, but she didn't care. It was an important part of the therapy she had planned for herself.

Maggie had just eased into a tub of hot water when Rambo barked and charged out of her room and down the hall, rousing Zach. Then she heard Nick's voice calling to her from the other side of the bathroom door.

"Maggie? I'm back. I swung by the office a little earlier and found a box on your chair. I brought it home for you. Looks like it's from John."

Oh, no! John had sent her the gift he'd promised. Yet, only hours earlier, she'd been kissing Nick like he was the last man on earth. How was she going to explain that? "I'm in the tub," she said. "I'll be out in a few minutes."

But she wasn't in any particular hurry. Nick's footsteps retreated, and she sank lower in the water. Strangely satisfied that he was home, she told herself she'd figure everything out tomorrow.

When Maggie was completely dressed and ready, she felt like a new woman. "This is symbolic," she told her reflection in the mirror. "I will live through this ordeal with Dr. Dan. I will continue to build my career. And I will find a man I can love, and who can love me and Zach. No more messing around with Nick Sorenson. I'm going to be completely open-minded to Brian Wordelly. Just because my mother had a hand in our getting together tonight doesn't necessarily mean he'll turn out to be someone I loathe, right?'' She gave herself a bleak, unconvincing smile, but squared her shoulders and went to the living room to find Nick sitting on the couch, tossing a soft football to Zach while watching the news.

Something squeezed her heart when she saw him so relaxed and at home on *her* couch, playing with *her* son. He looked good there, she thought. Zach was laughing and charging Nick after every catch, and Nick was flipping him onto his lap for a few tickles before sending him out for another pass. The scene definitely improved Nick's f.p. factor—so did the yard work he'd done this morning—but Maggie wasn't about to give him any points for it. In their ''after the frenzy'' talk, he'd made it very plain that he didn't intend to get emotionally involved with her or Zach. He wanted to remain free, and she wanted to get married, which meant she needed to quit begging for the moon and start looking elsewhere, this time in earnest.

At her approach, Nick glanced up, and Maggie felt a moment of pure female satisfaction when his jaw dropped. ''Wow! You look great,'' he said.

Zach called to him to throw the ball, but Nick didn't seem to hear him.

Maggie smiled. ''Thanks.''

''What's the occasion?''

''I have a date.''

His brows rose. ''You do?''

''Yeah. Don't sound so surprised.''

''I'm not *surprised*. I just thought, I don't know, you've never mentioned anyone.''

''Things change,'' she said, not wanting to go into the

whole embarrassing explanation about her mother's constant matchmaking.

"It's Friday. Don't you work tonight?"

"Jorge's covering for me. Besides, you seem to think you can come and go at the office any time you want. Why should I be any different?"

"I have another job."

Right. He was apparently a wedding photographer, but Maggie was starting to wonder about that. She never heard him schedule anything. He never talked about the weddings he attended. She never saw any of the pictures.

Picking up the phone, Maggie tried Mrs. Gruber again but there wasn't any answer. She stole another look at Nick, expecting him to be watching the news by now, but he was still staring at her.

She clasped her hands behind her back. "Any chance you could watch Zach for me?" she asked. "My date's going to be here at seven, and I haven't been able to reach Mrs. Gruber. I'm afraid she's gone to visit her son in Elk Grove and won't be back for another hour or two. She didn't know I needed her early tonight."

"Okay." He shifted on the couch and lowered the volume on the television. "So who's the lucky guy?"

"Nick, throw the ball!" Zach pleaded.

Nick tossed the ball, but he didn't watch to see if Zach caught it.

"His name is Brian Wordelly," Maggie said. "He's the son of one of my mother's friends."

"Looks like you went to a lot of trouble to get ready for him." Nick's gaze moved down her dress and over her bare legs all the way to her shoes. "You sure you want to wear that dress?"

"What's wrong with it?"

"Nothing. It's just a little…I don't know. It's kind of bare."

"What?" Maggie faced the narrow decorative mirror on the far wall. "What are you talking about? This dress has a high neck and comes almost to my knee. It's very conservative."

"It doesn't seem conservative to me."

Maggie frowned at him. "You're crazy."

"No, I'm not. That dress is sexy as hell, and you know it."

"There's nothing wrong with the way I'm dressed."

"Not if you want this guy to make some serious moves before the night's over, there isn't. Or is that the plan?"

What was he talking about? She'd never seen Nick behave so strangely. "I don't know what your problem is," she told him. "If I didn't know better, I'd think you were jealous."

"I'm not jealous. Why would I be jealous? We're just friends, remember? I *want* you to see other guys."

"Great. That's what I'm doing."

"Right."

She grabbed her purse and checked for breath mints. Blind dates weren't her forte to begin with, and now Nick had her rattled.

"Just making sure you got everything you need in there?" he asked.

Maggie sensed a strong undercurrent behind this question, but she couldn't put her finger on what it was. Nick said he wasn't jealous, but he was sure doing a good imitation of it. "Yeah," she said, deciding to take his question at face value to diffuse whatever was going on between them. "I think I'm ready to go."

"You must really like this guy."

"I don't know him yet."

"From the looks of it, you plan to get to know him pretty well before the night's over."

Maggie felt a blush creep up her neck. Was he saying all these things because of how eagerly she'd responded to his kiss? Did he think she was sex-starved or...or easy? "Are you trying to make me angry?" she asked. "Because if you don't want to baby-sit, I can call Darla—"

"No, I'll take care of Zach. We were thinking about ordering a pizza, anyway. And since I'm not going into work either, maybe we'll get some movies and popcorn and—" He paused as though trying to think of something more alluring than pizza and popcorn, then apparently gave up. "You go ahead and have your fun. We'll be fine without you, right, buddy?"

Then why was he making her feel so guilty for leaving them?

"Yeah, pizza!" her son cried and started running to throw his arms around Maggie's legs. At least, that was what she thought he was going to do. She opened her arms to receive him, but he swerved and jumped into Nick's lap instead.

Maggie stared at Zach in surprise, then made a face at Nick's victorious smile. "Don't get too attached," she muttered to Zach, "Nick's not going to be here long."

Nick didn't comment. He looked as though he was watching television, but she knew he was only feigning interest.

"Would you mind giving Mrs. Gruber a call in an hour or so and letting her know Zach won't be coming over tonight, then?" she asked. "She doesn't have an answering machine, or I'd leave her a message."

"Sure."

"Thanks." She glanced around the living room, suddenly remembering John's present. "Where's that box that came for me?"

"I don't know." Nick settled Zach more comfortably on his knee without taking his eyes from the television.

"You told me you brought it home."

He didn't respond.

"Nick, where's my present from John?"

"Open it later."

"Why?"

The doorbell rang, and he nodded toward the front of the house. "Because your date's here."

Maggie bit her lip, wishing, for a moment, that she didn't have to go out with a complete stranger, especially while Nick was sitting on her couch. She wanted nothing more than to snuggle up next to him.

Calling herself a weak fool, she started for the door. "Don't let him see you," she told Nick as she left the room. "I don't want to have to explain who you are."

Smoothing her dress and taking a deep breath, Maggie swung the door open, expecting to see a short, fat, balding man or someone with pockmarks and thick glasses, like most of the other men her mother had set her up with. Instead she saw a pleasant-looking dark-haired man about her own age wearing khakis and a golf shirt. Nearly Nick's height, he was thin and not particularly muscular, but he had a nice smile. Brian Wordelly reminded Maggie of an accountant or maybe a lawyer. She would never have pegged him as a plumber.

"Hi," Maggie said. "You must be Brian. I'm Maggie."

He grinned. "Your mother was right. You are beautiful."

"Thanks. I'm all set." She smiled and headed out, trying to drag the door closed at the same time, but something held it fast. Looking back, Maggie saw Nick's hand. The rest of him stood behind her.

Brian cleared his throat as Nick looked him over. "Hello, um, I'm Brian Wordelly," he said, sticking out his hand. "And you are…Maggie's brother?"

"I'm her roommate." Nick's gaze dropped to Brian's hand, then returned to his face. He extended his own just seconds before Maggie was going to elbow him in the ribs.

"What time will you two be back?" he asked Brian, ignoring Maggie's very pointed glare.

Brian cleared his throat again. "Um, I'm not really sure." Maggie was positive he'd almost ended that sentence with a "sir." "I just thought we'd go to dinner and then, possibly, a movie."

"So eleven o'clock?"

"Nick's baby-sitting for me," Maggie rushed to explain, refusing to let Nick intimidate Brian anymore. "He probably has a hot date of his own lined up for when I return, right, Nick? He likes things quick and easy," she told Brian. "No strings attached."

"I've never said I like things quick and easy."

Nick was still shaking hands with Brian, Maggie realized and stepped between them so they'd be forced apart.

"Maybe your actions were speaking so loudly I couldn't hear what you were saying," Maggie said but the tone of her voice did little to relax Brian Wordelly. Remembering her manners, she added, "Thanks for watching Zach."

"I'll expect you in—" Nick consulted his watch "—four hours, then."

What did Nick think he was doing? Her mother had finally sent her someone who could be a real possibility and Nick was trying to screw it up! Hadn't she told him she didn't want him to be seen? "Fine," she said and tried to shut the door again, but Nick wasn't finished with them yet.

"I wouldn't touch her if I were you," he muttered to Brian.

Brian's eyes widened. "Did you say what I think you said?"

"No," Maggie interrupted. "Nick's a big jokester. Ha, ha,

220                         DEAR MAGGIE

ha. Funny, funny. You'd better get back to Zach," she said and started Brian across the porch ahead of her so he couldn't hear what she was about to say to Nick. "Or you're going to be standing on my porch with your luggage again tonight, only this time you'll be heading in the opposite direction!"

NICK COULDN'T TAKE IT anymore.

He turned off the television and checked on Zach, who was sleeping peacefully in his room, then resorted to shuffling restlessly through the dark house, listening for the sound of a car out front. It was well after midnight. Maggie was nearly an hour and a half late. Where was she?

Remembering the condoms made Nick's stomach hurt. Had she purchased them for her big date? Were she and Brian Whatever-His-Name-Was back at his place right now?

God, he hoped not. Nick couldn't stand the thought of it.

Why hadn't he gotten Brian's license plate number? Or his driver's license? Then he could trace him if—

Headlights swung into the drive, and an engine shifted into idle. Nick went to one of the living room windows and watched from a crack in the blind as Brian got out, walked around the car and opened Maggie's door.

"Don't kiss her," he muttered. "Please don't kiss her."

Brian moved closer to Maggie, causing Nick's jaw to clench. If they kissed, and it was a deep, openmouthed kiss, he'd have his answer. If, on the other hand, Brian gave Maggie a simple peck on the lips, they'd probably saved the condoms for another day. Either way, Nick longed to toss Brian Brown Eyes back into his car and tell him to get lost. He felt Brian had it coming. The jerk said he'd have Maggie back at eleven, and he was an hour and a half late.

Nick heard Maggie say she'd had a great time as Brian walked her to the front porch, and wished he could say the same. He'd enjoyed Zach. Maggie's little boy was incredibly bright and sweet. But the minutes had dragged by, teeming with suspicion and angst, even a kind of pain Nick had never experienced before. He doubted he could survive many more of her "dates."

Changing windows, he watched from the front room as Brian and Maggie talked for a few minutes longer beneath the porch light at the front door.

"Any chance you'd be interested in going out with me again?" Brian asked.

"Over my dead body," Nick muttered.

"Sure," Maggie responded. "Why don't you give me a call?"

Nick winced at the cheerfulness in her voice. She liked him, all right, he thought grimly.

"You don't think your…um…roommate will mind?" Brian asked.

"He has no right to mind," Maggie assured him. "We're just friends."

"Say good-night and go," Nick said.

Evidently, Brian wasn't in any hurry. "*You* might think so, but *he* was acting suspiciously possessive. Are you sure he doesn't have any feelings for you?"

"Yes," Maggie said.

"No," Nick breathed. And that simple admission was enough to twist whatever it was inside him that was already knotted and hurting.

"That's good," Brian said, and then he dipped his head as though to kiss Maggie. Because of the angle of the window, Nick couldn't see where his kiss landed or how much Maggie participated, but it caused all the muscles in his body to bunch.

"Good night," he heard Brian say, finally leaving, and then keys jingled in the lock and Maggie came inside.

"Have a good time?" Nick asked, folding his arms across

his chest and leaning against the wall. He made no move to pretend he hadn't been spying on them. He was hoping she'd call him on it. He was spoiling for a fight; at this point, he didn't care.

"It was fine," Maggie said and started down the hall, but he could tell by her clipped sentence that she was as angry with him as he was with her.

"Fine? That's it?" he asked, following her. He wasn't willing to let it go. He couldn't.

"What more do you want to hear?"

"Did you kiss him?"

They reached the kitchen, and she flipped on the light. "Is it any of your business if I did?"

"No." He stabbed a hand through his hair. "Yes, dammit. You're driving me crazy, Maggie. I want you so badly I hurt all over, and yet—" He stopped. How did he explain why he couldn't have her? How did he tell her he was frightened to make a commitment he might not be able to keep? That he felt unsure she'd be able to forgive him for the deceptions of his job? Did he even have the right to ask?

She was staring at him, but now the look on her face spoke more of surprise than anger. "Why?"

"Why what?"

"Why me?"

"I don't know."

"Do you love me?" She asked the question softly, as though everything in their future depended on his answer.

Nick could hear his own heart beating in the silence. *Did* he love her? He wasn't sure. He knew he'd never felt this way about a woman before. Whether or not that meant he could uproot his life and make the changes in his work that a permanent relationship with Maggie would require wasn't something he could predict at this moment.

"I care about you," he admitted. "So much that I can't

think about anything else. I can't stand the thought of another man touching you. I thought I'd lose my mind tonight, wondering, imagining…'' His voice broke, and he fell silent as he tried to read her reaction. Would the truth be enough? Did she feel the same way?

"I must be the biggest fool in history," she said at last, "but God help me, I can't turn my back on you."

Nick let his breath hiss between his teeth and crossed the floor to take her in his arms. She felt so…right, like she belonged, like she would always belong. He wasn't making another mistake; he was sure of it.

"You won't regret this in the morning?" he asked.

"I can't even imagine tomorrow," she said. "There's only tonight." Then she slipped her arms around his neck and pressed her lips greedily to his, and Nick's response was so instantaneous and powerful and overwhelming that he knew he was lost. For better or worse…

# CHAPTER SIXTEEN

"WHY DIDN'T YOU BUY TWO?" Nick asked, frowning at the box of condoms on the dresser. "We're almost out."

Maggie laughed and pulled the sheet higher. She was so relaxed she could hardly rouse herself to speak. "I wasn't planning to use the first one."

"People don't buy condoms unless they plan to use them," he said, rolling over and pinning her beneath him in the bed.

Maggie gave him a challenging grin. "I was more interested in the brownies."

"Liar," he said. "The next time you go shopping for birth control, get—"

"There's not going to be a next time," she said between kisses. "From now on, that's your job." She didn't add, "until you leave." She didn't want to think about that. There were more crucial matters for the moment, like the fact that Zach would be up any minute. And Detective Mendez would be calling to see if she'd gotten the Fillmore letters. And Ben would want her latest article. And she had to write John and tell him what she'd done....

Poor John. She hadn't even opened his present. Not that she felt right about accepting it now.

"You have to go to your own room," she told Nick as he kissed her neck, then her nose. "It's six-thirty. Zach gets up around seven."

"That gives us half an hour."

"What if he gets up early?"

Nick groaned. "Can't *this* be my room?"

If he planned to marry her, it could. Maggie wanted nothing more than to spend the rest of her life with him. Regardless of everything she'd done to avoid it, she'd fallen madly in love with Nick Sorenson, and letting him into her bed as well as her heart had only sealed her fate. But she wasn't about to ask him for a commitment. She knew he had to come to that on his own. "No. I don't want Zach to find a naked man in my bed."

"Zach's three. He won't notice—"

"Yes, he will."

The telephone rang, and Nick slid to the side so she could answer it. Maggie was expecting it to be Ben or Mendez. She wasn't expecting her mother.

"Maggie, tell me you don't have a man living with you," Rosalyn Anderson demanded without preamble.

Oh, my gosh! What did Brian Wordelly do? Wake her mother up in the middle of the night to pass on that little tidbit of information?

"Um…"

"Who is it?" Nick murmured, wrapping his arms around her middle and pulling her backside into the cradle of his naked body.

Maggie stiffened and motioned for him to be silent. How could she explain the situation to her mother? "Mom, it's just a temporary arrangement," she said. "A friend from work needed a place to stay."

"Brian Wordelly said it looked like more than that to him."

Maggie couldn't care less what it looked like to Brian Wordelly. And she certainly didn't appreciate his reporting it. He'd been nice enough, but there'd been no chemistry. A half hour into their date, Maggie had known that a relationship between them would never go anywhere, regardless of what happened with Nick. Brian was very much a momma's boy, for one, and he liked to whine and complain. Maggie had played along because the date wasn't as bad as some her mother had arranged, but she had no intention of being anything more than a friend to him. Now she wasn't sure she wanted even that much of a relationship.

"Is it that man you told me about—John?"

Maggie ran a hand through her tangled hair, feeling a fresh wave of guilt at the mention of John's name. "No."

A pause, then, "I don't know about you, Maggie. What will your neighbors think? What kind of example does it set for Zach? You'll have to tell this man to move out and stay somewhere else."

"I'm going to get in the shower," Nick whispered. "I've got a lot to do today."

Maggie nodded and felt him slip away. "When did Brian call you?" she asked her mother.

"First thing this morning. He's not happy about the situation, of course. He told me if you want to continue dating him, you have to get rid of the man you're living with."

Maggie felt her eye begin to twitch. Why hadn't Brian had the guts to tell *her* that? He'd been congenial and soft-spoken. "Do you think your roommate will mind?" Then he'd run to her mother instead, as if he thought that would force her hand.

Maggie considered telling Rosalyn about Dr. Dan turning his sights on her and why she'd let Nick move in, but she knew it would only make her mother demand she pull up stakes and go back to Iowa. So she did what she should've done years ago. "Mom," she said. "I love you and I appreciate your interest, but I'm an adult now, and I can make these kinds of decisions on my own, thanks."

Shocked silence greeted this announcement. "But—but

what about Brian?'' she finally asked. ''He said the two of you are perfect for each other.''

''I'm sorry, but I don't want to date Brian again. And please don't set me up with anyone else, okay? I'm in love, Mom. I'm so in love I can barely think about anyone or anything else.''

''In love?'' her mother gasped. ''With whom?''

Maggie swallowed hard. ''With the man in my shower.''

''The one you said was *temporary*?''

Maggie winced at the horror in her mother's voice. ''I'm hoping he's not as temporary as I made it sound.''

The phone clicked and went dead, and Maggie realized her mother had hung up on her. She was trying to decide how she felt about that when it rang again. Aunt Rita this time.

''Your mother says you have a man living in the house,'' she said.

Maggie heard Zach outside her locked bedroom door and jumped out of bed to dress. ''Yeah, I do.''

''She says you're in love with him.''

''I am, Aunt Rita, madly.''

''Does he love you back?''

''I don't know.''

''Well, give him time. A man would have to be crazy *not* to love you. And don't worry about your mother. I'll talk to her, and she'll come around. I've never liked the Wordellys much anyway.''

Maggie laughed. She'd expected to feel more remorse for upsetting her mother, but now that she'd told the truth, she was hoping it would be the beginning of a more honest relationship between them. She was finally growing up. Maybe it was time her mother accepted that.

''WHAT DID YOUR MOTHER SAY?'' Nick asked when he got out of the shower.

Maggie was sitting on the bed, wearing a lightweight robe and reading to Zach, who was still in his pajamas. "She said Brian Wordelly won't date me any more unless you hit the road."

"Did you tell her Brian Wordelly was lucky to escape last night with all his body parts in good working condition?"

Maggie grinned, then shook her head. "No. I told her I didn't want to go out with him again."

Nick stood in front of the dresser, a towel wrapped around his waist, and combed his hair. "And her response was?"

"She hung up on me."

He looked at her in the mirror. "Just over that?"

Maggie shrugged. "That and the fact that I'm now living with you."

She said it flippantly, but Nick could tell that Maggie's mother had hurt her. Crossing to the bed, he sat down beside her, put his arms around her and kissed the top of her head. "We'll win her over," he promised.

Maggie didn't respond.

"Did you tell her about Dr. Dan?" he asked.

"No. I didn't see any point in upsetting her anymore."

"I'm sure the police are going to catch him soon," Nick said, wishing he could tell her who he really was. He'd almost done it a dozen times during the night. He hated the lies, hated knowing that his day of reckoning would come. But these feelings between him and Maggie were still so new and fragile, he feared the truth would destroy them. Besides, capturing Dr. Dan had to take precedence over everything else. The lab had gotten back to him just yesterday to say that the blood on the shirt he'd sent them from the park ranger's blazer had indeed belonged to Sarah Ritter. They found some of her blood on the leaves he'd gathered from the boat launch, too. Now if Nick could only find the man who'd left the shoe print outside the Ritters' window and at the river, he'd be able to place both murderer and victim at the scene. If only... Too bad they weren't having any luck with the leads coming in off the composite. Too bad that was such a big "if."

"Mommy, aren't you going to read?" Zach demanded, finally growing impatient with the interruption.

Maggie acted as though she didn't hear him. She was looking at Nick. "If the police don't catch him in time, if he... manages to get to me," she said softly, "will you see that Zach is taken care of until arrangements can be made to send him to my mother?"

"I thought you said your mother was getting old?"

"She is, but there's no one else."

Turning Maggie's head so they were face to face, Nick put his forehead against hers. "Nothing's going to happen to you or your little boy, Maggie," he said. "I won't let it."

"YOU'VE GOT TO get those letters." Maggie sat at the computer desk in her bedroom, the telephone pressed to one ear, the fingers of her right hand massaging her forehead while Rachel Nunez, intern at the *Seattle Independent* and her source for the Lola Fillmore information, sighed on the other end of the line.

"Maggie, I can't. I told you that yesterday. I don't dare go through her stuff again. It's all in storage by now."

"Then you've got to come forward and say what you know."

"No way. The police will subpoena the letters. If the *Independent* finds out I was snooping through Lola's desk, they'll never hire me, and I've worked my butt off for three years trying to get on at that place."

"I know, Rachel, but the police believe there might be something in those letters that will help them find this creep."

"There's nothing. I've told you that."

Maggie jammed a hand through her tangled hair. Nick had left more than an hour ago, but she hadn't had a chance to shower yet. She'd been returning her business e-mail and avoiding the inevitable—this call to Rachel. She believed the letters were as important as the police did, but she also knew Rachel wouldn't like being dragged into the light. "You said you only saw them once. Maybe there's something you missed. We don't know what the police have so far. Those letters could tell them more than you think."

"And what if they don't? I'd ruin my reputation and my chances at a career in journalism for nothing."

"Not for nothing. Dr. Dan's killed two women since he came to Sacramento. We have to do everything we can—"

"That's easy for you to say," she interrupted. "You're not the one who'll lose your dream."

"I could lose a lot more than that," Maggie told her. "Dr. Dan left me another message. He's been sending letters. He's stalking me, just like Lola, and if they don't catch him... I have a little boy, Rachel. I can't stand the thought of what'll happen to him if this maniac gets hold of me."

"So what are you saying?" Rachel demanded. "You're going to tell them who I am?"

"No. I can't do that. I've given you my word. I can only hope you'll decide to help. There are lives at stake here, mine included."

Rachel sighed. "If I thought these letters could really save someone's life, I'd do everything possible to help. You have to believe that, Maggie. But they won't help."

"Let the police be the judge of that."

"I can't let the police send a subpoena to the paper because of me."

"Then find a way to get copies of those letters on your

own. Fax them to me. I'll give them to the police, and I won't say how I got them. Then no one can fault you *or* the paper."

Rachel didn't respond right away.

Maggie prayed she'd finally convinced her.

"I'll see what I can do," she said at last and hung up.

Maggie sat for several minutes staring at the phone. She thought of calling Detective Mendez to let him know that she was making progress, then decided against it. She really couldn't say if Rachel would come through or not. All sorts of things could go wrong. What if she couldn't find the letters again? What if she couldn't manage a private moment to copy them? What if she changed her mind? What if, what if, what if! There seemed to be a "what if" attached to every-thing in Maggie's life right now. What if the police weren't watching her house carefully enough and Dr. Dan slipped inside?

What if Nick didn't love her?

Biting her lip, Maggie turned to her computer. It was time to take care of the second thing on her "dread" list—writing John. Whether Nick returned her feelings or not, Maggie's conscience demanded she tell John there was someone else, but she didn't know where to start. The last time she'd "spo-ken" to him, she'd told him Nick was gay. How he'd become her lover wasn't going to be easy to explain.

She clicked on the pencil icon and started:

Hi, John—
Your present arrived yesterday, but I haven't been able to bring myself to open it. I don't want your sweet gesture to make me feel any guiltier than I already do. Things have changed quite a bit in my love life over the past twenty-four hours. I should have seen it coming, and prepared you, but I didn't want to admit, even to myself, that there was someone else. Remember that roommate I mentioned?

The gay one? Well, he's actually straight and things have gotten pretty—

What did she say? She couldn't say "serious." Nick hadn't made her any promises.

—intimate between us. I'm very sorry. There are so many things I like about you. You seem kind and loyal and intelligent. I think I could have fallen for you, but there was just this other guy and… I'm sorry. I'll send your package back unopened. Maybe you can return it and get your money back. Otherwise, I'll be happy to reimburse you.

If I don't hear from you again, I'll understand. Please know I wish you happiness and success in everything you do.

Love, Maggie

Maggie shook her head as she read through her words. Her message sounded terrible, but she didn't know how to make it any better. She was in love with Nick, and there was no getting around it.

Squeezing her eyes shut, she hit the send button.

"I COULD HAVE FALLEN FOR YOU, but there was just this other guy…" Alone in his apartment, Nick crossed his arms and sat back to consider Maggie's e-mail to John. *He* was the other guy. Did that mean Maggie had fallen for the flesh-and-blood version of him?

He certainly hoped so. He'd never experienced anything like last night. He'd made love to other women, but never had he felt such an all-consuming emotional connection, such a desire to join and possess and enjoy forever. Maggie was the one woman who seemed to fit him perfectly, the one he thought he could mow the yard for—on a weekly basis. After drawing so close to her, he no longer feared that at some point he'd need to find the back door. He wanted a commitment, wanted to bind her to him. Bottom line, he wanted to marry Maggie, and once he caught Dr. Dan, he planned to do just that. He'd get a desk job and move to Sacramento. Since he'd met Maggie, traveling appealed to him less and less. He was more interested in fixing up her old house or buying them a new one, if that was what she wanted.

As long as Maggie didn't hate him too much for all the lies...

Nick steered his mind away from that thought. He couldn't deal with it now. He had to finish up the investigation, retain his focus. But first, he had to figure out what to do about John. Should he have him get angry at Maggie and not respond? Take him out of the picture completely?

No, not yet, he decided. John had a connection to Maggie that Nick, as himself, didn't possess. She trusted him, felt safe to tell him anything, and Nick wasn't ready to give that up.

Dear Maggie—
Keep the present. I bought it for you because I wanted you to have it, and I still do. I understand about your roommate. Sometimes things like that happen when you least expect them. You and I never had any commitments between us, so you don't need to feel guilty about anything. I've enjoyed getting to know you and hope we can still be friends.
Love, John

MAGGIE SHOOK HER HEAD as she read John's message for the second time. He had to be an absolute saint. There wasn't a hint of anger or reproach in his letter. He acted as though everything was fine, as though he cared about her and always would, regardless of the other men in her life.

"Who's that from?" Darla asked, leaning over the side of Maggie's cubicle.

Maggie lowered the volume on the cop radios that crackled on her desk and glanced down the hall to see if Nick had come into the office yet. He wasn't there. After last night, she couldn't get him off her mind. She missed him already, wanted to be with him. What was ever going to become of her? "It's from John," she said.

"You guys getting along okay?"

"We're just friends."

"Friends?" Darla followed Maggie's second glance toward Nick's desk and smiled sympathetically. "Okay. Now I see what's going on. You've got it bad, don't you?"

Maggie knew she wouldn't be able to hide the truth from Darla for very long so there wasn't any use denying it now. "Yeah," she said.

"Does he return your feelings?"

"He hasn't said."

"But has he *shown* you?"

Last night had been special. Maggie had never felt more loved, more cherished. And yet, without the words, she couldn't say for sure how Nick felt about her. "He got pretty jealous when I went out with Brian Wordelly," she said.

"That's a good sign. Was Brian any competition?"

"No."

"So what are you going to do about Nick? Let him stay at your place indefinitely?"

"I don't know yet. All I can say right now is that I'm going to give what I feel for him a chance."

Darla shrugged. "He can't be any worse than Tim, right?"

Maggie couldn't help laughing. "I guess that's one way of looking at it."

"And John seems to be taking the news okay." She waved at the message on Maggie's computer screen.

"Yeah, but I feel badly for him. He seems like a great guy."

The telephone rang and Maggie reached over to answer it. "Maggie Russell."

"Where's my article?" Ben demanded.

Maggie shuffled through the papers on her desk and uncovered her most recent piece on Dr. Dan, the one giving the make and model of the car that had followed her the night she'd gone to Darla's. Ever since she'd learned Dr. Dan had probably been driving the Geo Metro she'd seen in the parking lot at Safeway, she noticed every Metro on the road, regardless of color. "It's right here. I was just going to turn it in," she told him.

"I don't have all day," he said and hung up just as Maggie's call waiting beeped. She held up a finger to tell Darla she'd be another minute and switched to the incoming line.

"Maggie Russell."

At first there was no sound, no breathing, nothing. She thought she'd lost whoever it was and was about to hang up when Dr. Dan's high-pitched voice came over the line. "Hi, Maaaggieee, you know who this is, don't you?"

Maggie's heart lurched in her chest, and a cold chill went through her whole body. It was him, not a message. It was *him!* "What do you want?" she asked, quickly scribbling down Detective Mendez's cell phone number and mouthing for Darla to call him. "Why have you been following me?"

"Why do I follow any woman, Maggie? Because you're a lying, conniving bitch. I sent you a letter and told you to print the truth about the police and what happened in Seattle. So where's my article?"

"You're not going to get one," Maggie told him. "I decide what I write, not you."

He laughed softly. "Such a disappointment, pretty Maggie. You'd rather live the lie, just like everyone else, and believe the police can protect you. But they're idiots, and you're worse than Lola. You look so good and tease and tempt, and yet, when I get close you turn vile and putrid and vent your stinking anger in my face. But you won't be able to lie much longer. I'll fix that and leave you with nothing, not even air to breathe."

"Stay away from me," Maggie said. "The police are watching my house. They'll catch you if you even try to come near. And I'm going to let them tap this phone."

"It won't do them any good. The only thing they'll find is a pay phone. You're still dreaming Maggie, but it's time to wake up and know that I could slip into your little house without being seen and come to you in the night. I could caress you, bury myself inside you—"

"No! The police—"

"Won't stop me, Maggie. I know everything about you and your house. I know where your bedroom is. I know the color of your sheets. I know where you keep your underwear—"

"I won't believe you. You thrive on terrorizing innocent people, but you don't scare me," she lied. "And the truth is you know nothing about me."

He laughed softly. "Oh, yeah? We'll see about that, Maggie. We'll see."

ZACH FOLLOWED NICK around Maggie's yard, jabbering at his heels, while Nick used a flashlight to check the flower beds for any sign of footprints. The hot summer days had been dry, but the automatic sprinkling system the previous owner had installed turned the water on at night. If someone had been creeping around, peeking in windows, it was certainly plausible to think he might have left some trace of his visit behind. But Nick didn't find anything. Not that the absence of a print meant Dr. Dan hadn't been there. After the call Maggie had received earlier, Nick was sure Dr. Dan had visited her many times. He might even have been inside the house. And now that Dr. Dan was angry, Nick knew he'd be back. He just didn't know when.

"Did you know a s-s-snail carries-s-s his-s-s home on his-s-s back?" Zach asked, stooping to examine a snail he found in the dirt.

The moon was full and bright, casting everything in a silvery glow, but Nick shined his light on the creature so Zach could see it better. "Pretty convenient way to live, don't you think?" he said, pulling the light away long enough to check a broken tree branch for threads or fibers.

Zach poked his find with one chubby finger. "I think it would be heavy."

"Your house certainly would be. I know I wouldn't want to carry it."

The boy frowned at the snail. "Me, either. But I think Mrs-s-s. Goober could do it."

Nick smiled. "Oh, yeah?"

"She'd just put it in her purse."

"She packs a lot in there."

"Mrs-s-s. Goober can do anything."

Except drive, Nick thought, remembering the scrapes and dings he'd seen in the big Cadillac she parked out front. "Come on," he told Zach. "Mrs. Gruber is expecting me to bring you over so I can go to the office, but I want to check the garage first."

"Check the garage for what?" he asked, abandoning his snail.

"Anything that's not supposed to be there."

"Can I carry the flashlight?"

"For a few minutes." Nick handed him the flashlight and

watched its beam dart everywhere from the ground to the sky to the trees before they'd gone ten steps.

"Hold it steady," he said when they reached the garage. He put a hand over Zach's so he could direct the beam long enough to unlock the garage door.

The springs groaned as Nick lifted the heavy wooden panel, but before he could make out the shadowy shapes inside, Zach shined the light directly in his eyes to ask if he could see anything that wasn't supposed to be there. Momentarily blinded, he stepped back just as something came at them.

Instinctively, Nick threw his body on top of Zach to protect him, and rolled away with him, at last popping up in a defensive stance. But it was only an alley cat. Nick saw its white tail disappear around the corner of the house as he came to his feet.

Stunned and probably a little hurt, Zach was still on the ground. A second later, after the shock wore off, he started to cry.

"Come here, Zach," Nick said, lifting him up and into his arms. "I'm sorry. I didn't mean to hurt you. I thought..." He didn't know how to explain to a three-year-old, so he said simply, "It was an accident."

"No," Zach cried, adamant. "You did it on purpos-s-se!"

Nick tried not to laugh at the accusing look on Zach's face and hugged him close, marveling at how wonderful it was to hold him. Zach's small arms circled his neck and his round, wet cheek was pressed to Nick's. Evidently Maggie wasn't the only one making an impact on his heart. Zach was carving out his own place there.

"I would never hurt you on purpose," he told him. Then he said something he wasn't completely sure of at first, but as he spoke the words, he knew they were true. "I love you."

## CHAPTER SEVENTEEN

"I'VE GOT THEM."

Maggie held the phone closer to her ear, more grateful for those three words than for anything else in her life. Rachel Nunez was going to come through. Maggie would be able to call Mendez and turn the letters over to him tonight, and then, maybe, the police would be able to put a stop to Dr. Dan before he made good on his promise to slip into her house.

"How'd you do it?" Maggie asked.

"Lola wasn't married," Rachel replied. "So the *Independent* boxed up her stuff and sent it to her mother. I called and said the police thought there might be something in her files that would help them catch her killer. Her mother and I met once when she picked up Lola for lunch, so she let me come over and go through everything."

"Hadn't the police already gone through Lola's files?"

"Why would they? They thought she'd cooperated with them from the start. Besides, I dug through a lot of boxes. Maybe this was one that came from her house rather than the office. Who knows? Anyway, they're here now."

Maggie shoved her hair out of her face and took a deep breath. "Fantastic. Since you've got them, I'm sure the police will want the originals to check for prints, but before you send them, can you fax me a copy?"

"I don't have a fax machine, but my father bought me a scanner for Christmas. I'll scan them into my computer and e-mail them to you."

"That'll work. Thanks, Rachel."

There was a long pause. "You're welcome, Maggie. I hope they help."

Maggie closed her eyes and said a silent prayer. So did she.

"HI, BABE," Nick said, coming up behind Maggie at the water cooler and slipping his arms around her waist to kiss her neck.

Maggie turned and smiled up at him. "There you are. I've been wondering if you were coming in tonight. It's after eleven."

"You're here, aren't you? Where else would I be?"

"At your other job, I guess. You seem to have booked a lot of weddings."

Nick felt a twinge of guilt at the reminder of his double life and buried his nose in her hair so he wouldn't have to comment. She smelled so good. He couldn't wait to get her home and take off her clothes and—

"What's that?" he asked, suddenly distracted by the papers she held in one hand.

"Letters to Lola Fillmore from Dr. Dan. My contact in Seattle just e-mailed them to me."

"What are you going to do with them?"

"Turn them over to the police. Dr. Dan called me tonight, here at work." She shivered. "Talking to him in person is even creepier than hearing a message. He sounded crazy. I mean, he'd have to be, but it was disturbing to hear that odd quality in his voice."

Nick tensed but tried to keep his demeanor calm. "What did he say?"

"That he can get to me anytime he wants, basically. He prides himself on outsmarting the police. He wants to use the paper—and me—the way he used Lola and the *Independent*.

I'm supposed to portray him as beyond the law, too crafty for the police. But when I told him I wouldn't write something he dictated, he sort of lost it.''

"Can I read the letters?''

Maggie handed them over, and Nick instantly recognized the same computer font, paper and formal writing style Dr. Dan had used in his missives to the police and FBI.

The first letter disparaged the police in general terms. The second gave the details of how he'd stalked and murdered Tasha Thomas. He'd simply seen her and her husband at the movies, followed them home and watched the house over a period of several days, finally closing in one night when she was alone. He'd chosen her because he found her attractive. That seemed to be the only criterion Dr. Dan used. He killed women he found attractive before they could rebuff him.

The letters were interesting but provided nothing that would significantly help his investigation, Nick thought—until he reached the bottom of the third letter. It described several clues Dr. Dan had left for the Colorado police that they'd missed. Nick remembered some of them being listed in one of Lola Fillmore's articles, so he was sure James Jenson had already garnered what evidence he could along those lines. What caught Nick's attention was the fact that Dr. Dan claimed to have been pulled over by police while heading home from the scene of the crime. He said he had blood on his clothes and hands, and that the officer who stopped him didn't even notice. He simply ran his driver's license, gave him a speeding ticket and let him go.

"Why do you have that look on your face?'' Maggie asked, breaking into his thoughts.

Nick glanced up to see her staring at him and tried harder to cloak his excitement. "What look?''

"I don't know. You look…pleased, I guess.''

"This is interesting, don't you think?''

She grimaced. ''I think it's sick.''

''It is sick, but if this guy was pulled over, like he claims, there'd be a record of it somewhere, right? Maybe the police can use his driver's license and registration to catch him. If they can come up with his name and the city he's from, they can contact family members and friends to see if they've heard from him. They can also learn more about his personal habits, which can only help them narrow the search, right?''

''God, I hope so,'' she replied.

THE FOLLOWING MORNING was Sunday. The weather had cooled a few degrees despite the advent of July, bringing a slight reprieve from the stifling heat. Because Nick was home with her and she felt as safe as she could be under the circumstances, Maggie had the back windows open as well as the front. Zach was still at Mrs. Gruber's, but Maggie knew he'd be home soon and was enjoying the last of her time alone with Nick.

''Thank goodness for those Delta breezes,'' she said, getting up from where they'd been relaxing on the couch together, she still in her nightie and he in a pair of pajama bottoms, to check on the coffee brewing in the kitchen. ''Too bad it won't stay this way for long.''

''We're not going to have to worry about it,'' he said above the rattle of the newspaper as he turned the pages. ''I'm having air conditioning installed this week.''

Surprised, Maggie pivoted to face him. ''You are? But that's expensive—''

''I know how much it costs.'' He looked up from his paper and smiled at her, and Maggie felt something wonderful and warm fill her whole being. Nothing affected her more positively than his smile. It made her want to hold him and tell him how much she loved him. But she was afraid such a declaration would only frighten him away.

At least a two-thousand-dollar investment on his part gave her hope that he planned to stay with her. For a while, anyway.

Determined not to ruin the aftermath of their second night of lovemaking, Maggie pushed her insecurities to the back of her mind. She headed into the kitchen, where she poured them each a cup of coffee before returning to snuggle up with Nick. He put his arm around her and drew her closer, kissing the top of her head, and she realized that if not for Dr. Dan, she would've been happier than she'd ever been in her life. But the killer's threat cast a pall over her sense of well-being. There was a constant, inescapable tension; her eyes flicked to the window every time she heard a noise outside.

"Don't you think I can take care of you, Maggie?" Nick asked, watching her.

Maggie put a hand on his bare chest and caressed the appealing contour of muscle she found there. "I don't doubt you. I just..." She took a deep breath. "I'll just be uneasy until he's caught, that's all. Maybe we should get out of the house, go somewhere fun for the day, just you, me and Zach."

He frowned. "I'd love to, babe, but I can't. Not today."

"You're not going back to the paper, are you?" she asked.

"No, but I have other things to do."

What "other" things? Certainly not another wedding. If so, he had to be the busiest wedding photographer she'd ever met, which didn't seem likely.

Maggie felt the hooks of her insecurity dig a little deeper. Nick was gone an awful lot. Now that they were lovers, she hoped that would change. But he didn't seem any more inclined to stick around today than he had a week earlier. Was it possible he was still seeing his ex-girlfriend?

Maggie didn't even want to think about that. Especially

because he hadn't done anything to make her distrust him.
He'd been loving and kind and supportive. She owed him
the benefit of the doubt, didn't she?

"I'll have more time soon," he promised when she didn't
say anything. "Hey, what about that box from John? Aren't
you ever going to open it?"

"You don't mind if I do?" Part of Maggie wanted him to
say yes—a large part. The jealousy she'd witnessed over
Brian had helped convince her that Nick cared about her. But
his complete indifference to John undermined her confidence.

"I'm fine with it," he said. "Go ahead."

Maybe Nick didn't feel threatened because John lived out
of state and was only a screen name at this point, Maggie
thought. Or maybe he was just more confident in her feelings
for him than she was in his feelings for her. There was no
way to tell, but John had given her permission to keep the
present, and Nick had given her the okay to open it, so she
wasn't going to deprive herself. Retrieving the brown box
she'd seen in the front room, she sat down in the chair across
from the couch and ripped off the covering.

Nick looked on, still smiling as she pulled out a white
cotton sundress and a travel brochure on Cancun, Mexico.

"Do you like it?" he asked.

Maggie checked the label in the dress and was surprised
to find that John had purchased her exact size. "I love it, but
what do you think the travel brochure is about?"

"He was probably planning to take you to Mexico. But
now, I guess I'll have to do it." He set the paper aside and
came to her, kissing her long and deep. "Try it on for me,"
he said.

Maggie went to her bedroom to change, laughing when
she saw that Nick was following her.

"What's the matter?" she asked. "Think I might need
help with the buttons?"

He grinned. "I'm available for whatever you might need."

Maggie slipped off her nightie, trying not to turn away or blush at the low whistle Nick gave when she stood before him naked.

"Now this is a sight I'll never get tired of," he said. "You're beautiful, Maggie. I've never seen a more beautiful woman."

Moving close, he slid his hands up over the curve of her hips to her breasts, then helped her pull the dress on over her head. Sleeveless, with a loose neck that gathered and tied, it fell to just above her ankles.

"It's perfect. I want to photograph you in this dress," he said. "On the beach."

"Let's go there now," she said. "Half Moon Bay is only a three-hour drive. We could stay for a few days."

He ran his fingers through her slightly tangled hair. "Would you really leave town today?"

Maggie considered his question, tempted, then shook her head. "No, I wish I could, but Ben is counting on me to follow the Dr. Dan story to its conclusion. That's what a good journalist would do. And I'm determined to be a good journalist. I'm just hoping it'll all end soon—and that I'll be around to write the final article."

"You'll be here," Nick promised. "But not for long, because after Dr. Dan's caught and we can both get some time off, I'm going to take you away for a week."

It could be their honeymoon, Maggie told herself, wondering if Nick had thought about marriage half as many times as she had. She wanted to be his lover, his companion, his wife, and have more children—his children. She wanted Zach to have a father and siblings. But most of all, she wanted to know Nick loved her as deeply as she loved him.

The front door banged open and Maggie heard her son's voice. "Mommy, we're home!"

Rambo barked and met Maggie and Nick in the hallway before they could reach the living room. Zach and Mrs. Gruber came in behind the dog.

"You're not the only one who has a secret admirer," her neighbor announced, holding a box in one hand.

Maggie lifted her eyebrows. "How nice. Someone sent you a gift?"

"Yep. Left this box on my porch. And you'll never believe what's inside." Mrs. Gruber lifted the lid and pulled out a pair of bikini panties. "Pretty, aren't they? Not that they're anything close to my style. But I'm thinking this admirer is *so* secret, he doesn't even know what I look like. Or he got the wrong porch."

*I know the color of your sheets. I know where you keep your underwear…*

Maggie felt the blood drain from her face. "If he got the wrong porch, he meant to," she said. "Those belong to me. Dr. Dan's trying to tell me he's been inside my house."

NICK COULD HEAR James Jenson, the detective from Seattle, rattling papers on the other end of the line as he sat in his truck at a stoplight en route to his apartment. It had been difficult to leave Maggie and Zach in the care of the police officers watching their house today, but he knew he couldn't stay with them. He still had a job to do.

"I called the Colorado police and got the license plate numbers of everyone pulled over on March third, the day Jeannie Savoy was killed," Detective Jensen said. "But none were registered to a blue Geo Metro. And none of the drivers matched the description we have of Dr. Dan."

Gunning the accelerator as the light turned green, Nick bit back a curse. He'd thought the Fillmore letters would provide him with the link he needed to bring down this killer. Instead, the investigation had just reached another dead end. Dr. Dan must've been lying about being pulled over. Maybe that was why Lola hadn't printed anything about it in the paper. She might have checked his facts and found them lacking in validity. But dammit! What was Nick going to do now? The underwear Dr. Dan had delivered to Mrs. Gruber was meant as a message. He wanted Maggie. He wanted her to know it. And despite the protection she had from the police, Nick feared Dr. Dan would get to her in an unguarded moment. Or, if he couldn't get to Maggie, Nick felt sure he'd kill someone else. Dr. Dan's crimes were acts of rage. If Maggie wasn't going to bear the brunt of it, someone else would. Which meant Nick couldn't sit back and wait for Dr. Dan to come to him. He had to *solve* this case. And he had to do it fast.

"So now what?" Jenson was asking.

"You sure you followed up on all the clues he said the Colorado police missed?" Nick asked, stalling for time to think as he signaled and switched lanes in the light Sunday traffic. They'd already been over this. Jenson had assured him he'd left no stone unturned, but Nick felt they had to be missing...something.

"I was completely thorough," Jenson said. "I had Lola's article, the one she wrote from his letter, as a guide."

Nick rubbed his chin. Why would Dr. Dan claim he'd been pulled over if that wasn't true? Was it an outright lie? Or was it merely an exaggeration? "Okay, he said in the letter that he had blood all over him when he was stopped, but a police officer would probably have spotted that right away. What if there was no visible blood? What if he had a body in his trunk, instead? Or what if he was pulled over a day or two after the killing, while he was still in the same area? What do you think? Is it possible?"

"Hell, anything's possible. Worth a shot, at any rate. You

want me to run the plates of all cars that were pulled over in Boulder March 4th and 5th?''

"Go up to a week on either side, if you have to. If you find a blue Geo Metro or a driver matching Dr. Dan's description, let me know immediately. The task force I'm working with here have their hands full interviewing Marge Brown's friends and neighbors, but you can connect with them if you can't reach me.''

"You got it, boss. I'll be back in touch,'' Jenson said and hung up.

Nick entered the parking lot of his apartment building, found his space and cut the engine. He was just getting out when his cell phone rang again. This time he didn't recognize the number on his caller ID.

"Nick Sorenson.''

"Nick? This is Darla.''

"What's up, Darla?'' he asked, locking his truck.

"I want to talk to you about Maggie.''

"Okay.''

"I don't really know how to say this, but she's…sensitive and kind, and she's already been through hell with her ex-husband. We've been best friends ever since she came to Sacramento, so I know her pretty well.''

Nick frowned as he let himself into his apartment. "Where are you going with this, Darla?''

"I'm just saying I know you two have become close, and I don't want to see her get hurt.''

Neither did Nick. Unfortunately, considering the situation, the odds weren't really in Maggie's favor. Or his, for that matter. When she learned the truth, it would probably destroy all her trust in him—in *them*—and what relationship could survive without trust? "So you're looking for a promise?''

"I'm looking for something that tells me you really care about her.''

"I care, Darla," he admitted, "but my life's a bit confusing right now. Until things straighten out, we're just going to have to take it one day at a time."

Darla paused. Then she muttered, "Hurt her and I'll...I'll egg your truck."

NICK STRETCHED and yawned before slumping back over the files spread out on the desk at his apartment. Working all night with Maggie and loving her all morning had left little time for sleep. Now that he'd been up most of the day, as well as all night, he was beginning to feel the effects. But he had to come up with *something* that would nail Dr. Dan, and he was determined to dig through every single fact he'd amassed on this case until he did.

His cell phone rang, and he scrubbed his face with one hand before answering. Maybe he should give himself fifteen minutes to rest. A power nap might make all the difference...if only he didn't see that bikini underwear every time he closed his eyes and feel the clock ticking away. Every minute he lost was one more minute Dr. Dan had to plot his attack on Maggie.

"Hello?"

"Hi, gorgeous."

Nick smiled at the sound of Maggie's voice, wishing he could be with her. He wanted to see her, have dinner with her, hold her in his arms. "How's my girl?" he asked.

"Lonely. And bored. I haven't left the house for fear Dr. Dan will follow me. I certainly don't want to make things easy for him. So I've stayed put and vacuumed and dusted and made lasagna for dinner, and Zach and I have finger-painted and collected ants for his ant farm from the backyard. But now I need a nap and know you must be just as exhausted. Are you ever coming home?"

"I'll get there as soon as I can," he said, "but I don't

know for sure when that'll be. Are you going in to the office tonight?''

"Yeah."

"Then I'll be there to take you. How did Ben like your last article?"

"He was happy with it. He's already told me I'm getting a raise. And he said that the way I've handled the Dr. Dan stories has boosted his confidence in me. So when the question of an exclusive comes up again, I'll have a lot more credibility."

"That's progress, babe."

"Yeah. It beats the heck out of writing for a tabloid and feeling ashamed of what I'm doing."

"I'm proud of you."

"Thanks."

He could hear Zach in the background begging for the phone. "Let him talk," he said, logging on to the Internet just as Zach's voice came over the line.

"Hi, Nick. Is this-s-s Nick?" Zach asked.

"That's right, buddy. It's me. Are you and your mom having fun?"

"I want to play bas-s-s-ketball," he said. "Will you play bas-s-s-ketball with me?"

Nick saw that John had a message waiting from Maggie and clicked on it while he talked. "We'll play a game when I get home, okay?"

"When are you coming home?"

"Soon."

"Before bedtime?"

"I hope so. If not, we'll play tomorrow."

"But I want to do it now."

Nick chuckled. "So do I, except I've got work to do. Is Rambo behaving himself?"

"Yeah."

"Did you feed him his dinner?"

"Yeah."

"Good. Let me talk to Mommy again."

"Huh?"

"Let me talk to Mommy."

"Okay."

There was the sound of some telephone bobbling, then Maggie said, "I'll let you go."

"See you soon."

"Wait. Have you eaten any lunch?" she asked.

He hadn't. He'd gone straight to the apartment and spent most of the day there. He was as hungry as he was tired, and judging by Maggie's question he knew he didn't sound his best, but he wasn't letting Dr. Dan elude him any longer. "I'm okay."

There was a long pause. Finally, "You're not with Shelley, are you?"

Nick was so immersed in her message to John, a warm friendly thank-you for the dress and for his understanding, that at first he didn't recognize the name. "Who?" he asked.

"Shelley. Your ex-girlfriend."

Oh, *that* Shelley. Snapping out of his preoccupation, Nick cleared his throat and sat up straighter. "No. Of course not. No. I'm at a wedding."

"Pretty quiet for a wedding."

"The band's taking a break."

She paused. "You're going to lose your job at the paper, you know that?"

"Let me worry about my job at the paper."

"Okay," she said, but when she hung up, Nick wasn't sure he'd convinced her of anything. So he poured the tenderness he was feeling into John's reply to her message, then got back to work.

# CHAPTER EIGHTEEN

"LOOK AT THIS," Maggie said to Darla, who was painting her toenails in Maggie's bathroom. Zach was playing on her bed with his Power Rangers, and Rambo lay at her feet, yawning and gazing up at her every time she spoke. The blinds were drawn against the darkness—and anything else lurking outside—but Maggie wasn't going to bed. She'd traded Jorge Friday for Sunday. In another hour, she had to get ready for work.

"Look at what?" Darla said, hobbling out of the bathroom so she wouldn't smudge her fresh paint.

The odor of nail polish came with her. Maggie wrinkled her nose and said, "This message from John. He's got to be the nicest guy in the world. Do you think I'm crazy for giving him up?"

As Darla studied the computer screen, Maggie read his words again.

Dear Maggie—
I'm glad you liked the dress. I can easily imagine it on you. I still have your pictures all around my apartment. Sometimes I just sit and stare at them and think about you. You're beautiful and sexy and everything I want in a woman. And I've been thinking…you once asked me if I minded that you have a son. I've never minded, but now I see Zach as a positive thing. I already love him, just because he's such a part of you.

Let me know how things are going with your Dr. Dan stories. I'm worried about your safety. I don't know what I'd do if anything happened to you.

Love, John

"Jeez! He doesn't know what he'd do if anything happened to you? Are you sure this isn't turning into a fatal attraction? He barely knows you," Darla complained.

"He doesn't *barely* know me. He knows me better than most people. We've been writing each other and instant messaging for weeks. I've told him things about me I haven't told anyone else."

Darla looked wounded. "Even me?"

Maggie laughed. "Not you, silly."

"Still, he's never met you, but he's sure talking like he has."

"He's just a nice, sensitive guy. And I might be blowing it big-time by throwing over someone like him for someone who doesn't even want to stay home for two hours at a time."

Darla glanced back at Zach, who was busy having one of his plastic figurines karate-chop another. "Nick has a second job."

"So he says."

"At least he works."

"I guess."

"Anyway, he'll be home soon. You said he was coming to take you to work, right?" Darla was obviously trying to lift her spirits, but she sounded no more convinced of Nick's devotion than Maggie was.

"Yeah, but I'm starting to worry that I'm just one of many."

"I didn't get that impression."

Maggie pulled her eyes from John's message to stare at her best friend. "What impression?"

"I don't think Nick has another girlfriend."

An inkling of suspicion crept into Maggie's consciousness. "How would you know?"

"I'm just saying I don't think he—"

"But how would you *know?*" Maggie persisted.

"Oh, all right." Darla propped her hands on her hips. "I was going to tell you eventually. I called him, okay? I called him."

Maggie shoved away from her desk and swiveled to face her friend more fully. "You *what?* Here I am, trying not to smother him in the first few days of this thing and my best friend *phones* him?"

"Well, I was worried about you. I asked him what his intentions are."

"You're not my father!"

"I know, but I had to do it. I'm all you have, out here, anyway."

Maggie dropped her head in her hands and rubbed her temples, determined not to let her irritation with Darla hurt her friend's feelings. Darla meant well, but Maggie wished she hadn't interfered. Still, after a moment, she couldn't help asking, "So what did he say?"

Darla looked sheepish. "He was pretty noncommittal. I didn't feel any better after we'd hung up."

Great! More doubts about Nick. At least John seemed capable of making a commitment; he also seemed ready for one. "If Nick loved me, he'd say so," Maggie said. "Wouldn't he? I mean, what could possibly be stopping him? Have I gotten myself involved in another one-sided relationship?"

"I have wondered if you've checked your phone bill lately," Darla said with a grimace.

"He's not using me for that," Maggie said. "He's paying two thousand dollars to install an air-conditioning unit this week, he's already given me a check for the rent and his share of all the bills, and he hasn't been to the video store once."

"Then he can't be all bad," Darla said, sounding genuinely impressed. "A girl could do a lot worse. Nick's good in bed—"

"Who said he was good in bed?" Maggie interrupted.

"Are you kidding? It's written all over your face."

Maggie smiled. "Okay, I'll have to give you that one."

"And he's generous with his money," Darla went on. "You should be happy, kiddo."

Maggie looked gloomily at the underwear that was still sitting on her dresser, the pair Dr. Dan had sent to Mrs. Gruber. "Oh, sure. I'm sleeping with a guy I'm madly in love with, but I don't know where he goes most of the time. I'm writing off a kind, sensitive guy who could probably love me like Nick can't. And I have an insane killer out to rape and stab me. I can't imagine why I'd be having such a bad day."

Darla put her arm around Maggie. "Don't worry, Mags. If anything happens to you, I'll be sure and take care of Nick. I mean Zach," she said with a wink, and they both laughed.

When Nick went to pick Maggie up for work, his reception was cool. He tried to draw her into conversation a few times, but she seemed reluctant to talk, and he was too exhausted to push her. At this point, he was so deeply immersed in the investigation, that ensuring her safety was all he felt capable of doing. Which meant their relationship would have to be sorted out later.

They both said hello to Ed, the security guard behind the reception desk, as they entered the *Trib*'s lobby and started up the escalator. At the top, Maggie thanked him for the ride and turned resolutely toward her desk.

Nick watched her go, tempted to confront her about whatever was bothering her, but he knew that if he did, they'd probably end up in an argument. His nerves were so taut, he couldn't spin the kind of convincing lies it would take to calm her down. She knew something was up; she just didn't know what.

He went to his desk and sat down to rest his burning eyes and think. He'd be able to explain everything to Maggie soon, he told himself. Not that the thought of coming clean brought him any comfort. He'd be able to reassure her that there was no one else in his life—like his mysterious nonexistent girlfriend. But he'd made love to Maggie while she thought he was someone he wasn't—a photographer, not a cop. That wouldn't go down easily.

On the positive side, he'd made progress in his profile on Dr. Dan. After placing numerous calls to the lab, the coroner and FBI headquarters, some things were becoming apparent. The women in Boston and Missouri were killed on Friday nights. The two victims in Colorado were murdered on Saturday nights. Because of the timing, Nick had originally guessed that Dr. Dan had a job that kept him busy all week and left him free only on weekends.

But then the killing pattern had changed. Lola Fillmore was killed on a Monday, and the victims in Sacramento were killed on two different days, Friday and Sunday. Suddenly Dr. Dan seemed to be rambling from city to city, striking at will, regardless of day, which suggested he was now unemployed. However, after speaking to Lalee Wong, the profiler who'd prepared Dr. Dan's original report, Nick was again convinced that Dr. Dan needed a paycheck in order to survive. He wasn't someone who lived on the street. He wasn't independently wealthy. He probably worked off-hours, nights and weekends, and his employment was flexible and blue-collar enough to make finding work easy. Which meant he wasn't a surgeon or a doctor, even though he was skilled with a knife. A cop wanna-be wouldn't go through eight years of med school. No, Dr. Dan was a hunter or a survivalist or a trained soldier or…what? What else could he be?

Nick thought back to the last letter Dr. Dan had sent Maggie, which had started out "To the Public" and blasted the press for disseminating erroneous information fed to them by the police. Dr. Dan tried to set the record straight according to his own twisted mind, insisting that the women he'd killed had deserved to die. Then he ranted about his own brand of justice, boasting several times about his superior intellect compared to everyone else, especially Mendez and Hurley. Soon after the opening, however, the letter became almost incoherent. Dr. Dan's sentence structure deteriorated until he was using mostly fragments that didn't make sense. His letter sounded like the ravings of a lunatic, which meant, according to Lalee Wong, that Dr. Dan was growing angry and irrational. Maggie hadn't cooperated the way he'd wanted her to. In his mind, she'd turned on him, just like Lola. And now that there was a squad car parked in front of her house, he couldn't act on his desire for revenge, which increased his level of frustration.

He'd make a move soon, Nick thought. Dr. Dan's emotions were running too high for him to hide out for long—

Nick's cell phone rang. Taking a deep breath, he sent a fleeting glance at Maggie, who was busy on her computer half a room away, and answered. "Sorenson here."

"This is Detective Jenson. I've got something for you."

Nick sat up straight, his fatigue miraculously gone. "What is it?"

"The Boulder police pulled over a blue Geo Metro the day after the murder. The driver matches Dr. Dan's basic description, at least for height and weight. Name's Daniel Murrill.''

Yes! He'd been right. The name, if not the car, confirmed it. Dr. Dan *had* exaggerated. "And?"

"He's originally from Boston."

The place of the first murder. "Does he have a record?"

"Served eight years in the state pen for kidnapping and rape. Got out three years ago."

"Any friends or family?"

"I haven't been able to gather that information yet, but I've got a detective in Boston, the guy who investigated the first murder, helping me out. He's going to ask a few questions and get back to me tomorrow."

"Perfect. Let me know what you turn up."

Nick punched the end button and sat back in his chair, feeling a measure of relief for the first time in days. He was getting close. Dr. Dan—Daniel Murrill—might feel invincible. He might think he could taunt Maggie and punish whomever he wanted to, but it wouldn't be long now before Nick brought him in.

MONDAY MORNING the HVAC company arrived to install the air-conditioning unit Nick had promised. It took two men working most of the day, but by late afternoon, the house was several degrees cooler.

At first Maggie swung Zach around in the kitchen, marveling at the difference. But her elation didn't last. Air conditioning was only air conditioning, after all, and Maggie was worried about something bigger. Nick hadn't slept in her bed when they returned from work. He'd driven her home, crashed on the couch for a few hours—then he'd left.

Finally surrendering to the despondency that hovered over her, Maggie cursed herself for falling in love with him, for letting him move in, for wanting him so badly. In an effort to make herself feel better, she exchanged e-mails with John, who commiserated with her and told her if she ever got fed up with Nick, he'd be willing to take his place. But that wasn't enough. Maggie doubted anyone could take Nick's place. She picked up the phone to call Darla at work, thinking she'd use the announcement of her new air conditioner as an opener, when the doorbell rang.

Zach dashed from the lunch table to answer it, but Maggie called him back before he could reach the front room.

Rambo beat her to the door and stood there, stiff-legged and barking at whoever waited on the other side. Maggie could see a squad car parked across the street but still wasn't going to open the door without checking the peephole. Stretching up on tiptoe, she saw Detectives Mendez and Hurley.

She released the bolt, and threw open the door. "Tell me you've caught him," she said.

A regretful expression appeared on Mendez's face. "Uh, no, not yet. But we think we know who he is now. Can we come in?"

Maggie stepped back to admit them, then waved them to the couch. "So who is he?" she asked, sinking onto the loveseat.

"He's an ex-con—"

The door opened again and they all looked up as Nick walked in.

Maggie blinked at him in surprise. He'd left a check for the air-conditioning company; she hadn't expected him back before dinner. "What are you doing home?" she asked.

Zach skirted around her and reached for him, demanding to be held, and Rambo wagged his tail so hard his whole back end moved. They were all crazy about him, Maggie thought.

"I had a few minutes, so I decided to stop by and see how

it went with the air conditioning. Feels good." Nick lifted Zach into his arms as his eyes flicked over Mendez and Hurley, then returned to Maggie. "What's going on?"

"These are the detectives heading up the Dr. Dan case. They think they know who he is."

Carrying Zach, Nick crossed the room and sat next to Maggie, holding her son on his lap and simultaneously giving Rambo the attention he craved. "Who is he?" he asked.

"Daniel Murrill," Mendez said. "He served eight years in Massachusetts for rape. Released three years ago. Comes from a broken home. Has a background of abuse. We believe his rage against women stems from his relationship with his mother, who sent him to summer camp when he was twelve and—if you can believe it—moved away while he was gone. As far as we know, she hasn't contacted him since. He went into foster care at that time, but never lasted long in any one household. He was out on his own by the time he was sixteen."

"How old is he now?" Maggie asked.

"Thirty-four."

On a personal level, Maggie tried to digest this information, to create a more complete mental picture of the man who wanted her dead, hoping to see him as human and fallible. On a professional level, she sought the details she'd need to write her next article for the paper. "Does he have a wife, kids?"

"He's never been married, but he has a son who's being raised by a woman named Roxanne Rodinsky, who had a brief relationship with him. Evidently there've been problems there, too. She moved away without telling anyone where she was going, and she took their son. Her co-workers say she did it to escape Murrill, that he was abusive. He went a little crazy when she up and disappeared, just like his mother."

"When was that?" Maggie asked.

"A little over a year ago."

"You think that incident might have been what triggered the murders?"

Hurley spoke for the first time. "Probably. But Murrill went to prison for rape, remember? He has a history of violence."

How could she forget? Dr. Dan now saw her as a betrayer like his mother and girlfriend. Only he knew where she lived.

"Why didn't he go after this Rodinsky person or his mother? Why is he taking his anger out on complete strangers?" she asked.

"Some murderers are completely cowed by the very people they deeply hate," Mendez said. "In any case, Murrill's problems started way back in grade school. He fought regularly, was expelled again and again—one time for sending his teacher a drawing he'd made of a man stabbing a woman—and was teased or avoided by the other children. Generally there isn't a single event that defines a person like Murrill. His psyche grows out of a combination of factors and experiences."

"So he's crazy?"

"I wouldn't say he's crazy. I'll leave that for the defense attorneys and psychiatrists to argue about."

"What kind of work does he do?"

"He's a diener."

"A *what?*"

"A diener. It's a German word for servant but it's actually a person who assists in performing autopsies."

Autopsies? Maggie was beginning to feel a little queasy imagining Dr. Dan cutting up dead bodies. Nick must have sensed her unease because he took her hand and threaded his fingers through hers. "So that would explain his talent with a knife," she said.

"You bet."

"Is he a doctor of some sort, then?"

"No. The Dr. Dan bit was probably his attempt to feel as powerful as those who exercise authority over him. Dieners generally have no formal training. But many have some background in the funeral industry. It seems that one of Dr. Dan's foster families owned a funeral home, so that's probably where he got his start."

"What is the life of a diener like?" she asked.

"It's not pretty," Mendez said. "They do a lot of the dirty work, load the body onto the table, open the chest cavity, that sort of thing."

Maggie made a face. "What would make anyone accept such a job? Are they well paid?"

"Not especially, but management tends to leave them alone, so they have more autonomy than other workers at their pay-grade and level of education. We actually found the hospital where Dr. Dan's been working here in Sacramento, but he had an argument with one of the pathologists three days ago and was fired."

Maggie's heart sank. They'd come that close and missed him? "He's been working at a hospital here in town? Why didn't anyone recognize him and call in?"

Mendez shrugged. "Why don't we find more perps through composites? They grow a beard or wear a wig or dye their hair, and they no longer resemble the two-dimensional picture. And it's not like the whole hospital staff ever saw him. Being a diener is pretty solitary. Murrill went in late at night and spent the majority of his time with one, maybe two, pathologists, who were concentrating on the job at hand. They may not have seen the paper or paid attention to the story if they did. There're a lot of possible reasons."

"But can't the hospital give you his address? It should be on his application for employment."

"It was a bogus address. No one bothered to check."

"So what did his co-workers say he was like?"

"Strange, secretive, quiet," Hurley said.

"Maybe he'll be moving on now that he's lost his job. Maybe he already has," Maggie said, wishing she didn't sound so hopeful.

Mendez exchanged a look with Nick that Maggie didn't quite understand. "We don't think so. He called you after he was fired. We don't think he'll go away until he comes for you."

Until he came for her? Maggie knew Dr. Dan wanted to hurt her, but hearing Detective Mendez say something like that just seemed so fatalistic. She tightened her grip on Nick's hand. "What are you saying? We sit back and wait?"

Mendez glanced at Nick again. "Actually, we have an idea we'd like to put into action, something we think will draw him out."

A tremor of foreboding skittered up Maggie's spine. Drawing an animal out of its den required some sort of bait; humans weren't much different. And she knew perfectly well whom Mendez wanted to use as bait. "What's your idea?" she asked.

"We know from his letters that it's extremely important to Dr. Dan to appear smart and elusive, but we also know he's already been caught by the law once and done some hard time, so he's not as brilliant as he thinks he is. Anyway, if you print everything we just told you about him and take special care to make him look as weak and pathetic as possible, we think his anger will override his caution. He's recently been fired. He hasn't been able to get close to you because of our protection. He's got to be frustrated as hell. In the same article, we want you to say there's been another woman murdered, this time in Los Angeles, and that police are linking her slaying to suspect Daniel Murrill. Authorities believe he's left the city, etc., etc. We'll pull back on our surveillance around this house to make it believable—''

"You'll what?" Maggie cried.

Mendez held up a hand. "Don't worry. We'll still be here. As a matter of fact, I'm going to—" he shifted and glowered at Nick "—dress up as a woman, as your friend Darla, and come over this Sunday night."

Maggie wondered, fleetingly, if he somehow held Nick responsible for something. It didn't make sense that a photographer from the *Trib,* or a wedding photographer, for that matter, would have anything to do with Mendez, but there was some kind of tension between the two men. They certainly didn't behave like complete strangers. Had they met?

"And you think you're going to make a believable woman?" she asked.

"From a distance, I will. I'll have the wig, the makeup, the whole get-up."

"And you're coming next Sunday because it's my night off."

"Right. Dr. Dan will be angry and eager, but he'll need the cover of darkness, so he'll most likely strike the first night you're off."

"I'm off tonight. I work Tuesday through Saturday."

"But we need some time to make a believable show of it, to back off the security, etc. On Sunday, we'll have the lady who watches Zach come and get him and the dog, so Dr. Dan will think you're here alone with Darla. Two women won't frighten him. He'll think you're vulnerable."

As far as Maggie was concerned, she *would* be vulnerable. What if Dr. Dan overpowered Mendez? What if he brought a gun instead of a knife and simply shot them both? Or what if he decided to hurt her by following Mrs. Gruber and going for Zach instead? "How do we know he won't hurt Zach? If he feels I'm too risky he—"

"Don't worry. We'll be taking Zach and Mrs. Gruber somewhere safe."

"How would we notify your friends on the force if we need help?" she asked Mendez.

"They'll know because they'll be watching from a few discreet locations. And I'll have my gun under my, um, dress."

Every time Mendez mentioned wearing a dress, Hurley smiled. When Maggie sent him a questioning look, he shrugged and said, "I'm too big to be a woman. There isn't a dress or a wig that would convince anyone."

Judging by his smugness, he was happy about that fact. "So that's the plan?" she asked. "What about all the things that could go wrong?"

"If you get into trouble, flip the lights off and on a couple of times," Nick said, breaking his silence. "The police won't be able to see everything. That should help notify them that there's a problem."

Maggie twisted to face him. He'd said, "that should help notify them that there's a problem," but it sounded more authoritative than she would have expected. "What stake do you have in this?" she asked. "What's going on?"

He looked uncomfortable. "I just think it's the safest way to stop him, Maggie. If Dr. Dan can't get to you, he'll go after someone else. The police have no idea who that someone will be, so another life could be lost. But if they can draw him here, they can get him off the streets once and for all."

Suddenly Maggie's unease turned to suspicion. Was she crazy, or was Nick somehow involved in this investigation?

# CHAPTER NINETEEN

WITH BEN'S APPROVAL, Maggie wrote the article Mendez and Hurley had told her to write, but waited until Saturday night to print it. The detectives wanted it to appear in Sunday's paper, so Dr. Dan's anger would be fresh and fierce that night, and Maggie had no doubt it would be. The story she'd written would make the front page and would chronicle a troubled little boy who'd grown into a social outcast, making Daniel Murrill appear as pathetic and pitiable as he probably was.

Through the week, Nick continued to be vague about his activities and whereabouts. When she asked whether or not he'd ever met Mendez before last Monday, he said he'd seen him around town once or twice. When she pressed him about his other job, he clammed up. Maggie was becoming more and more convinced that he played some part in the investigation, but she wasn't sure exactly what. He could be involving himself because he cared about her. Or he could be a more important player.

Maggie wanted to believe the former because the alternative was so painful—that everything between them was a lie—but Nick's behavior was quickly eroding her confidence. He hadn't shown up at the office all week, hadn't made love to her since the morning he'd announced he was buying her an air conditioner and whenever she spoke about their plans for Dr. Dan, he always took the side of the police.

Sunday came quickly, far sooner than Maggie wished, although she longed desperately for the whole thing to be over. She was tired of feeling frightened, tired of listening to every creak or noise as though Dr. Dan was trying to break in. And now that she had central air and no longer needed to open her windows at night, she wanted to take off all the bars so she could paint the outside. She wanted to wallpaper, too, and live like a normal human being again.

Maggie spent Sunday afternoon playing with Zach, but she couldn't stop herself from watching the clock. The whole idea of leaving herself so vulnerable to a man who'd be crawling into her house with a knife terrified Maggie. And she hated how remote Nick had become. He seemed more focused on what they were about to do than she was. He spoke with the police, worked out details, lent them his support—which only confirmed what she didn't want to believe in the first place: he was a cop.

John, at least, seemed sympathetic. He wrote her several times telling her how much she meant to him, how beautiful she was, how special. She'd confided in him and Darla, telling them what she was going to do, and they were the ones who pulled her through the week leading up to the big show-down. But on Sunday night, just before Nick left in anticipation of Mendez's arrival as Darla, he took her in his arms and held her close.

"Be careful," he murmured in her hair. "Flash the lights if anything goes wrong. And no matter what happens—" he pulled back to gaze down at her "—no matter what happens, Maggie, remember this. I love you."

He kissed her before she could respond, then walked out of the house, leaving her to wonder at his strange behavior. She'd been thinking she'd lost him, that their whole relationship had been a front, a lie. And then, out of the blue, he announces that he loves her? Who *was* Nick Sorenson? Could she believe anything he said?

Something clunked against the back of the house, causing Maggie's nerves to tighten into what felt like a steel ball in her stomach. She was home alone now. Zach had left with Mrs. Gruber nearly an hour earlier, gone to whatever safe place the police had arranged. Nick had just left, and the patrol car that normally sat out front had disappeared, too. At Mendez's request, she'd listened to her voice mail a few minutes ago to see if Dr. Dan had left a response to her article. But his eerie voice wasn't among her messages.

Daniel Murrill was being awfully quiet, she thought. She hadn't heard a word from him since he'd called more than a week earlier to share his disappointment that she hadn't printed his letter. Maybe she wouldn't hear from him tonight.

*Wishful thinking...*

Another thunk drew Maggie to the kitchen, her eyes sharp and alert, her heart beating fast. What was that? Mendez hadn't arrived yet. It wasn't even dark. But someone was out there...

*Please let it be the police, secreting themselves away.*

Maggie checked the doors and windows to make sure they were all locked, but that did very little to improve her sense of security. She'd inflated Dr. Dan's fearful abilities in her mind and kept expecting him to pop up behind her.

Foreboding descended on Maggie as she returned to the kitchen window and studied the backyard. She wished Mendez had let her keep Rambo home. Zach wasn't the only one who'd grown fond of Nick's dog. Despite her earlier reluctance, she was now glad to have him as part of the family and knew he would've been an asset tonight. But Mendez— and Nick—didn't want anything to frighten Dr. Dan away. They wanted him to fall quickly and easily into their trap.

So did Maggie. Holding her breath, she listened carefully, her eyes affixed to the garage. She thought she saw a shadow pass behind its shiny window, but with the setting sun reflecting so brightly off the glass, she couldn't be sure. Her anticipation of the night's events was probably fueling her fear, causing her to interpret normal daily sounds as threats, to see things that weren't there.

The telephone rang and Maggie turned to answer it. Maybe Mendez was phoning to say he was on his way. Maybe Nick was calling to tell her to remain calm and safe. She longed to hear his voice even though he'd left her only minutes ago.

But no one responded when she said hello. She waited several seconds, listening to the beating of her own heart, then finally hung up.

Something was wrong. Where was Mendez? Nervous and impatient, she dialed his cell phone.

"Detective Mendez here."

"Where are you?" she asked without bothering to identify herself.

"Maggie?"

"Do you have any other big dates tonight? I'm home alone here, and I'm terrified. What's taking you so long?"

There was a lengthy pause. "I can't get these damn panty hose up," he grumbled at last. "I think I bought the wrong size."

If she'd felt less threatened, Maggie would have laughed at the image his words created. Mendez was one of the least feminine men she'd ever met. But she was too agitated to laugh. "Then shave your legs and forget the panty hose, but get over here and don't forget your gun."

"'Don't forget my gun.' What do you think I am?"

"A cop. So come over and start doing your cop thing."

"Give me fifteen minutes."

He hung up, leaving Maggie standing in her kitchen feeling as though fifteen minutes equated to an eternity. How long did it take to break a window and stab a woman?

Remembering Mendez's description of a diener's job, she

opened her utensil drawer and took out a butcher knife. She wasn't sure she could use it, but she certainly wasn't planning to stand in her kitchen and wait without a weapon.

The phone rang again, and again no one answered when she said hello. Maggie hung up and thought about calling her mother. She wanted to make peace, in case things went badly tonight. Rosalyn hadn't contacted her since learning about Nick, and Maggie didn't want her feeling guilty if they were never able to speak again.

But neither did she have any desire to hear "I told you so" if her fears and insecurities about Nick happened to come tumbling out. She and her mother needed to have a heart-to-heart. Before that, though, Maggie needed to decide what stand she wanted to take, regardless of Nick, and what she was willing to sacrifice in order to achieve it. So she called Darla instead. She didn't want to notice the house noises. She didn't want to see shadows outside in the garage. She didn't want to answer the phone and hear only her own voice.

"Darla? It's me," she said as soon as her friend picked up.

"Maggie, are you okay?"

"I'm fine."

"Tonight's the big night. What are you doing calling me? Have the police changed their minds?"

"No, Mendez can't get his panty hose on."

"What?"

"It's true. And Nick, Zach and Rambo have already left. So other than the policemen who are supposed to be hiding around the neighborhood, I'm alone."

"Jeez, what's Mendez thinking?"

"That he should have considered the size-grid on the back of the box."

"I wish he'd have let me help him," Darla said. "He came

over here to get a better idea of what I look like and what I'd wear, and I offered to get him ready, but he thought he had it dialed in.''

Maggie's call-waiting beeped, and she purposely ignored it. "I think someone's in the garage," she blurted out. "I'm hoping it's a cop.''

"What? You mean it might not be? I'm coming over," Darla said. "I'll leave when Mendez gets there, but I don't want you—''

"No," Maggie interrupted. "You can't do that. It'll ruin everything if Dr. Dan sees two Darlas come to the house at the same time."

"So you think he's watching."

"Yes."

"How do you know?"

Maggie shivered. "I can feel it."

The phone beeped again, indicating another incoming call, but Maggie let it go. "And I think he has a cell phone," she went on, "and that he keeps calling me."

"You're giving me the creeps," Darla said. "I want you to phone Mendez and demand that he or someone else get over there right away. Call Nick and tell him you've decided not to cooperate with the police."

What if Nick *was* the police? Maggie backed away from that thought as quickly as she had all week. If he was the police, he'd gotten involved with her for only one reason— to further the investigation. And if he'd done that, he didn't care about her. And if he didn't care about her...

*Stop!* "I don't think he'd support me in calling it off," she said, trying to simplify the situation, even in her own mind.

Call-waiting intruded yet again. This time, Maggie told Darla to hold and switched over. She expected the silence she'd already experienced, but Nick's voice came over the line.

"Dammit, Maggie, why haven't you been answering the phone?"

"Because someone keeps calling me who doesn't say anything! And it's scaring me!"

"That was me," he said. "My cell phone's been cutting out."

Maggie breathed a sigh of relief. "Thank God."

"I'm just down the alley in back, babe," he responded. "I'm watching the house and the yard. I won't let anything happen to you. I couldn't live with myself if I did."

Nick's words were intended to comfort her, but they made Maggie's heart sink a little further. "You said you loved me," she said, trying to hang on to that much.

"I did."

"Do you mean it?"

"Without a doubt."

"Then why have you been so secretive, Nick? When are you going to tell me what's going on?"

He didn't speak for a long minute. "Now's not the time to go into it, babe. You'll understand soon. Just promise me…"

"What?"

"Nothing."

"You're not making any sense."

"We'll talk about it later," he said. "Hang on…"

After a short pause, he said, "Mendez just pulled up in Darla's car. He's got her key to the house and he'll let himself in, but I wanted you to know he was coming so you wouldn't be frightened."

"Okay."

"It won't be long now," he said, and then he was gone and Maggie could hear a key in the lock out front. She switched back to Darla and told her she had to go just as Mendez came clunking into the living room, wearing high heels, a print dress, a long blond wig, and bright red lipstick. He looked like a prostitute on steroids.

"It's a good thing Darla isn't here to see this," Maggie said.

A wounded expression claimed Mendez's face. "What do you mean?"

"Never mind. Looks like you got your panty hose on."

"I wasn't about to shave my legs."

"Where's your gun?"

He hefted whatever padding filled the cups of his sizable bra. "Right here."

"That would explain why one's lower than the other."

"Really?" He approached the mirror on the far wall and attempted to adjust himself. "Oh, well," he said when all efforts proved futile. "Steel weighs more than toilet paper. Nothing I can do about that."

Maggie shrugged and put her butcher knife away before she cut herself. "Works for me. So what do we do now? Paint a big red target on my forehead?"

He adjusted his panty hose. "That sounds like fun, but don't distract me. I've got to open the back windows."

"Yeah, I can see that would require a great deal of mental energy," she said, following him to the far wall and watching as he unlatched both windows.

"Don't you want my mind on my work?" he asked.

"Don't *you* think Dr. Dan's a little too smart for this?" she replied. "I've kept the house locked up tight ever since he came on the scene. Why would I, all of a sudden, relax my security and unlock the windows without bars?"

"It's not all of a sudden. Darla's here. You're having a good time and feeling safe because you haven't heard from him for a while. The police think he's moved to L.A., where all good criminals eventually go. And you think you're in the clear. What's so unbelievable about that?" The windows squealed in protest as he lifted them partway. "Turn on some music, will ya?"

Maggie had to admit she was feeling calmer by the moment. If Dr. Dan ever got a good look at Mendez, he'd run the other way, not come busting into her house.

On the other hand, if he was hiding in the garage, as she feared, and hadn't seen the detective lumber up to her front door, the costume might just work—if it was seen through the windows and from a distance...

She looked at Mendez again. "Nah, I'm perfectly safe."

"What?" he asked.

"Just talking to myself," Maggie said.

"Nick doesn't mind if you do that occasionally?"

"I think he spends more time with you than he does with me."

She was testing Mendez, but aside from a fleeting glance at her face, he kept his comment neutral. "He's a busy man."

"How would you know?" she pressed.

This time Mendez studied her for several seconds. "You'd know better than I would," he said at last.

"If you say so," she grumbled.

Sinking ponderously onto the couch, he snagged the remote control and started flipping through stations.

Maggie wrenched it out of his grip when he settled on a karate movie with subtitles.

"Hey, what're you doing?" he complained. "I like a good fight show."

"We're not watching that. You're supposed to be keeping your mind on your work, remember?"

"But it's early yet. Dr. Dan won't be showing up for some time."

"Close your legs," Maggie told him. "A woman doesn't sit like that."

Mendez scowled but obeyed.

"How long are we going to give him before you take off that ridiculous costume and go home?" she asked, flipping the channels herself.

"I don't know. It's not up to me when we pull the plug."

"Then who's it up to?"

He didn't answer. His attention was on the TV. "Wait, what was that?" he cried when she flashed through a channel that had a car chase going on.

"It's a rerun of 'Magnum P.I.' Don't tell me you want to watch it."

"Don't you like Tom Selleck?"

Maggie shook her head. She'd been worried about tonight for nothing. Mendez looked like an idiot and was more interested in watching television than catching bad guys. "Aren't you supposed to check the perimeter of the house or something?" she asked.

"I can't do that. It would tip our hand. We want our man to come to us. And he will," he said with certainty. Despite that, four long hours passed without a hint of trouble, and just after midnight Maggie's eyelids became so heavy she couldn't stay awake.

"I'm going to turn in," she announced at the end of their second HBO movie. "I don't think we'll be having any visitors."

Mendez nodded and swallowed a mouthful of Doritos before responding. "Go ahead and get some sleep. I think I should turn off the television and the lights, anyway. A little darkness might encourage our boy."

She watched Mendez finger the bra cup that held his gun and wondered if she should get her knife. The hallway to her bedroom was looking awfully long and dark, as was the yard outside her windows....

She knew Mendez would protest if she carried a knife to bed, but Maggie didn't intend to let that stop her. Circling around to the kitchen, she retrieved the butcher knife and concealed it in the waistband of her shorts before passing him again on the way to her room.

"Good night," she said.

"Good night," he replied, snapping off the television. "Leave the music on. Covering sound makes an intruder feel safe. But hit the lights, will ya?"

*Hit the lights.* Maggie swallowed hard. She'd nearly convinced herself that Dr. Dan wasn't going to fall for this little ruse, but the thought of turning off all the lights was still a scary one. "Darkness makes an intruder feel safe, too, right?"

The wicker couch Mendez was sitting on creaked as he lay down. "You got it."

"You're looking pretty comfortable there. You're not going to fall asleep, are you?"

"Hmm?" he said, adjusting a throw pillow beneath his head.

"You're not *really* going to sleep, right?"

"What do you think?"

What Maggie thought was that he sounded tired. She turned off the living-room lights, wrapped her fingers around the handle of her knife and made her way slowly down the hall. Irrational as it was, she half expected Dr. Dan to be waiting under her bed, or in her closet, or behind the door....

Swallowing to relieve the dryness of her throat, Maggie listened for movement or breathing or anything that shouldn't be there. She heard nothing but still couldn't bring herself to sleep in her own room. Going past it, she used the bathroom in the hall, then turned off the rest of the lights and climbed into Zach's toddler bed with her clothes on.

Lying on her back, now wide awake, she stared at the patterns shifting on the ceiling, her knife still clutched in one hand.

In the living room, she heard Mendez get up and move around—possibly checking the windows? A few minutes later, he returned to his place on the couch, judging by the creaks. Except for the soft strains of ''Classics from the 80s'' still coming from her CD player, everything fell silent.

MAGGIE WASN'T SURE how much time had passed. She must have fallen asleep—although she hadn't thought she ever would—because when she awoke, the color of the night had changed to purple. A glance at the Pokémon clock on Zach's nightstand confirmed the approach of morning. It was after five o'clock.

What had awakened her? Momentarily disoriented, Maggie blinked at the glimmer of metal on the pillow beside her and realized it was the butcher knife she'd brought to bed. Then the night's plan came tumbling back with frightening clarity: She was in Zach's bed, and Mendez was in the living room, waiting for Dr. Dan to make his move.

Had the detective fallen asleep? Maggie strained to hear any sign of him breathing or snoring or moving around. But the house was silent except for the CDs she'd set on continuous play hours ago.

Slipping out of bed, she considered taking her knife with her. But she decided that creeping up on a cop while carrying a butcher knife probably wasn't a good idea. Especially when he was expecting a murderer—a murderer who'd never showed. Evidently Mendez and Hurley had been wrong about him. Daniel Murrill was smarter than they'd known and had probably found his way into someone else's bedroom while the police were watching her.

Maggie shuddered at the thought as she crept, barefoot, into the living room. But there she stopped cold. Something was wrong. One of the windows Mendez had cracked was now open wide. She could see the outline of its wooden pane in silhouette, could hear the rhythmic slap of the blind as the wind gently stirred it.

Refusing to turn her back on the room, she slid sideways until she could reach Mendez and shake his arm, but he didn't move.

"Mendez," she whispered, her eyes still roving over the dark living room in case Dr. Dan came at her. She wanted to turn on the light but was afraid to cross the room to get to the switch, afraid her footsteps might alert an intruder. "Wake up. I think we might have company."

No answer. Confused, Maggie risked a glance at the detective's face and thought he was still sleeping. Then she lowered her gaze far enough to see something dark and wet covering much of his dress.

Blood! She felt its warm, sticky wetness and thought she might be sick. Dr. Dan had killed Mendez, a trained police officer, right in her living room and with scarcely a sound. Which meant she didn't stand a chance against him. And now she was alone.

A creak down the hall drew her attention. Dr. Dan was looking for her, most likely in her own bedroom, but now he seemed to be coming back. Had her timing been slightly different, she might have run into him on her way to the living room.

Terror turned Maggie's blood to ice as her eyes flicked toward the back door. Could she reach it before Dr. Dan reached her? Both the front and back doors had old-fashioned bolts that required a key. The key was on the counter. But with her hands shaking so badly, Maggie doubted her fingers would be nimble enough to fit it into the lock. And her legs felt almost too weak to stand, let alone run.

Dr. Dan would catch her before she could unlock the door, she thought, panic nearly overwhelming her. She couldn't even reach the window.

If she flashed the lights, would the police arrive in time? She briefly considered the knife she'd left in Zach's room, but retrieving it or another one was hopeless now. She doubted she'd have the upper body strength or the nerve to use it, anyway.

The gun! What about Mendez's gun? Judging by the way he was lying, he'd never even drawn it. Which meant it was still there, in his bra.

Summoning every ounce of courage she possessed, Maggie crouched low and slipped her hand down the dress to search through the wads of toilet paper. Much of it was soggy with blood.

Where was it, where? The left cup? Maggie was so frightened, she couldn't remember. Dr. Dan's tread was nearly in the living room now, and everything in her mind was turned around. Her hands were cold and unwieldy and shaking uncontrollably. Her heart was hammering so hard it was difficult to breathe....

Finally, her fingers closed around the warm steel of a small handgun. Mumbling a silent prayer of thanksgiving, Maggie took it and launched herself away from the bleeding Mendez toward the back door—and the light switch—just as a dark-clad figure flew at her from the hall. It was too late! She wasn't going to make it, she realized, as a hand grabbed hold of her hair and pulled her down to the ground.

"Maaggiiee," Dr. Dan crooned above her. "What's the matter, Maggie? Didn't I tell you I'd be paying you a little visit? Nice trick with the drag queen, by the way, not that it fooled me. You must think I'm an idiot, Maggie.''

He smelled of cheap cologne and body odor. Swallowing hard, Maggie tried to shift so she could free the hand that held the gun, but he had a knee to her back, and she couldn't move. ''The police are watching,'' she said, stalling. ''You'll never get away from here.''

He laughed. ''I got in, didn't I?''

The CDs Mendez had told Maggie to put on before she went to bed started over at the beginning. Dimly Maggie recognized Janice Joplin's voice singing that she had nothing left to lose and felt exactly the opposite. She had everything to lose—Zach, possibly Nick, and a thriving career. She wasn't going to die now. She wasn't going to let Dr. Dan cheat her out of her future.

He'd turn her over eventually. And when he did...

''You're pathetic,'' she told him. ''You like to pretend you're smarter than the police and everyone else, but when it comes right down to it, you're just a rejected little boy throwing a violent tantrum. And it can't last forever, you know that, don't you? Someday you're going to jail and from there to the electric chair.''

Pain exploded in Maggie's head as he struck her. The blow hurt so badly, she wasn't sure he hadn't used his knife. But then he turned her, as she'd expected, and there was no time to worry about pain or anything else, only survival. Her hand now free, Maggie fired the gun.

The noise seemed deafening and the weapon's recoil surprised her. It jerked her arm back and smashed her elbow into the hardwood floor, sending shards of pain shooting down to her fingertips. At the same time, she felt Dr. Dan's hold give way.

No longer able to grasp the gun, she dropped it and cradled her throbbing arm as she scrambled to the far wall, where she flashed the lights several times, finally leaving them on before realizing that she'd fired and missed. The shot had merely surprised Dr. Dan, and now he had the gun.

Pressing herself flat to the wall, as if she could somehow make herself less of a target, Maggie closed her eyes, expecting him to squeeze the trigger. It was over. There was nothing more she could do to save herself.

But when the explosion came, she felt no pain. Opening her eyes, she saw Daniel Murrill crumple, instead. Nick was half-inside the open window and held the gun that had shot him.

# CHAPTER TWENTY

IT WAS AS SHE'D SUSPECTED. Numb, Maggie sat on the couch as the last of the police and EMT people who'd been tramping through her house for over an hour finally headed for the front door. Dr. Dan was dead and on his way to the morgue. There'd be no long, expensive trial for him, no chance of his escaping and hurting other women. Nick's bullet had killed him instantly. Mendez, though, was still alive. Unconscious and losing a lot of blood, he was in critical condition, but the paramedics had been optimistic about his chances for survival. The knife wounds in his chest were deep, but the gun in the left cup of his bra had deflected Dr. Dan's blade away from his heart.

Nick and the paramedics had wanted Maggie to go to the hospital along with Mendez, just to be checked out, but she'd refused. She had a bump on the head and a sore elbow; that was all. The only part of her that had been truly injured was her heart, and she knew there was nothing anyone could do for that. Experience had taught her it would eventually heal. Only this time, she feared it would take years. Long, long years...

Closing her eyes, she shook her head. She'd come face to face with a man who'd raped and killed eight women. She'd fired a gun, something she'd never done before. She'd watched Nick kill Daniel Murrill after her shot had missed him. And she'd believed Mendez was dead, too. So much in one night. So much terror and violence.

And now she had to face the truth that Nick wasn't the man she'd thought he was. Everything he'd told her, everything they'd done together, was a lie. He was more than a cop. He was an FBI agent, for God's sake, and he'd used her as a…a pawn, a prop in his investigation.

She heard Hurley ask him how much longer he'd be staying in Sacramento and wondered the same thing. Would he pack up and move back to Connecticut, or wherever he was from, tomorrow? The next day? She didn't know. He spoke to someone else and never answered Hurley.

"You okay?" Nick said, coming to sit beside her after shutting the front door behind everyone else.

Maggie nodded.

"How did you come so fast when I flashed the lights?"

"I'd just discovered a downed cop and knew something was wrong. I wasn't taking any chances. I called for backup, then raced over here."

"How did he get in?" Maggie asked. "Why wasn't Mendez watching the windows?"

"He probably was," Nick said. "Dr. Dan used a glass-cutter and came through the kitchen. He took Mendez by surprise."

"But the living-room window was open wider than when I went to bed."

"Mendez probably did that, hoping to entice him."

Nick tried to put his arm around her and draw her close, but she pulled away. "Don't touch me," she said. "I feel like enough of a fool already. I knew something was going on. I just didn't want to face it—"

"Maggie, you're no fool. I—"

"You what?" she demanded, her scrambled emotions giving a rare edge to her anger. "You didn't lie to me? You didn't use me?"

"I'm sorry," he said. "I didn't mean for us to get

so…close. One thing led to another, and I simply couldn't help myself.''

"Tell me something. Why did you first ask me out?"

"You know why."

"I want to hear you say it. I want to hear you speak the truth for a change."

He stared down at his hands, loosely clasped between his knees. "For the most part, I did what I had to do, Maggie."

Ignoring his answer, Maggie went on, "The last time I asked why you were interested in me, you said it was because I'm beautiful and driven and a little shy, and you liked that combination. Isn't that what you said? But that wasn't it at all, was it? Somehow you knew Dr. Dan would contact me because of my job and because of what happened to Lola, am I right?"

He looked at her before responding. Finally, "It was a hunch."

"And if you could get in my pants, too, well, that would be a bonus, right?"

"Don't even think it, Maggie. That's not how it was," he growled.

"Funny, I'd swear I'm finally seeing things clearly," she replied. "You were determined to bag your perp any way you could, and if you bagged me at the same time…" She couldn't finish.

"I know you're hurt," he said, obviously trying to rein in his own emotions. "I was afraid it would come to this. I knew it would. But I can only say one thing, Maggie. I loved you when we made love for the first time. I love you now. My job doesn't change that."

Maggie squeezed her eyes shut, wishing she could believe him. But the trust was gone. She'd closed her eyes to the truth, but now it was staring her right in the face, and she knew, even if Nick stayed for a while, he'd eventually leave.

He had a whole separate life wherever he lived, family, friends—maybe even a wife!

"Just tell me you're not married," she said. "Or is that where Shelley comes into the picture?"

He scowled. "I'm not that much of a lowlife, Maggie. There is no Shelley. I made her up so you'd let me move in with you."

Maggie shook her head. What *could* she believe about him? About them? What was real? "I think you'd better pack your things and go," she said at last.

"You don't mean that, Maggie. Take a few days to think about it. We'll talk when you're ready. I don't want to let go of what we have—"

"What we have?" she echoed. "We have nothing. I'm going to bed. When I get up, I want you gone." The words, even as she spoke them, sliced through Maggie. But she knew it was better to end their relationship quickly and move on. She refused to drag things out for months, living in constant fear that today was the day Nick would decide he didn't love her enough to give up the life he lived elsewhere. She had Zach to think about. Somehow, she'd lost sight of what was best for her son. She'd let her own needs take over and felt a terrible guilt about that, on top of everything else. *Remember f.p.?* she thought sadly. She'd just started to believe that Nick had all she could ever want of good fatherhood traits. But now? She didn't even know who he was.

"Goodbye, Nick," she said, standing. "I mean it when I say I don't want to hear from you again."

GOD, THAT HURT. Nick sat on Maggie's couch, feeling as though she'd just slugged him in the stomach. He'd been so frightened when he'd found that cop on the ground and realized Maggie was in trouble. His emotions had run from anger and fear to complete relief when he arrived in time, and now he just felt spent.

Dropping his head in his hands, he heard Maggie in her room getting into the bed they'd shared and he wanted to go and plead with her to reconsider. He wanted her to welcome him back into her arms and make love with him and say she'd be his wife. He wanted to sleep for the next twenty-four hours with her curved against him. But he knew she was in no shape to withstand an emotional onslaught. They'd both been through a great deal. What he needed to give her, more than anything, was time. Then, maybe…

Slowly, he stood and went to Mrs. Gruber's room to pack his things. When he finished zipping his suitcase, he walked slowly to the door, but something on the dresser caught his eye. It was the framed picture of Maggie he'd taken at the river. Pausing, he opened his luggage and slipped the photograph in with his things. He had the pictures she'd sent him, but they were taken before he'd come on the scene. This one meant more to him, and he wasn't about to leave it behind, just in case it was the only thing he'd ever have to remember them by.

MAGGIE?
I haven't heard from you in over a week. Are you all right? I'm worried about you.
    John

Maggie sighed as she read John's latest message on her computer at work. It was late, and she was nearly alone in the office, with only the crackle of her radios to keep her company. Her follow-up article on Dr. Dan was laminated and hung above her desk. It had run front and center in the Sunday *Trib,* the issue that had the widest circulation, and was her crowning achievement. Soon she'd be moving to days, thanks to a raise and a promotion from Ben in recognition of her work. But that was in September. Right now, in the middle of another hot August night, with Nick's desk empty and cleaned out just down the corridor, she was feeling weaker than usual. She missed him, longed to talk to him, and knew it would be all too easy to fall for John on the rebound. Which was why she hadn't written him since Nick had moved out. He was a good guy and deserved more than second-best.

But it was a slow night, which made it that much more difficult to occupy her mind, and her fingers itched to return his message. John had been good to her. What could it possibly hurt to continue their relationship? To accept a little support? As long as she made it clear that she was only interested in friendship…

John—
I'm sorry I haven't written. I haven't been at my best and didn't want—

An instant message popped up on her screen.

Mntnbiker: There you are. Where have you been? I've checked and checked and you're never online anymore.

Maggie sighed. So much for avoiding close contact.

Zachman: I've been…

What did she say? Heartbroken? Lovesick?

…busy,

she wrote at last, deciding to keep things as neutral as possible.

Mntnbiker: You've had a lot going on in your life.
Zachman: At least the FBI took care of Dr. Dan.
Mntnbiker: That's got to be a relief.

It *was* a relief—except that Maggie had been happy then, despite Dr. Dan and his threats. She'd been with Nick, content and in love… But she wasn't about to explain all of that.

Zachman: Yeah.
Mntnbiker: How are things with that roommate of yours?
Zachman: Nick?

*As if she didn't know who he was talking about!*

Mntnbiker: Do you have another roommate?
Zachman: No. I don't even have him anymore. He moved out.
Mntnbiker: Are you glad?

Glad? She'd give almost anything to have his arms around her again, if only he felt as strongly about her as she did him.

Zachman: I think it's for the best.
Mntnbiker: That's not really an answer.
Zachman: What is it you want to hear?
Mntnbiker: Don't you care about him?

Maggie wanted to tell John that it was all over between her and Nick, but she knew better.

Zachman: I care about him.
Mntnbiker: Does that mean you're in love with him?

Zachman: Are you trying to make me miserable?

Mntnbiker: No.

Zachman: Then let's talk about something else.

Mntnbiker: Just tell me if you love him.

Zachman: I do, all right? I want to have his children, wash his clothes, cook his meals. Am I sick, or what?

There was a long pause.

Mntnbiker: That's the most incredible thing I ever heard.

Evidently John didn't care about her any more than Nick did.

Mntnbiker: What if he loves you back? Would you marry him?

Zachman: I don't want to talk about this. It doesn't matter, anyway. I have to think about what's best for my son. I can't get involved with someone who works for the FBI, lives halfway across the country and is always away on dangerous assignments.

Mntnbiker: What if he took a desk job?

Zachman: He's not the type.

Mntnbiker: How do you know? Maybe he's ready to settle down. Maybe he's finally found the right woman and the right boy and the right town.

Zachman: And maybe he hasn't. Listen, I've got a dispatcher sending out a call for officers. A 7-Eleven just got robbed. I've got to go.

Maggie, wait—

Maggie didn't hesitate. She signed off the Internet, grabbed her briefcase and headed out.

A DOZEN RED ROSES arrived the following day, and the day after, and the day after that. By the following Sunday, Maggie's house was beginning to look like a florist's shop, but as yet, no one had claimed credit for sending them. Each new batch arrived with a card that said simply, "I love you."

"Do you think they're from Nick?" Darla asked, closing the door as the flower deliveryman left.

Maggie frowned at her fifth batch of roses. "No. They didn't start coming until after John wrote me the last time. They must be from him, although Mrs. Gruber insists they're from our 'nice' garbageman."

Darla chuckled. "She's something else. She was a trooper through everything that happened with Dr. Dan."

"I don't know what I would've done without her. She supported me every step of the way and she's helped me so much with Zach."

"I'll bet she's relieved it's all over."

Maggie grinned. "Just don't come up on her from behind. She still keeps a frying pan handy, just in case she has to knock someone silly."

"I hope I have that much spirit when I'm her age."

"Me, too," Maggie said, leading the way into the kitchen.

Darla paused at the table while Maggie searched her cupboards for something to put the flowers in. "So what do you think?" she asked.

"About what?"

"About who's sending the roses. Maybe now that Nick's gone, John sees this as his chance to get his foot in the door. Have you asked him?"

Fresh out of vases, Maggie filled a quart jar with water and began to arrange the flowers. "I've written him a couple of times, but he hasn't responded."

"Then maybe it *is* Nick."

"No. I haven't heard from Nick since he left. And why would he, all of a sudden, start sending me flowers?"

"Mommy, where's Nick?" Zach demanded, hearing his name and glancing up from his place on the floor in front of a Disney movie. She and Darla moved into the living room and placed the flowers on the coffee table. "He had to go away," she told him, sorry she'd mentioned Nick in his presence.

"But when's he coming home?"

Maggie didn't have the heart to tell her son that Nick probably wasn't ever coming back. Zach had asked for Nick every day since he'd moved out and frequently begged her to let him call. "He lives far away from us now," she said.

"But when's he coming back?"

Zach didn't understand that things were better for them this way. When Maggie opened her mouth to explain that sometimes people have to leave, Darla answered for her.

"Soon, if these flowers are from him," she said.

Maggie gave her a look that told her not to get Zach's hopes up as she opened the card that had come with the flowers. She expected the same three words she'd received so far, only today there were four—*Will you marry me?*

She stared down at the card in surprise.

"What does it say?" Darla asked.

"I can't believe this," Maggie said, showing her.

"He wants to marry you?" Darla's eyebrows shot almost up to her hairline. "Oh, boy! It's gotta be Nick."

"There's still no signature." Maggie shook her head. "But it can't be Nick. He hasn't even tried to call me."

"Well, it's only been a couple of weeks."

A couple of weeks that felt like forever. At least she and her mother were speaking again. Maggie had called her shortly after Nick's departure. She hadn't said anything about what had happened with Dr. Dan—it seemed pointless to frighten her mother now that it was all over—but she'd tried to explain that she was a responsible adult and Rosalyn needed to respect her choices. She wasn't sure very much had changed, though. Her mother's attitude hadn't improved until she told her that Nick was history. Then Rosalyn had asked if Maggie was going to call Brian Wordelly, which led to a whole discussion about Maggie taking care of her own love life. In the end, it hadn't gone as well as Maggie had hoped. But at least they were on speaking terms again. And Rosalyn had promised not to set her up with anyone else.

"If Nick cared about me, he would have been in touch by now," she told Darla. "He's probably on his next assignment and has forgotten all about me."

"I don't know," Darla mused, still staring at the card as though she could decipher the riddle. "Reese let me sweat this last break-up for over a month."

Maggie nearly dropped the coffee she'd started pouring for herself. "Reese is back?"

Darla gave her a devilish smile. "He showed up last night to say he's working at Sam's Club. That's where he is now, until four o'clock." She held up both hands, fingers crossed. "Let's hope it holds."

"You're a slave to your heart," Maggie told her, but she knew the same held true for her. If Nick ever walked back through her door, she doubted she'd have the strength to tell him to leave a second time.

"Reese and I have our problems, but we love each other. We're going to see if we can work things out."

Impulsively, Maggie hugged her. "I'm happy for you, Darla. I love you."

Darla returned her squeeze. "I love you too, Mags. Now let's get online and see if we can coerce John into telling us whether or not he's the one sending the flowers."

Maggie settled herself at the computer while Darla lounged

on a corner of her bed. The usual sequence of tones sounded as Maggie's modem connected. She hadn't received a message from John for almost six days, but there was one in her mailbox now. The caption read, "So what's your answer?"

Her answer? That couldn't mean what she thought it meant... "Oh, no," she said as she read his message, "they *are* from John. What am I going to do?"

Darla leaned over her shoulder and read the message aloud.

Dear Maggie—
How do you like the flowers? Have I convinced you to marry me yet? You'd better say yes, or they'll keep arriving, every day until I get the answer I want. I love you. Will you be my wife? There may be some things I can't tell you, but I promise I'll never lie to you again.

There was no signature.

Maggie blinked at the message. John loved her? John wanted her to marry him without ever meeting? This was crazy. She'd just told him she was in love with Nick. How did he expect her to respond to this? And what did he mean by promising never to lie to her again? What had he lied about so far?

"He's nuts," Darla said. "And I introduced you to him. Tell me he doesn't have your address—"

"Wait. There's an attachment, a .jpg file."

"A .jpg file is usually a picture."

"I know." Had John finally broken down and sent her a photo of himself? Maggie clicked on the download and waited nervously for the image, then couldn't believe what filled her screen. It was a photograph of Zach, the one Nick had taken the morning they were playing basketball. How had John gotten hold of that?

"Look," Darla said, pointing to the caption at the bottom of the screen.

Can we be a family, Maggie? We love you, and we love each other—Jonathon Nicholas Sorenson and Zachary Taylor Russell (hopefully soon to be Zachary Taylor *Sorenson*).

Jonathan Nicholas Sorenson! Nick? Nick was John?

It had to be true. How else could John have the picture Nick had taken?

Darla seemed to arrive at the same conclusion, only a second after Maggie. With a scream, she grabbed Maggie, but anger, confusion, hurt, and hope converged on Maggie all at once. Hadn't Nick told her enough lies? Was John just another avenue he'd used to get close to her? How had he managed it?

Maggie remembered all the questions John had asked her about Dr. Dan and Lola Fillmore and her contact at the *Independent*. She remembered the mysterious call to Atkinson's house and how well "John" had taken the news when she'd told him about her relationship with Nick. She'd thought he'd been kind about it because he was such a nice guy. Now she knew he'd only been giving her up to himself!

*Of all the dirty, rotten—*

"What's wrong?" Darla demanded. "Nick loves you. He wants to marry you. Why aren't you jumping up and down?"

"I don't know what to say," Maggie told her helplessly. "How could he lie to me like this? How could he make love to me knowing—"

Darla grabbed her by the shoulder and gently shook her. "Maggie, don't. You love him and you know it. Here's your chance. Forgive him, and wipe the slate clean. He's an FBI agent, and he was doing his job. Chalk it up to that."

Before Maggie had a chance to answer, an instant message appeared on her screen.

Mntnbiker: What do you say, Maggie? I'm going crazy without you. Do you still love me? Can you forgive me?

Maggie stared at the words. How did she fit all the pieces together? How could she attribute the right motives to Nick's actions?

Zachman: Nick?
Mntnbiker: Yes.
Zachman: You lied to me again.
Mntnbiker: I did it for the investigation, Maggie. I did it to save lives. Surely you believe that.

Maggie couldn't deny that she was grateful for the way Nick had looked after her. She was proud of him, too, for finally getting Dr. Dan off the streets. Clearly he was a good agent. But after they'd become close, he should have trusted her enough to tell her who he really was—shouldn't he? If he didn't trust her, how could she ever learn to trust him?

Zachman: You could have told me at some point. You could have trusted me.
Mntnbiker: I couldn't tell you, Maggie. I can't tell anyone certain things regarding my job. But that doesn't mean I don't trust you. As a matter of fact, I'm trusting you with something that frightens me a lot more than the details of a murder investigation.

Maggie held her breath, waiting for him to tell her what he was trusting her with, but he didn't volunteer the information. Finally she couldn't wait any longer.

Zachman: What's that?
Mntnbiker: My heart. Is it enough?

Finally Maggie felt a smile come from somewhere deep inside her and couldn't stop it from bursting across her face.

Tears filling her eyes, Darla put an arm around her and squeezed hard. "Go for it, Mags," she said, and Maggie laughed. She was going to marry Nick.

Zachman: Your love is all I've ever wanted. Come home so I can show you how much.

## EPILOGUE

"HOW'S OUR BABY TODAY?" Nick asked, sliding a protective hand over Maggie's rounded middle and curving his body around hers in the bed. He'd always found Maggie attractive, but now that she was pregnant with his child, he thought her more beautiful than ever, and he couldn't keep his hands off her.

"Your baby kept me awake most of the night, kicking and squirming," she complained, but a sleepy smile told him she wasn't upset.

He kissed her forehead. "I think I should make that up to you, since I slept like a rock."

She raised her finely arched brows. "How are you going to do that? Let me sleep all day?"

"I'm going to take you to Carmel-By-The-Sea. You can sleep on the drive. I want to take some shots of you and Zach on the beach."

"You've already taken a ton of pictures of us on the beach," she said.

Nick hadn't forgotten. He and Maggie had gone to Mexico for their honeymoon, but Darla and Mrs. Gruber had taken turns keeping Zach, so he wasn't with them. And Maggie wasn't pregnant then. Nick wanted to get her walking along the seashore, the swell of his baby evident beneath her sundress, their son playing in the background. It was the only way he could improve on his initial vision for the cover of his book.

"I like taking pictures," he told her, sliding his lips up the soft skin on the inside of her arm. She tasted so good, smelled so good… "It's my hobby."

"When are you going to start doing it professionally?" she asked.

He shrugged. Photography was a nice dream, but he was still enjoying the bureau too much to make the switch. When he'd moved to the Sacramento office, he'd wondered if he'd miss traveling, but he didn't. He couldn't wait to get home to Maggie at the end of each day and had no desire to leave her or Zach, even for one night. "I'm not in any hurry to make a career change."

Maggie turned to face him and ran her fingers through his hair. "Should we go to Utah and see your family for Thanksgiving? We'll have the baby by then."

"Will your mother mind if we don't come to Iowa?"

"We could go there for Christmas. She and Aunt Rita aren't growing any younger. And now that we're getting along better, I'd actually enjoy spending the holidays together."

"You think Darla and Reese will take care of Rambo while we're gone?"

"With three cats?"

"What about Mrs. Gruber?"

"She'll do anything for Zach. We'll have him ask her."

"Daddy, I'm hungry," Zach called from the living room. He'd gotten in bed with them an hour or so earlier, and fallen asleep on Nick's arm. But Rambo had woken him a few minutes ago, wanting to be let out. Now boy and dog were together, watching cartoons in the living room.

"I'll be right back," Nick told Maggie, slipping out of bed to take care of Zach.

She stopped him with a hand on his arm. "I love you, Nick," she said. "I was wrong about your f.p. factor."

"F.p. factor?"

"Fatherhood potential. I didn't know it when we were dating, but yours is off the charts."

He smiled. "I didn't know it, either," he said. "I only knew what I know now."

"What's that?" she asked.

"That I can't live without you."